CW00376932

Life on the Margins

and other stories

Scottish Arts Trust Story Awards

Volume 2: 2019-2020

Edited by

Sara Cameron McBean and Michael Hamish Glen

Scottish Arts Trust

ISBN: 9798693586345

Other publications from the Scottish Arts Trust

The Desperation Game and other stories from the Scottish Arts Trust Story Awards 2014-2018 (Volume 1)
Edited by Sara Cameron McBean and Hilary Munro (2019)

Rosalka: The Silkie Woman and other stories, plays and poems
By Isobel Lodge (2018)

Dedication

For Maurice Roëves

Life on the Margins is dedicated to the memory of Maurice Roëves, the stunningly powerful actor and great supporter of so many of our story award events at the Scottish Arts Club.

On Friday 27 November 2020, we launched *Life on the Margins* via a wonderful online show with readings from the anthology by some of Maurice's friends and fellow actors. We are grateful for the magic they created as they brought these stories to life, enabling us to share in such a fitting tribute to Maurice's memory.

Our thanks to:

Alan Cumming who performed *A Christmas Surprise* by Peter Kelly and *Armed and Semi -Dangerous* by kerry rawlinson.

Alli McGraw who performed *Judith* by Jupiter Jones and *Flash Point* by Sherry Morris.

Maureen Beattie who performed *Gust in the Gusset* by Jo Learmonth and *Life on the Margins* by Shaun Laird

John Bett who performed *I've Killed George* by Bob Shepherd, *Our Ghostly King* by Sandy Forsyth and *fourteen* by Paul Walton

Contents

Acknowledgements

Alexander McCall Smith was the chief judge of the Scottish Arts Club Short Story Competition from its inception until 2019. We are grateful for his encouragement and support, and delighted to welcome and thank Andrew O'Hagan who took over as chief judge in 2020. Our thanks also to Sandra Ireland who continued as chief judge in the Edinburgh International Flash Fiction Awards to 2020.

We are grateful to John Lodge for the donation that enables the Isobel Lodge Award, which brings such encouragement to countless unpublished short story writers in Scotland. In 2020, thanks to a donation from Mark Jones we were able to introduce the Golden Hare Award for Scottish Flash Fiction – which seems to have sparked an increased interest in the flash format in Scotland.

Thank you to all our readers who give their time, energy and passion to reading and re-reading the stories entered in our competitions. Their passion for discussing, debating and making the case for the stories they love is a sheer delight. We are also indebted to Dai Lowe who works tirelessly as our story awards administrator and to Gordon Mitchell whose wonderful paintings give the Scottish Arts Trust Story Awards their distinctive visual style. Shaun Laird's clever flash fiction story *Life on the Margins,* included in this collection, provided the perfect title to blend with Gordon's beautiful *Two to Tango* painting, and give us a memorable cover for this anthology. We are grateful for the contributions of Michael Hamish Glen who designed the interior pages.

Our thanks to the Scottish Arts Trust and the Scottish Arts Club Council, who have collaborated on the story awards from the beginning. We look forward to being able to resume those sumptuous Story Award Dinners and Flash Bash Suppers. Specific thanks are due to Vanessa Roëves, Linda Greig and Cate Howell who joined me in 2020 in organizing the Flash Bash and putting together our online events – the Story Awards Show and the *Life on the Margins* event that launched this anthology.

Finally, a huge thank you to all the writers who have imagined, drafted, written, re-written and submitted stories over the years.

Your stories are the stuff of dreams, of inspiration and a towering, irresistible creative spirit. We look forward to reading more!

Sara Cameron McBean
Director, Scottish Arts Trust Story Awards
Edinburgh 2020
www.storyawards.org

Overdue
by Gail Anderson

Winner, Scottish Arts Club Short Story Competition 2019

When their eyes locked over the cheese dip at the Bodleian Library's Christmas party, Alexandria Pergamum and Constantine Celsus felt the stirrings of something long overdue.

Constantine, a cataloguer for the Medieval Dentistry collection, worked in the south sub-basement. Alexandria, a more senior member, worked reference in Special Collections, third floor north. Dark and light, day and night. It is truth that cataloguers and reference specialists are the oil and water, the Montagues and Capulets of the library world. Their paths had never before crossed; and the fact was that Constantine was married, that Alexandria, after a series of vivid disappointments, had embraced celibacy.

And yet.

In the new year, Alexandria received a series of book requests written in a bold, forward-leaning hand:

The yearningly interrogative 823.44 – *One Sign of Love?* (Fiction; 19thC, English).

The deliciously bawdy 641.509 – *Take Ye This Luscious Tart* (Cookery; 17thC, Baking).

The boldly instructive M93.E00206 – *Undressing the Union* (Labour; Political Activity).

Constantine returned from lunch to find a daring request to reclassify a title within his own subject area – *Fill the Cavity* – from 617.62 (Role of Dentistry) to 617.634 (Endodontics, Early).

The following morning Alexandria received a citation enquiry that stole her breath: 808.80369 – *The Pop-up Book of Braille Erotica* (Literature: Esoteric). She returned the form stamped in red ink: *This Item Long Overdue – Urgent Action Required To Meet Patron Need.*

That these were rash, wanton acts both of them knew – and they were not deaf to the voices of stigma and scandal. This could not be seduction in the stacks, coitus among the carrels. It was time to move beyond the walls of the Bodleian – but where? The Buttery in Broad Street was out of the question, as was Browns in the Covered Market. Both were too popular, too well-thumbed by colleagues from both sides of the divide. Finding a rendezvous in Oxford which was *not* right around the corner from one of the twenty-nine Bodleian branch libraries was a task requiring almost superhuman research abilities.

At length, Alexandria slid a set of requests into the pneumatic tube and sent it sucking away to the sub-basement:

PN.U65.B90 GOW DVD – *Go West* (Comedy Films; Marx Brothers);

X07.E00990 – *The Other Side of the Tracks* (Fiction; World War One);

X00.H00289 – *Paddy* (Prejudices; Boston, Irish Americans);

Mus. Pop. E.1903.166 – *Out He Went At Seven In The Morning* (Employment; Songs).

Thus it was that before work the next day they met at Mick's Transport Cafe, tucked behind the railway station. There, over chipped mugs of steaming strong tea and surrounded by blaspheming cabbies wolfing Full English, Constantine wasted no time.

"There's something I need to do with you," said he in a low voice laden with intensity.

"Yes?" Alexandria's throat was tight.

"Something my wife won't even consider."

He leant forward, elbowing the sauces masterfully to one side. For Alexandria, the sheer electricity of the moment blurred the chequered, oiled-cotton table cloth beneath her into something resembling a barcode.

Constantine's secret passion – long held, closely guarded – was for Medieval stained glass. Specifically, for a design so rare that it occurred in only a handful of locations in England: the *Lily Crucifixion*, depicting the Saviour martyred on the outstretched fronds of a lily.

"A lily," said Alexandria, stunned.

"*Lilium candidum*," he clarified. "*The Madonna Lily*."

Alexandria, lured with an explicit promise of carnal pleasure and now confronted with the flower of virginal purity, was two heartbeats away from walking out. But as Constantine spoke – explaining how, by tradition, the yellow flower had turned white as the Madonna picked it – she reflected. So many empty nights spent holding nothing warmer

14

than a cup of orange pekoe. There was passion in his zealot's eyes, certainly – and therein, perhaps, the makings of a quest. And so she vowed, over their shared plate of Number 12 (Beans on Toast), to accompany him in visiting all five of the ancient windows on his list.

They travelled.

At the Church of St Edmund in Effing Badger, Shropshire, they stood side by side beneath a gothic window, bathed in coloured light, their fingers barely touching. At St Dunstan's in Great Fossick, Cornwall, they made so bold as to hold hands. At St Barnabas in Tooting Bottom, Yorkshire, they kissed, shyly. But it was at St Hermione-in-the-Wilderness in Chipping Marrow, Oxfordshire, that opportunity stirred and opened one eye. For it was here that Alexandria discovered that the key had been left in the lock on the inside of the church door.

It was a heavy, ornate key. It was festooned with a tassel of the deepest scarlet. As Constantine made his way towards the apse, clutching a pamphlet (*50p in aid of the Font Restoration Fund*) Alexandria took this key in both her hands and turned it, locking the door behind them.

Constantine was seated on the edge of a raised granite tomb, gazing silently at the tracery, when her shadow fell across him. She laid her hands on his shoulders, pushed him gently onto his back across the polished surface of the granite and slid herself over him. He watched her as she teased open the buttons on his shirt. He fumblingly helped her undo the buckle of his belt before laying back on the tomb and spreading his arms in mirror of the lily glass over their heads. Then they were in the throes: jolting, thrusting, an apocalypse, the coming of the rapture. Spine arching, head thrown back, Alexandria opened her eyes and found herself staring directly into the unblinking lens of a CCTV camera.

For a week they waited for facial recognition technology to forge a damning link between recent activities and their driving licence photographs; but the authorities were, presumably, more interested in metal thieves. The dreaded call – from the police, from church elders, from the Bodleian – never materialised. The blow, when it fell, came from an entirely unexpected quarter.

The video – *LOL Lively Recumbents Get Medieval in Oxfordshire*

Church!!! – went viral, breaking all previous YouTube records in just fourteen hours. And while their gyrating sacrilege spread across the globe, closer to home medieval churches were inundated with tourists, and the more enterprising of local teenagers were selling souvenir condoms at a profit.

That Monday morning, Alexandria's usually peaceful reference room was crowded with chortling undergraduates; she didn't care. What mattered was that she and Constantine now despaired of completing their quest, of seeing their fifth and final Lily Crucifixion. They hadn't the heart to brave the crowds.

Not far away, in peaceable Charlbury, the local Women's Institute Chapter had finished their tea and biscuits, concluded their review of the last meeting's minutes and were engaged in a lively discussion of short courses in Architectural History. Their fervour led them first to Oxford University's Continuing Education website, and from that safe harbour into the choppy waters of the wider internet. The Chapter Secretary, whose interests extended barely beyond jam-making, dismissed each suggestion as it was made. Art Deco (*licentious!*), Brutalism (*beastly!*), Rococo (*naked cherubs??*), Roman (*oh my dears – orgies!*). The membership, restive, put it to a vote; and only then was the phrase 'Medieval Churches' typed with martyred reluctance into the search box by the Chapter Secretary – a woman known to her few friends as 'Dear Felicity', but more generally known as Mrs Constantine Celsus.

Constantine spent the next several weeks withdrawn from circulation, camping in dark corners of the Bodleian sub-basement, his shoes and effects shelved in among 947.073 (War: Civil; English). Alexandria met him again for their regular tryst at Mick's. They could have met at the Buttery or anywhere, as they had no more secrets to keep; but old habits die hard. They warmed themselves over their plate of Number 12, and Alexandria saw that Constantine's eyes were shining, his inadequately shaven cheeks were glowing. He slid a magnolia-coloured citation card across the table, face down. She turned it over.

DT 298.C7 Rb – *The End of the Siege* (Constantine; Algeria, History)
306.88 Ru – *Liberty at Last* (Monograph; Divorce)

And stamped below in black ink: *The resource is now available.*

They didn't miss seeing their final Lily Crucifixion – at St Michael at the North Gate, right there in Oxford. They stood before it, listening, as an adaptation of the Bodleian Oath was read out: *Do you pledge to preserve this precious volume?* Reference specialists on the bride's side of the aisle, cataloguers on the groom's. Alexandria and Constantine each carried accession bouquets, *lilium candidum,* bright as dazzling white trumpets.

Rip
by Donna Rutherford

Second Prize, Scottish Arts Club Short Story Competition 2019

Rip (noun) – a stretch of fast flowing and rough water caused by the meeting of currents.

Rip (verb) – to tear or pull something quickly or forcibly away from something or someone.

[Oxford English Dictionary]

***

There are 11 steps from your bedroom to the front door, and six mail boxes till the end of our street. It takes 17 minutes to walk to St. Clair beach, and the café has 25 chairs with a view of the ocean. I am 45 years old, and today is your 19th birthday.

Early December, the doorstep of summer, yet the sun seethes like a tied dog. The air is hot asphalt and the soles of my feet spike and burn as I shadow hop under shady trees along Bird Street. Cars laden with children and boogie boards pass on Victoria Road. A solo surfer rides an old bike, one arm loped over the board as he negotiates traffic and pedestrians.

The Esplanade is a people watchers' paradise; kids in togs playing in the water fountain, couples strolling, hands within hands, dogs on leads desperate for the ocean, and the bench bound elderly, setting memories adrift with the tide. I walk to the rail and watch the water.

White Island stands sentinel beyond the breaks. A hunk of rock and guano beneath our horizon. Out at the edge, surfers float waiting for the ride. Waves break and crash in foamy sets of seven, beating the sand, push pull, push pull. Children paddle at the ocean's edge, delighting in waves that rush around dimpled knees. Three shirtless boys throw a rugby ball, sprinting and diving, tossing and catching, eyes trained on bikinied girls sunning like sleepy cats.

The wooden rail is warm under my palms. I close my eyes and breathe. They say the first step to escape the mind is the simple act of breathing. The smell of fried fish and garlic blends with briny air and suntan lotion. I breathe, but a car passes, and Bob Marley is singing *Stir it Up*, the stereo base beats underfoot. I can't open my eyes, because my breath is gone, and my mind forever looking backward has taken over. I grip the rail till the car passes and the music fades.

"Ari, I've had enough." His room was musty, stale socks, sweat and something else. Something I decided to ignore till I knew how to address it. My heel squished a cigarette butt. I didn't bend down.

"Good for you."

I opened the curtains roughly. "Ari Tipene, get up, and get dressed! We're going to church." He turned his back and pulled the duvet over his head. "I mean it Ari, this can't go on." I hovered by the bed, surveying the lump under the covers. "I'll stand here until you get up."

"Go ahead."

When did this man-child take the place of my boy? Distant and disrespectful, dark eyes and dark moods.

Angry men in rock bands glared from postered walls judging me. *You're messing it up they say. He's going astray. Sort it out Mrs Tipene.* I was sure he just needed time.

"Come on Ari." A few thick black curls stuck out from under the duvet. I reached to touch them, but he recoiled like a snake. The backs of my eyes stung, "Ari, please, would you just …"

"Leave me alone Mum. Just leave me the fuck alone."

I did as he asked, and left the room closing the door too hard. Bob Marley's Redemption Song answered my footsteps as I descended the seven stairs and left for the beach to watch other people's sons in the sunshine and surf.

***

It's nice to walk. The air is a balmy, and tension fades as my muscles stretch and warm. I walk in the hard sand where the tide pushes cool water around my toes. I keep my eyes forward, past the row of disappearing groynes, past the dunes of St Kilda, out to the headland – Ōruawairua.

I must walk to the end where the gulls nest in rocky crevices, and maidenhair seaweed whips and turns with the tide. Each step toward the headland brings the same stew of joy, grief and anger. Memories jagged like oyster shells prick my eyes and I stop, frightened by the sting. I push the heels of my hands into my eyes and colour bursts as silhouettes form then dissolve in turquoise and cerise. I see you; a flash

19

of white teeth, and toffee skin, your father closed and dark, and me – a pale outsider. *Our words are not yours,* he'd say. But I try to make them mine, Ari. I try with my pākehā tongue to weave a rope of words that lead me to you.

The beach is dotted with families. Parents, children, friends, couples and lovers, so many variations on together. We follow the instinct to gather and group, to avoid the curse of loneliness. I never asked how you felt when our whānau became two. Was that the beginning of our rip? Unlike my numbers, there are no rules to shape what comes next.

I remember the gentle tone of the school counsellor. We understand there's a change in circumstance Mrs Tipene … does Ari see his father? There's been a shift in his behaviour, we suspect marijuana. I could have told them the shift was when they locked up your father. I could have said I was afraid, should have asked what to do. Instead, I thanked him and said nothing.

Ōruawairua extends in a gentle nod to the ocean. Gulls wings glint in afternoon sun, hovering on pockets of air. They glide where groups gather to admire the view, pointing out to Tomahawk beach and beyond. Below, the waves are deep and desolate, thrashing on the rough rock that once resembled the profile of a man.

When you were little, we'd cycle on summer nights. When heat blanched from the sky and radiated from asphalt, we'd ride along John Wilson Drive. You would fly along the flat, giddy with speed till you reached the incline. We'd push our bikes to the top, lay them on the grass and go to the lookout. You said ghosts flew around the cliff, singing sad songs at night. Kids at school told you – kēhua of those who'd jumped.

***

"Excuse me?" I start, lost in thought. A young mother looks to me, shading her eyes from the sun. "Do you know what time it is?"

It's a little thing, feeling useful, but it's nice. It brings me back and reminds me to breathe. "It's twenty-two, after two."

"Thank you," she squints into the glare. Her slender arm gestures to the water, "My boys have been in there for hours." I follow her gaze to where two boys play on boogie boards, kicking and paddling, riding to shore on white wash.

"Enjoy. This is Dunedin, the weather will have changed by evening."

"Yes," she sighs. "It probably will." Something ripples below her skin, and her eyes widen and limbs jerk and tense. She runs to the water shouting a child's name. In seconds she's waist deep, staggering through sloshy waves. A child screams, clinging with one hand to his board, waving furiously with the other. Each wave propels the board and his small body backward, further out into the angry current of a rip. Sucked quickly into the tide her head jerks toward me, eyes pleading above the pitch of her voice.

"Please help me!"

The ocean sucks the shore from under my feet as a swell washes over, drowning her pleas. There is danger in delay, but I'm frozen with fear as the traitorous tide pulls the boy with each wasted second.

The other child is out of the water, crying and shivering. "Stay here!" I shout, fierce with fright wading into the shock of icy water. My chest tightens in the effort to breathe as I focus on the diminishing figure of the boy. For a flashing moment I'm the eyes of the hovering gull. I see me, the mother and the drifting boy flailing in waves that push us back and draw him away.

I swim, skirt dragging, sunglasses balanced like useless high beams. "Sideways" I pull an arm from the water to signal right. "Kick sideways!" But the words catch the current and are gone. He doesn't kick sideways but clings in desperation to the board. "Let the rip take you!" I shout to the mother, pointing out to the boy. She must reach the board and hold on, or panic will pull her under. My life funnels to this single moment.

"Help us, please help us." Her voice between the rise and fall of waves, face contorted by a mother's worst fear – she can't save her child. Her fear ignites, flickers and ripples, travelling in a direct line to my heart. I fight for control within the power of the rip, thinking if I can do this one thing, it hasn't been for nothing.

"Hold on to the board." My voice is shrill, cawing the command again and again. The boy holds. Closer, I see his eyes clamped shut, cheek pressed against the yellow board. The rip has dragged his mother to him. She grabs the board but is panicking and thrashing. "Kick to the right! Kick! Kick!" Her ears are filled with the ocean. She does not kick. Takaroa. Have mercy.

My chest is packed tight in terror. That life can flip so suddenly, chaos from calm, death replacing life, no explanation. Anger swells mixing with fear, fuelling adrenalin. Time is opaque.

I reach the board and grab it, flipping on my back, eyes to the sky, kicking sideways, kicking and kicking and kicking. The screaming and crying mix with salt water in my ears and I watch the sky. I ask now. I ask like didn't before. Save the life of this boy. A boy whose day is not today. My breath comes ragged, legs weary and weak. A wave breaks over our heads and Ōruawairua appears. Gulls and ghosts on the headland. I watch the contour where land meets the ocean and say your name. *Ari.*

The undertow has changed, from pull to push. A gentle eddy of undercurrent bobs us forward. Three drenched, shaking bodies drifting back to shore. We are free of the rip and the tide returns us. My joy is clear and cold as the water. The rough sand is heaven as we stumble from the shallows. I'm on my knees. The sobbing mother embraces me, the boy too. Three drenched, tangled bodies lucky to be alive. Sandwiched in the middle of their relief and gratitude, intensity of feeling takes form, becomes physical; he wairua. It passes in embrace from them to me and I know what to do. I'll bring it to you.

I waste no time retracing my steps home. 17 minutes from beach to home, six mailboxes to pass. seven stairs to your bedroom. I knock on the door. Ari? You don't answer, you never do.

I am 45 years old and today is your 19th birthday.

I sing happy birthday and I know this will surprise you because for two years the singing has stopped. Reminded of the capacity for gratitude, the fight to hold and treasure life – I open the door.

The room is bright and light, golden yellow from the kowhai tree by the window. I breathe, and I breathe. Your picture on the shelf smiles reluctantly. You were 17. I hold the frame, sit on the bed and sing rā whānau ki a koe, and out at Ōruawairua you fly with the gulls.

***

Glossary:
Kēhua – ghost spirits.
Ōruawairua – place of meeting spirits.
Pākehā – New Zealander of European descent.
Rā whānau ki a koe – birthday greeting.
Takaroa – Māori god of sea.
Whānau – extended family group.
Wairua – spirit which exists beyond death.

Sammy, the Queen and the Nice Lady
by Liz Treanor

Winner, Isobel Lodge Award 2019
Third Prize, Scottish Arts Club Short Story Competition 2019

Sammy didn't like the Queen one bit. Her picture had hung above his Granny's fireplace since before he was born and he'd stared at it many a time wondering how the Queen had managed to sit on the Frone for 25 years. Granda sat on the Frone every Sunday afternoon for ages and this annoyed the rest of the family so much that Sammy thought that the Queen's family must really hate her. *And* she took people away. He heard Auntie Maggie telling her friend Jean that Daddy had gone to be a guest of Her Majesty for six months and he thought the Queen could not be a very nice person at all if she took Daddies away to her house where she just sat on the Frone all day. She was coming to Belfast soon and Sammy was going to find her and ask her did she not have a Daddy of her own and could she please send his Daddy back before he started school in September.

When Mammy said they were having a party in the street for the Queen's Silver Joogalee, Sammy was less than impressed, but it hadn't been too bad so far. The other Daddies had been busy all day making a long, long table for everyone to sit at and there had been sandwiches and sausage rolls and red lemonade and orange jelly. Everyone wore hats with The Flag like the wee pointy flags that the other Daddies had hung from the lampposts and played games all day.

The whole street was there – apart from Daddy and one family that lived at the far end of the street where Sammy wasn't allowed. Auntie Maggie said there was no point in asking them seeing as they were Kafflicks and would probably poison the Guinness anyway. His big brother Andy was nine and knew everything so Sammy had asked him what was a Kafflick. Andy said he'd never actually seen one but he had heard that they killed babies and were smelly and had pictures of Jesus on the wall instead of the Queen. Mammy had told Andy to stop filling the wean's head with nonsense but Sammy now thought that Kafflicks were even scarier than Daleks and he thought the Queen must be a Kafflick with her Frone and her house full of Daddies.

Sammy was bored now that the games had stopped. It was getting dark and the music had started. Charlie Thompson's sisters were pretending to be Abba and were singing into lemonade bottle microphones. They were trying to get Charlie and Andy to join in but the boys were too busy drinking the dregs of the Daddies' Guinness. Sammy was worried that they were going to try him next but he didn't like Abba so he hid under the table and that's where he saw Charlie's new puppy, Paisley. Sammy loved Paisley. He was fluffy and funny and very fast. Some days Sammy would play with him for hours and hours. He hoped that Daddy might bring him a puppy when he came back from staying with the Queen.

The music was getting louder now and so were the Mammies and Daddies. Charlie's big brother and his friends had brought out their flutes while two sweaty Daddies had started to drag a big, big drum across the street. Paisley didn't like loud noises and neither did Sammy so when Paisley ran away, Sammy ran too-all the way to the end of the street.

The music was farther away now and so was Paisley -in fact Sammy couldn't see him anymore. He stopped running and looked around. He wasn't very sure where he was. He didn't recognise the houses and there were no flags. He could still hear the thundering of the big, big drum and he could see light from a bonfire, but they seemed far away. He had drunk too much red lemonade and he really, really needed a wee. He knew his house was far away and he couldn't do a wee in the street because the last time he had done a wee in the street Daddy had told him it was wrong even if nobody could see you. Sammy missed Daddy.

Sammy saw a house with a light on and wondered if the people who lived there were Strangers because, if they weren't, they might let him use their toilet. Sammy knew you shouldn't talk to Strangers. Andy said they took you into their house to look at puppies or kittens and then skinned you alive. Sammy decided to knock on the door anyway and if they asked him to look at puppies or kittens he would run away really fast and wee in the street anyway. Daddy wouldn't know.

He knocked the door as hard as he could. A lady looked through her curtains. Sammy waved at her and she came to open the door. She smiled and said "Hello, Sammy isn't it? I've seen you walking to nursery with your Mammy. I like your hat. Are you lost, Sammy?" She wasn't a Stranger – she was a Nice Lady! Sammy tried to tell her he wasn't lost he just needed a wee but the words wouldn't come. Just the tears and then the wee running down his leg. The Nice Lady said "come in Sammy" and she picked him up and carried him to the bathroom. She said "you're about the same size as our Brendan," and she brought him some pants with Superman and a pair of blue shorts. Sammy loved Superman and he told her that while she helped him dress. The Nice Lady told him she loved Superman too.

"Would you like a biscuit?" she said. "Custard Cream?" Sammy said yes please they were his favourites. Downstairs a boy about the same size as him was watching TV with his big sister. The girl said "Who are you and why are you wearing our Brendan's shorts?" The Nice Lady said he was lost and had spilt his drink and she was taking him home to his Mammy after he'd had his biscuit.

"Why are youse not at the party?" asked Sammy." It's great so it is. There's sandwiches and sausage rolls and orange jelly and you could be in Abba instead of Charlie and Andy."

"The party is only for Pwods," said the boy.

"What's a Pwod?" asked Sammy.

"They kill babies and they never smile and they can't sing" interrupted the girl.

"No" said Sammy, I amn't a Pwod".

He had never met a Pwod and he hoped he never would because they sounded like no fun at all.

"Mary, stop filling the wean's head with nonsense," said the Nice Lady. On the shelf Sammy saw a photo of a man who was hugging the Nice Lady and the boy and girl. "Is that your Daddy?"

"Yes, but he isn't here."

"Did the Queen take your Daddy away too? She took mine."

"No, he's a astwonut and he's away in space but he'll be back soon and I'll be five then and we're going to the zoo," said the boy.

"That's where we're going when my Daddy gets back from the Queen's House," replied Sammy.

"Come on Sammy," said the Nice Lady, "I'll take you back now.".
Sammy yawned. "I'll carry you". Brendan, Mary, you can walk." She
picked him up and he buried his head deep in her shoulder. She smelt
like Mammy. Parma Violets, smoke and stardust.

As they were leaving, Sammy looked over the Nice Lady's shoulder
and that's when he saw it. The picture of a man with a beard and a
heart. "Who's that?" asked Sammy. "That's Jesus" said the Nice Lady.
Sammy smiled to himself and put his head back in her shoulder. He
couldn't wait to tell Andy that it couldn't be the Kafflicks that had
pictures of Jesus because the Nice Lady had one in her house and sure
how could she be a Kafflick when she smelt like Mammy and had
custard creams and loved Superman?

They walked along the street, with the Nice Lady singing softly in
his ear – the same song that Daddy used to sing to him about the old
woman who swallowed a fly. Daddy always made him laugh with his
silly voices. The music was getting louder now and he could hear the
Mammies and Daddies singing the song about the 400 children and a
crack in the field. He heard Andy calling his name but he didn't look
up – he just kept his head in the Nice Lady's shoulder and she kept
singing softly in his ear.

"You picked a fine time to leave me ..." sang the Mammies and
Daddies and then they stopped dead. The flutes fell silent too. One of
Charlie's sisters dropped her lemonade bottle microphone. A shattering
of glass then absolute silence. The crowd slowly parted as the strange
little group edged towards Mammy: Sammy with his head in the Nice
Lady's shoulder, Brendan and Mary holding each other's hands tightly.
Auntie Maggie muttered that the Theenian must have stole the wean.
Sammy was pleased that he knew the Nice Lady's name now even if
Auntie Maggie was wrong about her stealing him.

"Hello Sally," said the Nice Lady to Mammy. "I found your Sammy-
he's had a wee accident. I'll bring his clothes round tomorrow when
I've washed them." Sammy was pleased that she hadn't told Mammy
he'd done a wee in his pants again. She would have been very cross.
She had been cross a lot since Daddy went away but if she thought he'd
only been in an accident she wouldn't be so cross. Sammy loved the
Nice Lady.

She set him down and Sammy gave her a big hug. Charlie's Daddy asked him if he wanted a hot dog but Sammy didn't like the sound of that at all. He would never eat any kind of dog. He looked around anxiously and was pleased to see Paisley fast asleep in Charlie's arms.

The Nice Lady turned to walk away from the silence, holding Brendan and Mary by the hand. "Deirdre," said Mammy. The Nice Lady stopped and turned around. "Thanks for bringing him home – will you and the weans not stay for a drink?"

Auntie Maggie spat out her Guinness all over Granda.

"Maggie," said Mammy, "Get some lemonade for the weans. Vodka all right for you Deirdre? I'll put a wee drop of Coke in it for you. She held out a flag cup to the Nice Lady and she reached out her hand to take it. "Thanks Sally," she said.

An Evening with Casper Roth
by Michael Callaghan

Shortlisted, Scottish Arts Club Short Story Competition 2019

Despite its location in central London, it's unlikely you will have heard of the Desmond Hotel. The Desmond (not its real name – I have changed that much for the purposes of this narrative, although the real name is just as dull and flat-mat as that) is a hotel for a particular clientele. It's for those who require discretion. Serious discretion. Secrecy is its USP. And around its tables corporate takeovers are concluded, bank mergers plotted, political betrayals hatched.

And so it was that three weeks ago I found myself waiting there at the invitation of one Casper Roth. Roth does not appear on any published list of the world's most wealthy but in my experience few possessors of true wealth do. He was officially CEO of EmeraldCore International but my own sources suggested that he had made his fortune primarily from an online app that had been quietly sold to one to one of the internet behemoths twelve years earlier and from which he continued to receive payments. The invitation said simply that he *had need of my expertise,* which is the reason why most people seek me out. I am a wine authenticator. And one whose expertise is matched, I would say, by about three other people in the world. My reputation in certifying wine can make the difference in sales running into hundreds of thousands of pounds.

Roth's invitation was a surprise. He was not known as wine collector.

I had just ordered a mineral water when I spotted Roth emerge through the doorway. Simultaneously, he saw me and strode towards me, without waiting for a guiding waiter. We shook hands, exchanged pleasantries, and – since we were both gentlemen – we postponed the business purpose of our meeting until after we had dined. We chatted amicably enough as we ordered and ate. I studied him as we did so. Roth had a look of slightly faded handsomeness. Early forties, he had a broad, craggy build and that air of restless aggressive power that you associate with successful people. The overall impression was that of a former athlete who had kept himself in shape. Yet it was clear that something was troubling him. He looked slightly gaunt, and the skin hung slightly loosely on his face, as if he had lost weight too fast. He ate politely, methodically, but I got the impression it was an effort.

Finally, the meal ended, our polite chitchat stalled, and. I waited, as Roth lit a cigarette (The Desmond has no truck with anti-smoking laws) and drew on it.

"They say that you are a cold man, Mr Lawrence," he said, finally. "You have no family, no friends, no emotions. You are impervious to anything but cold rationalism."

I nodded. That reputation was not undeserved. Cold rationalism, indeed, is my guiding mantra. Generally, the rational choice is the right choice and is the key to a less ... *troubled* existence. In relation to having no family, until I was eighteen, I did have a family. I lived with my parents and three sisters. That all changed when a lorry ploughed through our Land Rover when we were visiting our holiday château in Provence. Only I, miraculously, survived; and survived almost intact, save for a scar across my left cheek and the loss of my left eye, scarcely noticeable through its glass replacement.

Perhaps my experience explains my inability to form any kind of relationship. There is a certain pop psychology plausibility to that. I suspect however, that I was simply born a man content with his own company. The more lasting, practical consequence of that event was an early inheritance of my father's European vineyards and through which I developed my knowledge and understanding of wine.

"I have need of that cold rationality." Roth continued. He then lifted a hand and gestured, as if to capture someone's attention. I turned to see a man in a charcoal suit and thin black tie emerge from one of the Desmond's gloomily lit tables, and approach us. He was carrying something. When he reached us, he said nothing, but placed in the middle of our table a glass bottle, about the shape of a milk bottle but slightly smaller. Nodding slightly to Roth, he immediately retreated.

"Tell me what you think," said Roth. "You can study the bottle. Lift it up. Do anything except drink the wine."

Not drink the wine. Curious condition for someone like me. But I have often written that ninety eight percent of any decision I make is made before I let the wine touch my lips. Authenticating wine, at least the way I do it, involves little actual tasting.

I picked up the bottle. It looked old, and the glass was dirty to the point of being opaque. It also felt oddly warm. No label, of course. No markings or engravings. Heavier than I had anticipated. *The glass must be thick.* I thought. Nonetheless I held it like a baby. Whatever was happening I felt that I really didn't want to drop this.

I tipped it on its side. I could, just, make out the rise of liquid within. Despite myself I felt a curious chill. At the top there was no cork. Instead, there was a wax seal; thick, discoloured. Instinctively, I raised it to my eyes. As I did so, I pressed on the wax. At this point Roth motioned with his arm, to stop me. Too late.

The wax yielded slightly, and gas emitted in a spray, causing me to jerk my face back. Not fast enough though, to avoid droplets landing on my face. I rubbed my face instinctively. But there was no pain. Whatever was inside the bottle wasn't toxic. Roth however reached out, and retrieved the bottle, placing it back on the table.

"Tell me what is going on Mr Roth," I said, wiping my face with my napkin.

He nodded. "Have you heard of the Cana wine?"

"Cana?" I said. "The first miracle of Christ? Where he turned water into wine at the wedding?"

Roth nodded. "But have you heard of the Cana wine *legend*?"

I began to feel horribly disappointed. I had a bad feeling about where the conversation was headed.

"I have heard," I said, neutrally. "Casks of the miracle wine were saved, and been hidden and protected over the centuries. Some bottles survive to this day." I looked again at the bottle on the table. "But surely ..."

Roth smiled: a thin, damaged smile.

"She's dying." he said.

I remained impassive.

"I'm sorry. Who is she?"

"My daughter. Anya."

I reproached myself internally. I had researched Roth's business but been sketchy on the private life details. I remembered his marriage to an Irish actress a decade earlier. I vaguely recalled talk of a child. But nothing more.

"Cancer. In her brain, lungs, and lymph nodes," he continued. "No hope. I have sought enough medical opinions. I tried …everything. So you see why I have taken an interest in the Cana wine legend. I am told there are three surviving bottles. One in the Vatican, one in America … and this one. The bottle in front of you could be mine. The cost would be one hundred million US dollars."

I shivered. I remembered my careless handling. But there was more. My fee was a percentage of the concluded price of the bottle. Agreeing the authenticity here would net me twelve million dollars.

I reached out and turned the bottle round. Again I saw, faintly, through the glass, the liquid beneath swirl and merge. It seemed to glow, the patterns mixing hypnotically as it moved towards the neck of the bottle. Could it conceivably be what Roth hoped it was?

"I understand scientific principles," said Roth. "There are too many unknown variables. You cannot confirm that this is the wine that is claimed. I ask you to confirm merely if it is possible. I am a rich man. There is no shortage of people willing to take my money for worthless cures. This … is different. I have received no promises or assurances. Quite the reverse. But I ask you … is it *possible*?"

I considered the bottle again from my chair. I glanced around at the various darkened tables, wondering how many other eyes were upon me. I looked at the desperate, agonised anticipation of my companion.

I thought: twelve million dollars.

I leaned forward.

"I can make a case for this, Mr Roth. It would have been the custom to save wine from the wedding feast. And, as Christ's fame grew, you could see how it could be recognised that this wine, the first of His miracles, was something to be … prized. And when he died, and acquired the status of … Messiah … well it was already the custom to acquire relics of holy men when they died. Rumours of other relics of Christ persist. Why not this? And, yes, the legend says that the bottles have been kept through the ages. Waiting until some suitable price was paid to acquire them."

His face seemed to lift. He was hoping. I continued quickly.

"So yes, it is possible. Yes, if you consider Dan Brown novels fact. If you believe in Ouija boards, in horoscopes, in magic crystals. Yes, in other words, if you see the rational world and are unable to accept it, because to believe in things that cannot be is the easier option."

"The bottle is glass," I said. "Wine would not have been stored that way, then. The shape also dates it from hundreds of years later. So you are having to accept that the wine would have been later decanted into this container. But regardless, wine that old would have long ago turned to sediment. You are looking for a hope I cannot give. This wine is not authentic."

Our business had thus concluded, and I stood up, and offered my hand. Roth did not take it. Not out of rudeness. He had simply stopped seeing me.

***

I have had no further contact with Casper Roth. Last week there was small piece in the *Times* business section about his resignation from EmeraldCore in order to care for his terminally ill daughter, but that was the last I heard.

But there is one final matter however, which I feel obliged to mention. Within days of my meeting with Roth, the scar that had been with me since childhood faded, and within a week had disappeared completely. That much I can accept, and put down to the fortuitousness of time. I do however recollect that spray of wine, which contacted my face over the scar and over my glass eye. More troubling is that when I opened my bedroom curtains last week, I felt a sharp shard of pain from the light that entered. In that same glass eye. Moreover, in the intervening days, I found, with a feeling of lurking horror, that that eye could make out shadows, and indeed, since yesterday, actual shapes.

I appreciate, of course, that there will be a … rational explanation for all of this. I am not impervious to diseases of the mind and I am sure that any competent psychologist could explain what is happening, or what I think is happening, in terms of some nervous hysteria or the like. But I find myself curiously reluctant to take that step. Further, I have taken to scrolling through the contacts in my phone, until I come to Roth's name. My finger hovers, then I put it away again, scolding myself for my weakness. But I still find myself thinking back to that evening, my mind gnawing and picking at the bones of what happened. I think of the blank, broken face of Roth. I think of the dying little girl I never knew. And I think of that strange bottle, of those curious patterns swirling underneath that warm glass. And I must … I must confess that I am troubled. Oh yes – yes indeed – I am troubled.

Last Day at the Archive
by Ian Plenderleith

Shortlisted, Scottish Arts Club Short Story Competition 2019

First, they send down the pallid teenage intern, late in the afternoon. As though this wasn't a big deal. A slightly scuffed and undersized navy-blue suit advertises his piteous virginity, hand shaking as he passes the written request through the small hatch in the Perspex shield that separates us. I scan it for a second. They want just a single page from the millions of documents behind me, but it must be securely sealed. The paper's appropriately stamped and signed, by the highest authority. I pass it back to him.

"We are not authorised to release original documents," I say. "I can only give you a copy."

He must know this, because he nods and turns away, but then he remembers what his superior said before he took the lift down. *Don't come back without it.* He turns around and approaches the counter for a second time. I have deliberately moved away and am pretending to be occupied with another piece of paper, which is in fact a flier that says, 'Special offer, takeout only – deluxe Sushi platter for £8.50!' I have plans for dinner.

He coughs, and I ignore him. "Excuse me," he says, and slowly I look up. "Sorry to disturb you again."

"Yes?"

"They told me that you could probably make an exception."

"Did they?"

He nods, perhaps hopeful that I will be sympathetic towards the unpaid summer hire endeavouring to make an impression.

"When I was your age," I say carelessly, "I spent my summers smoking weed and sucking on the bodies of any woman, or man, who'd give me the signal."

I look him in the eye through the divide and he winces, then looks down at his feet. He half-opens his mouth, but I know that he's nothing to say.

"There are no exceptions," I say. "They know that. And now you know that too. You're welcome."

His pout and suddenly wet eyes betray a scantling of anger and I hope that he can summon the dignity to swear at me before he leaves. Instead he pulls himself together and remains my subject. "Thank you," he mutters, and walks to the door that leads to the lift that elevates him back to the people who sent him down.

Eight minutes later (I time it), a young woman hurries through that same door, holding the same piece of paper. She is smart in every sense of the word. In my youth, the echo of her heels alone would have marshalled my obedience. She carries off a cracking smile and breezily announces, "Bloody intern, can't do anything right. Can you sort this for me? It's kind of urgent and we need to get it sorted before EOB."

Yes, I'm surely that stupid. A gust of Chanel, two breasts and a smile, and off I'd happily go. Handing it over with hope in my groin. It *is* nearly EOB. Fancy a drink in The Plumber's Pipe with a 47-year-old divorcee?"

"I can only give you a copy," I tell her. She's still trying to smile. "I think that you know this department is never authorised to hand over original documents."

"Yes, yes, of course," she says. "It's just that in this particular case, you know …"

She tails off. I know, but I look blank. "What?" I ask.

"Oh come on," she says. "You *know*."

"It's not relevant, whether I know," I reply. "Now please stop asking me to break the law and risk my job."

The smile and the false sexual promise are all gone. "Look …" she starts again. Then she gives up and mutters, "For Christ's sake," and leaves, less breezy now. I can still smell the Chanel.

Next comes the delegation. It's taken a further 17 minutes to summon a team of three. It's ten to six, and almost time for me to leave. The Archive used to be open until midnight, but the people now standing before me cut back the hours to save money. If my now redundant colleague Alan McCauley had been standing here, the problem would have been solved already. McCauley could be flexible when it came to meeting requests for original documents. Now he lives in Cyprus, watching the waves.

The intern and the perfume didn't work, so now I am faced with three well-tailored public servants of a certain age and an improved authority.

"As a matter of urgency and national security, we require the original copy of this document," says one, thrusting the now familiar paper through the gap. "Now."

"I am afraid that I am not authorised …"

"Now!" booms the second man. He is taller, thicker, with baby blond curls and an unnatural sneer. Rugby player. I can imagine how this played out upstairs. "Come on, Colin, you're a big chap. Come down and growl at this obstinate bugger."

"I am not authorised to release any original documents from the Archive."

The third public servant sighs, then comes forward with a condescending smile.

"It's Alan, isn't it?" he asks.

"No, sir. Alan McCauley was made redundant last March," I say. This throws him for a second. He'd obviously heard that McCauley would see you alright with a little soft compensation.

"And you are?"

"The assistant general manager of the Archive, sir."

"Yes, yes, but what's your name, man?"

"I am the assistant general manager of the Archive, sir," I repeat. His wiry, creviced face turns rubicund. "Look …" he begins again, but all of a sudden the rugby lad roars and throws himself head first at the divide, causing nothing but self-harm and a brief shudder of the reinforced window. He falls back on to the floor and his two colleagues attend to him briskly. They pick him up by the shoulders and carry him back out through the door. If I still had a sense of humour, I'd probably laugh.

It's now five minutes to six. I start to clean up my desk and to turn off the lights. At one minute to six, the phone rings. It's Ellen Giles, the Archive's director.

"Stay open until they come back down," she says. "Then give them what they want. I'll take care of the trail."

"I'd rather not, Ms Giles," I say. She has never asked me to do something like this before. I'm struck by a sinking desire to leave immediately and get drunk.

"I wouldn't normally ask you," she says. "I'm sorry. If I wasn't in Cardiff, I'd do it myself."

"It's strictly against the law …" I start, but she interrupts.

"Do it." Then she immediately hangs up, as though ashamed of her own command.

My colleagues forgot the document release order when they carried 'Colin' off for medical attention. I take a picture of it with my phone. Then I turn all the lights on again and walk briskly through the looming stacks of dead documents, most of which will never be read again, but many of which would disgrace the nation. I know exactly where to locate the single sheet of paper requested by the prime minister's office, because I already looked it out earlier this afternoon. I re-read it. It's short, but memorable. I break the law again by taking another picture with my phone, this time of the letter that the current prime minister sent to one of his constituents, 23 years ago, when he was a rowdy young backbencher.

I try to send the copy to myself by email, but as usual there's no signal down here. I'm about to take the letter and make a hard copy of it when the bell rings, very impatiently. Someone's back at the front desk. I replace the letter in its file. Now my hands are shaking like the intern's.

It started with a small item in the latest *Private Eye*, claiming that in the distant past the PM was known for writing letters to his constituents late at night when in a 'tired and emotional' state. In responding to a man who had complained about too many foreigners coming into the country, the honourable but upstart member for Tillington South had used numerous racial epithets no longer considered appropriate. The constituent's former wife was the source of the story, although she had no physical proof. The recipient himself, still loyal to his party of choice, denied any knowledge of such a letter. The magazine, though, knew that many members of parliament duplicate their correspondence for posterity, perhaps one day imagining their publication to an awed world. In the case of the current PM, this conceit had been carried through by his former secretary, despite the inflammatory content. So far, we as a government had stifled all its requests to see the letter that had been filed under the Freedom of Information Act. We were claiming that it did not exist.

On my phone I now have the evidence to bring down the most powerful man in the country. And behind the Archive's front desk stands this same most powerful man, unaccompanied. He's looking serious. Then when he sees me approach, he has the decency to wear an embarrassed smile.

"Awfully sorry to keep you late," he says. "Ridiculous business."

"Sir?"

"I was young and very, very stupid."

"We can all sympathise with that, sir."

"Indeed. Exactly. So glad you understand. Could we take care of it? Loyalty of course brings its own reward in the end."

"Loyalty to whom, sir?"

His face loses patience and subsides to a grimace. He has no idea how close I am to breaking. Power rubs off on me too. Right at this second I would love to put the PM out of his misery. To become his quick friend and trigger his oleaginous gratitude. A wink and a handshake and a future promotion. Why not? McCauley would have been in the pub by now, laughing up his sleeve.

I'm on the cusp of succumbing when he shouts, "For God's sake, man! Just one stupid bloody letter I was too shitfaced to know I'd even written. Can't you just …?"

I'm already pulling down the blind. "Sorry, sir, we're closed," I say, "but my colleague will be able to help you again tomorrow morning at eight." He thumps the screen and orders me to open up. He apologises, cajoles, then rages again. I record it all on my phone, then turn out the lights, lock up and leave.

As soon as I'm up at street level, I check for a phone signal. Because of all the high buildings around me the screen shows only a single, intermittent bar, so I start to walk towards the nearby park where I always eat my lunchtime sandwich. Or maybe I should get a cab straight to *Private Eye*? I almost break into a run, feeling more alive than I have for years, as though I could just float upwards to find better reception.

Then out of nowhere several large people block my path, including a bruised 'Colin', his two colleagues, and several policemen. "This is the man who hit me, officer," he says. My arms are yanked back and handcuffed, my phone falls to the ground, and two of the policemen push me towards a waiting, unmarked car, dictating my fading rights and charging me with assault. I protest and they ignore me. A struggle is pointless.

From the car I see 'Colin' retrieve my phone from the pavement as the others walk back into the building. He holds it up, then smiles. As the vehicle moves off he parodies a sad face and waves me goodbye.

Backtrack
by Richard Newton

Shortlisted, Scottish Arts Club Short Story Competition 2019

Fresh flakes will soften the clarity. The wind will sweep away the central scene. After the thaw, nothing will remain. For now, here it is for the reading. A story written in snow.

Legibility is meaningless without the particular literacy for tracks. These are not bookish eyes interpreting the mud-marbled imprints of two vehicles on a narrow, rising farm road. Set within a weathered face, they are attuned to the fleeting messages inscribed in the landscape. Farmer's eyes.

"Both going up, both coming back. This morning, looks like." He says, unselfconsciously. His sheepdog listens. Identifying no words to react to, the dog resumes his search for scents in the odourless snow.

The next words don't reach even canine ears. "Land Rover and a car. Thin tyres on the car. Not much grip." A short way up the road, the evidence shows that the car slithered to the brink of the snowbound verge before regaining purchase. The farmer nods in vindication.

The beginning of the story has fallen into place by the time he reaches the gate at the top of the road. He also has pieces of the ending.

So.

The car stopped short of the final incline. The Land Rover continued to the top, turning to park. One person stepped out. By the size of the prints, a man. He waited beside his vehicle, kicking his heels. Zigzag fragments of compacted snow are strewn over a small patch of tramped-down, crinkled ice.

The car apparently arrived later. The occupant walked up the road. Smaller prints. A hint of styling in the shape of the sole. A woman. The man walked down to greet her, then returned to the Land Rover while she waited. They walked in close step to the gate. They pulled it open, closed it, and continued on the public right of way.

The farmer ushers his dog through and clanks the rusty barrier shut. He requires no statutory right of access beyond the law of ownership. This is his gate, his land.

As the couple walked across the field, they scattered the sheep. Musky warmth still lingers here in the corner where the flock bedded down for the night in the lee of a limestone wall. The flattened snow is pitted with hoof prints and sullied with excretions and wisps of wool.

The couple's tracks overlay the ovine spoor. The churn of hooves radiates through the pristine snow of the downward slope to all parts of the field. The flock has since coalesced and settled in the valley.

The farmer scans for lone animals, and sees none. No broken legs to deal with. No lambs prematurely dropped in the stampede. From distance, he is satisfied that his flock is collectively plump and healthy; lambing is a fortnight away. He leaves them be, continuing his walk in ghostly company.

The couple's strides are firm, purposeful, youthful. Their prints faithfully trace the footpath concealed beneath the snowy blanket. They are close together, perhaps hand in hand. The farmer knows they didn't end that way. They left the field separately. When they drove down to the village, the Land Rover turned right. The car reversed, three-pointed at the bottom, and went left.

Was this a final assignation? The farmer is jolted by a reawakened memory. He had buried it in this field. He had conditioned himself to tramp over it without a second thought. For twenty years it lay beneath sight or feeling. Now it envelopes him.

A man and a woman walked hand in hand along the path. The air was textured with insects and pollen. The ground was hard. The two people left no mark on it. He and Kathy, that summer. For a dizzying moment, his experiences of this place conflate. The years of his lifetime meld. All seasons become concurrent.

Here he is playing cricket with his brother, just the two of them, with a pile of stones for stumps and the wall for a boundary. Here, in full flourish, are trees long since storm-toppled and chopped for firewood. Here are the snatches of view that have latterly been screened by the saplings he planted in haphazard batches during half a century. Here is the field ploughed for crops, and here at harvest. Here it is fenced for his herd of Herefords. Here it affords the open space for him to fly kites with his brother's young children. Here it adapts to the rigors of sheep. And here it is under snow, releasing its spectres.

He walks on, temporarily uncertain of which story he is following: a couple from this morning or a couple from two decades ago. The stories are interchangeable. A man and a woman entered the field together. They left separately.

The hidden path tacitly leads the fresh tracks down into a gully and up the other side. Centuries of farming and the deposits of weather are merely a veneer on this land. The dominant authority is geological.

Snow scrunches squeakily under the farmer's boots as he climbs the steep hill. Cold dampness seeps into his sock through the thorn-sized hole that punctured his right boot while clearing a hedgerow before the snow came. He huffs with effort that will be rewarded. It always has been. Almost always. He evades recollection of the one exception by looking for his dog. There he is, meandering happily in the gully.

Cresting the hill, walkers slow their stride, recover their breath, and accept their prize. The landscape tips its contours, providing a vista that spreads pleasingly in three directions. It is never the same view twice. Sometimes everything is blotted by mist, and he makes do with the knowledge of clearer days. Days like today, when he can see the church tower in Stow, ten miles away, and, eight miles over there, the rigid lines of Bourton's rooftops.

He once flattened rugs here and enjoyed summer picnics. The picnics ended twenty years ago.

It was an abrupt transition without design. He didn't recognise it at the time, but from one day to the next he switched from gregariousness to solitude. The instinctive retreat to the comfort of his own company became permanent. Paraphernalia of happier times was shunted into a barn, all of it now covered by a tarpaulin that has not been lifted for years.

It seems inevitable that the story of this morning's couple should hinge on this spot. This is where he stood with Kathy. He can visualise his hand reaching to her cheek, smoothing away a tear with his gnarled thumb.

"You're right," he said. "It's for the best." With that simple submission, he allowed a shadow to be cast over the rest of his life.

She left him here. He waited for an hour or more, staring blindly with his back to the view. There was no sign of her on the way home.

Not the slightest trace was etched for him, or others, to read. She evaporated from his life, and nobody knew. Villagers attributed the shift in his personality to financial trouble, or middle age. He retracted behind his own door, and no attempt was made to winkle him out. Communal life continued more or less without him.

Rooted in the past, he steers his attention back to the present, and to the tangle of the couple's tracks. They were here for a while. He can imagine the conversation. He recalls his own version of it word for word. Were there tears this time? Probably. Then they forged separate trails back to their vehicles.

The story has played out as he anticipated, exposing within him fissures of self-pity. He has learned over the past twenty years to smother his emotions, just as the snow now smothers the landscape. He expects no catharsis, no redemption. It is too late for that.

His right foot is uncomfortably wet. The leaden cold has breached his worn coat. He calls for his dog. "Brock!" There he is, down the slope, rolling in something. "Brock-boy! Heel!" Thus summoned, the sheepdog stops writhing, bolts to his feet, and trots to his master.

The farmer no longer gives any care to the couple's story. His course out of the field dissonantly weaves across theirs. It is the author's privilege. The narrative was his own composition, informed by personal prejudice. He interpreted the tracks. He imposed the meaning.

When he reaches the outlying houses of the village, he is safe once more under the carapace of solitude. He keeps walking when a neighbour, scraping her driveway clear, pauses to wave to him. He twitches his head by way of reciprocation. Undeterred, she starts talking. He is too close to pretend not to hear. "Was that Robert and Jane I saw driving past earlier?"

He stops to face her, slipping a hand under his flat cap to scratch his balding head. "Robert and Jane, you say? No. Haven't seen them."

"I was so sorry to hear the news. Such a difficult time for you all."

"It's life," says the farmer with a brusqueness that does not strike the neighbour as being in any way out of character. Another episode of rudeness will be added to the village's collective litany.

Back in his kitchen, the farmer strips his feet of boots and socks. His bare soles find little relief on the cold lino, which has served as the flooring since the 1960s. Most of the fixtures are of a similar vintage. The room reeks of fried breakfasts, working clothes, stale footwear.

The farmer absently hangs his coat on the back door. He is preoccupied by the exchange with the neighbour. So it was Robert and Jane up the field. His nephew and niece. Why there? Why today?

The funeral must have been last week. Phone calls from an elderly cousin had kept him informed, up to a point. He volunteered no questions. He betrayed no concern, no emotion. The cousin kept things brief.

In threadbare slippers, the farmer pads through to the sitting room, which is slightly more up-to-date than the kitchen, having been redecorated in the 1980s. "Brock!" The sheepdog is scratching himself on the rug in front of the fireplace, beating a cloud of fine dust from his coat.

Realisation is instantaneous. His brother's death. The two children meeting at the gate and hiking up the field, carrying something that Robert had retrieved from his Land Rover. Brock rolling in the snow, coating himself with the scattered contents.

It had been Edward's lifelong wish to end up there. It hadn't entirely gone to plan. Some of his ashes are now settling on a rug in the house he had vowed never again to enter. They catch in the throat of the brother from whom he had severed all contact.

The farmer can't help but smile. He sacrificed himself to lonely penury for the sake of his family. There had been no acknowledgement, no appreciation. He cut himself loose, and received nothing but contempt from his unforgiving sibling. And here is that sibling now, reduced to flakes of ash settling on the floor, like snow.

The medium of a story is immaterial. Whether it is told in words, tracks in the snow, or in a light dusting of human ashes, it exists only in the perception of others. In pure solitude, there are no new stories. Imagination atrophies. Emotion withers. Homes become frozen in time.

Released from two decades of purgatory, the farmer wastes no time. Familial duty has suppressed love for too long. The obligation has lifted. He picks up the phone, and for the first time in years he dials his brother's number. A familiar voice answers. The thaw begins with two words: "Hello, Kathy."

Gust in the Gusset
by Jo Learmonth

Editor's Choice, Scottish Arts Club Short Story Competition 2019
Longlisted, Scottish Arts Club Short Story Competition 2019

Ishbelle Mary was slumped on the kitchen table. Her expansive bosom spread like scone dough, amongst the breakfast crumbs. Absent- mindedly, she turned the clothes pegs over in the pocket of her sprig muslin pinny, staring into space as the wind whistled through the ill-fitting glazing and slammed rain against the window.

It was gone seven, the tea in her mother's Paragon teacup had long since gone cold and still she hadn't been out to peg the pants on the line.

Heaving herself up from the table, Ishbelle Mary stumbled a little as her bosom slid into place. She trailed her hand over the clothes in the untied bags as she made her way across the kitchen to the backdoor, the peculiar smell of black bags and washing powder comforted her. She pulled on a boucle coat from the nearest bag. It wasn't the ideal choice, what with the rain but there was life in it yet and the fit was better than she cared to admit.

Ishbelle Mary firmly knotted a checked headsquare under her chin and lifted the ancient serge pants from their hook. Three generations of Campbell women before her had hung these pants on the line at Gaothar for the daily gust in the gusset ritual, a weather predicting tool the family had come to rely on. For the past seven weeks, Ishbelle Mary had wearily shouldered the responsibility, hanging the pants out each morning gave her a little victory in her tussle with unrelenting apathy. Her character and stature were, under normal circumstances, like her shoes, stout, ideal for surviving and occasionally thriving in uncompromising conditions but this apathy was proving to be an unpleasant lingering bedfellow. As she emerged from the shelter of the house the wind worried at her headsquare and the rain stung her cheeks.

The clothesline was at the back of the croft house, strung parallel to the shore, to catch the air. Ishbelle Mary trudged along the sheep track through the heather and rocks and across the moss to the line.

Here on the most westerly island of the archipelago, wind was the dominant meteorological feature. The very reason why the ritual had evolved.

Ishbelle Mary pegged the substantial pants in the middle of the line and stepped back respectfully to watch their flight. She expertly assessed the angle. 38 degrees. Today would be a good day. Any angle of pant flap less than 90 degrees is a good day in the West.

The wind turbine's frantic whirring on the hill above the croft caught her eye. It must have been there a good two years now, no three; could it really be three years?

It was, she remembered now, it had been that Hogmanay, how could she have forgotten? She'd been home from Glasgow and the possibility of putting up a wind turbine was the talk of the village. Campbell hill, their hill was, it transpired, the most suitable site for it. Her mother had railed against it from the outset; she hated the idea of the turbine looming over the croft, its long flickering shadows probing right into the house. Ishbelle Mary had eventually persuaded her to let the project go ahead but not without some ferocious rows that knocked the wind out of them both. Ishbelle Mary now regretted her lack of patience, ashamed by the way she'd dismissed the elderly woman's concerns. She'd behaved badly and that was that. Tears stung the back of her eyes.

The wind turbine was part of the fabric of the place now, generating power to pump water from the loch up to a header tank which supplied the whole village. Her mother had no truck with this alchemy of wind and water and resolutely continued to draw water from the loch every morning, hirpling down the track with her wooden bucket until she was well into her dotage. The taste, she proclaimed, was far superior.

The screeching of gulls wheeling overhead startled Ishbelle Mary and brought her reminiscing to an end. Oh what a calamity, the hazards of living on the coast. Guano slid slowly down the pants' navy-blue shirring and into the moss below. Ishbelle Mary's gusset had been sullied. It was sure to need a boil wash now. She pulled the tainted briefs from the line and stomped back into the house cursing those birds.

The very thought of boiling the guano-covered pants and the accompanying smell of herring it would bring made Ishbelle Mary shudder. She held the pants behind her back in the hope that would delay the rank smell wafting into her flaring nostrils. It didn't; she boaked.

A good soaking, that's what was needed. Mentally running through all the containers, she would be willing to sacrifice for such a purpose, Ishbelle Mary drew a blank. The stench hit her again, galvanising her into action. She rushed through to the bathroom, lifted the lid on the toilet cistern and unceremoniously dumped the pants in. The ideal place. With each flush the water would be changed and the guano would be washed away in no time. Ishbelle Mary was gleeful she had happened upon the perfect solution.

The last time she could remember the gusset being sullied was that Hogmanay three years before, when she had gone bird watching with Donald John. The invitation had been unexpected. They'd got chatting at Willie the Boat's, where most of the village had gathered for a ceilidh. Separately they had made their way to the front room, to escape the singing. It was only themselves in there so chatting had been required but thankfully, not a song. Despite no interest whatsoever in birds, Ishbelle Mary had accepted his offer of a walk to the cliffs at Ness, keen to be away from her mother for a while.

Surprisingly, the day had been glorious; just the two of them, amidst the maelstrom of skirling birds. She was sure she'd seen a Shag on the horizon.

Even now, the slightest whiff of rubberised waterproofs took her straight back to that day. It had been romantic, Ishbelle Mary was sure of that, hadn't Donald John brought a picnic? Thick slices of black bun left over from Hogmanay. She had taken a wee ginger bottle full of her homemade blaeberry gin. It stained their lips and loosened their tongues. Although her legs were cocooned in three layers of outdoor garb, Ishbelle Mary had been acutely aware that she was touching Donald John as they lay on the sparkling gneiss.

Donald John. Donald John MacIver. The very mention of Ishbelle

Mary's neighbour made her cheeks glow like the slap of sleet in a south-westerly.

Donald John ran, cycled and laughed through her earliest memories, assuming a lead role in what, in reality, was only a bit-part. He was a couple of years older of course, the same age as Angus and Jamie. As children they'd run wild over the shore and the hill, before self-consciousness descended abruptly. Ishbelle Mary could still see the shadow of the boy although Donald John was well through his fifties now. He was tall and straight-backed with just a smattering of hair and all his own teeth. Unlike Ishbelle Mary and her brothers, Donald John had never left, content with life on his piece of land between sea and the sky.

Ishbelle Mary stared wistfully out of the rain streaked windows, across the peat hags to Donald John's in-bye, hoping for a glimpse of him, or even Tess his collie would suffice. Some other living thing. She missed the stir and the possibilities Glasgow had proffered and now seriously regretted the fact that she had partaken in precious few.

The view from the window reminded her of a badly executed watercolour painting where tiny hints of colour bleed together into a sweep of muddied brown. Today an unfamiliar block of colour stood out; bright red, a van, the Post van. Surely Donald John must be having a delivery. Elspeth the Post was parked by the byre again.

Next morning Ishbelle Mary lay late in bed, loathe to face another day. She was contemplating the intricacies of the spider's web in the greying lace trim of the lampshade when a loud rap at the door scattered her thoughts. Ishbelle Mary threw the warm eiderdown aside, mortified she'd been caught having a lie in. She keeked round the side of her curtains, wiping a swathe of condensation from the window with her sleeve: Donald John was standing outside her porch.

Ishbelle Mary quickly rummaged in the bottom drawer and extracted a bold blue jumper with the word FABULOUS emblazoned across the front in a jaunty orange. She whipped it on, over the top of her winceyette nightie, and made for the porch.

She took a moment to arrange herself in an alluring manner amongst the damp waterproofs and wellies, her heart thumping so hard that she felt certain that Donald John would hear. Ishbelle Mary knew her moment had come. She opened the door.

"Oh, it's yourself Donald John, good morning to you" she breathed.

"Have you water?" he demanded. This was not the opening gambit she had been hoping for.

"What?" Asked Ishbelle Mary, sure she'd misheard.

"Have you water in your taps?" Donald John tried to make his question crystal clear, rather like the missing water.

"Well, I'm sure I don't know Donald John, I'm just this minute out of bed." For Ishbelle Mary, the atmosphere was electric, sparks were flying. Indeed they were. The stiff breeze coming in at the door was rubbing her winceyette nightie on a cagoule, creating a static storm to rival the aurora borealis.

Years of stifled emotions and pent up lust threatened to overwhelm Ishbelle Mary but oblivious to anything other than a slight fire hazard, Donald John broke the moment.

"Aye and the pants aren't out. Elspeth says she'll not be knowing what strength of hairspray to use. If she ever gets her shower that is."

Ishbelle Mary's eyes narrowed. Elspeth the Post. Elspeth the bloody Post. So Donald John was availing himself of the comprehensive range of services the Western Isles postal service offered. Slowly Ishbelle Mary intertwined her fingers and rested them across her bosom. She composed herself, by inhaling deeply, before replying, "Oh, why now that I think of it, Donald John, I have plenty of water thank-you, it's a pity you have none yourself." The trace of a wry smile flickered across her lips.

Without giving him a chance to respond she shut the door and went through to the kitchen. Picking up her mother's boucle coat she buried her face in it and sobbed, quietly at first.

It was gone seven by the time she'd pulled herself together. The weather-predicting pants were still in the cistern. Ishbelle Mary went through to the bathroom. She heard the water before she saw it. Looking out the small square panes of glass in the bathroom window she could see a torrent of water cascading from the overflow down the outside wall.

She lifted the lid of the cistern and saw the pants draped over the ballcock, wedging it down. No wonder there was no water.

She gently replaced the cistern lid and went to look for her mother's wooden bucket. There were definitely still traces of guano there, the pants would need to soak a while longer, a good while longer.

A Very Anxious Case
by William Neilson

Longlisted, Scottish Arts Club Short Story Competition 2019

Bewigged, bothered, and bewildered, here we are, scrambled like fighter pilots, me in the chair, first time in all my years as a senator, Davie on my right, solid fellow, and on the left-wing that whippersnapper, what's-his-name, youngest ever on the Bench, but keen … A last-minute scratch team.

Have barely had time to read the papers. Brothel-keeping, procuring, knocking-shop … appeal against conviction and sentence … Have heard a lot about the madam, face a shade familiar, yet not intimate with the premises myself… Seventy, according to the sheriff's note, widowed, well preserved.

Only an 'extra' division, mind you, raked up at the last minute by the clerk, trawling judges' rooms, head round the door, phone calls at bedtime, twisting arms in the car park this very morning; usual excuses: cases overrunning, 'flu … Better make the most of it. Never likely to attain the regular First or Second now. Packed with neophytes.

Father would have been proud, though, if only for the day. Once occupied this very seat himself. Dreamt of a judicial dynasty, but our son Jack put paid to that. Went to the bad. Girls, boys, drugs. Worry and shock finished his mother off. Good thing the old man didn't live to see it.

Never mind, perhaps an undeclared pre-marital scion, sired in my callow youth, has somewhere, sometime, gained his spurs. Strait-laced parents, girl's father a 'very reverend', preferred to send her away … unhappy at prospect of progeny scarcely six months into shotgun wedlock. Like that in the 'fifties. Short-back-and-sides decade. And she was happy to go. Scorned my entreaties. Last saw her on a tram heading for the station.

Abortion, still birth, full term, boy, girl? Never heard another word.

Best forgotten. Flighty besom, younger then than the delectable Miss Fairpoint, representing the appellant today I see, properly dressed, as the Dean demands, in a kinky variation of the male attire. Hair off the ears, swept up behind her virgin, snow-white wig. Black stockings, not visible below her gown of course, mere surmise, but definitely something on suspenders.

"If your Lordship pleases ... represent appellant ..."

Sensible enough, I suppose, to instruct a female if you're a madam. Sisterhood, all girls together.

No wonder the lady's appealing. Standard disposal, judging by her previous, seems to have been a monetary penalty every six months or so, meekly borne and set off against the tarts' earnings. Thought there was a tacit agreement on that ... turn a blind eye ... worth it to keep them off the streets. Mind you, 71 Rhine Gardens, engraved in the standing orders of every battle fleet in the Western Hemisphere ... US sailors queuing at the door. Not popular with the local *nomenklatura*. Constabulary has to do the needful now and then.

"My very learned friend, the Lord Advocate, has had a word with me. Happy to concede the right of first address ..."

Fairpoint is exceedingly deferential.

... big gun booming on my lower right ...

Lord Advocate in person, preaching *ex tempore*, thumbs in waistcoat, now we're for it. Only in Caledonia. What other nation on earth has its chief Law Officer appearing in a case like this? Treason, espionage, terrorism, yes, but keeping a bawdy house? Better let him go first. Otherwise the lovely Fairpoint lisps a few sweet submissions, hardly worth noting, and then we have the LA boring on into the afternoon. Difficult time that, especially on a Friday – post-prandial narcolepsy – martyr to it.

"Your Lordships, thought it would be helpful, in my capacity as Senior Law Officer, if I were to open, review the law pertaining, in a totally impartial manner of course ..."

"Your client happy with this arrangement, Miss Fairpoint?"

The Madam herself nodding acquiescence, not to her legal team, but to the Bench direct. Sly old biddy. Seems to have her eye on me.

"Very well, Lord Advocate. We shall hear you first."

Pen in hand, hovering over my jotter, eyes down, open, shut, or half-roads over, no-one will ever notice. Should be able to stay awake, it's only quarter to eleven.

Here's the usher now, struggling up to the Bench with a weighty tome for each of us. King James version … pulpit size … Deuteronomy, Leviticus … All three desert faiths so hard on fornication, can't blame them: tribes wandering the wilderness … food, water in short supply … wouldn't want a baby boom.

… flip through my copy and pretend to read …

What's up with Davie, ripping the pages in his haste to find the reference? Been rather jumpy all morning ... broke his pencil, in two pieces … bit of a sweat on … sickening for 'flu by the look of it. The Madam is eyeing Davie, as though confirming something. And as I look down, she looks up, at me again. Something's afoot. Can't guess what.

The Advocate's speaking up for the madam's peevish neighbours (all great, or good, goes without saying, nary a pimp, ponce, or pander among them), their evidence a hilarious farrago for some, but not your average prune-faced burgher. Reported verbatim in the press, well almost, lots of asterisks, family newspapers.

Hallelujah! Winding up, at last …

"May it please your Lordships, that concludes my submission, unless perhaps I can be of further assistance."

Amen! Please God young what's-his-name doesn't put some question. Speak quick and don't give him the chance.

"Thank you, Lord Advocate. We have listened with great interest. So much law in the *Good Book*. Justiciary Cases, Law Reports …, all redundant. Time for a spot of lunch. Back at 1.45."

… halfway to my feet …

"If your Lordship pleases …"

The delicious Fairpoint straining her suspenders again, clutching a note.

"I have to inform your Lordships that I must withdraw from the appeal. The appellant wishes to forego our services. She insists on addressing the court herself."

Davie's wriggling in his seat, and it's not piles.

Now the madam's on her feet.

"I shall address the court, I know what I have to say, and I shall say it."

That voice … Determined type. Davie turning purple. Young what's-his-name all agog. Better get off the Bench *pdq*. Thank God it's lunchtime and the usher's holding the door open.

"Very well, madam, but we shall rise now."

God knows what the madam intends to say this afternoon. No chance of her arguing the law … well-enough settled long before the Advocate's sermon this morning, but the sentence? Could be more than a simple plea for leniency.

In the clear myself. Since Jack then his mother died, never bothered much. Changed days when contemplation supplants consummation and is satisfying enough. But what's up with Davie? He and his wife seem happy together, still eager for each other, rushing home early from parties and the like, so I've heard.

Davie the Orphan. Rescued from a London orphanage by an elderly couple, long since deceased … Best education money could buy, just like son Jack, but Davie did well, a First at Oxford, then Edinburgh to tack on some Scots law, glittering career at the Bar, now on the Bench, never seen him looking as leery as this before.

"We've got ten minutes Davie, let's take a turn in the Hall, mustn't talk shop in the mess."

Get in step, unrobed, de-wigged, tail-coated, black beetles rearing on hind legs, parading under a lofty hammer-beam ceiling, stout receptor of many a secret swirling around its ancient rafters … nice sight for the tourists. Photography strictly prohibited of course.

"Not a patron of that palace of varieties in Rhine Gardens are you, Davie?"

"She's my mother! I'm sitting on my own mother's appeal!"

Almost broke step there. Davie must have 'flu … fever … delirium. About turn … pick up the step … not easy the way Davie is … traipse back towards the Great Window … stained glass … nice colours. Guide books on sale at the desk.

"It's true. Long after the old couple died, I tried to trace my natural parents. No evidence of the father – unrecorded – but the mother's trail led to number 71, and the only one on the premises old enough? Her ladyship!"

"A desperate business, Davie!"

"Couldn't face it, never made contact, never saw her even, until this morning."

Should have stood down of course, declared an interest, but how could he? Find a familiar litigant before you, own a *tranche* of shares in his corporation, or your brother-in-law's on the Board of Directors, declare, withdraw, pat on the back, impartial judiciary, and so on, but what would the prattlers make of a declinature in an appeal by the local Madam?

"Sure about this, Davie?"

Redundant question. Proof's in the pudding. See it now … always a touch of the Levant about Davie's nose – not Jewish, mind, just a hint of Araby. The madam has the same characteristic, and skin, a sexy tint of olive, just like Davie. Thought he got it on his yacht, brings back memories.

"The Clerk caught me coming in the door this morning. No time to get up an excuse, and there's none I could have offered. You know what the gossip's like in this place. Sweetie-wives, every one of us."

"Davie, you can't be party to sending your own mother to jail!"

"That's why she's dismissed her counsel. Wants to show me up. Shame me! Claim me! Probably call me 'Sonny'."

And the way she gimleted my learned self this morning, which term of endearment might she reserve for me?

"Davie, tell me something, what's your date of birth?"

"Second of March 1954: just done, as they say, the big Five-O."

That settles it. Coronation night plus 39 weeks! Black and white television, nine-inch screen, seven-hour ceremony, bored to lust by the end of it.

No call for DNA. Family affair. Break step, lead the crumbling Davie back to the robing room, *tout de suite*.

"Davie, I know what we have to do this afternoon, won't take five minutes."

"Resignation for me. Fall on my sword."

"Not at all. Panic uncalled for. Shoulder to shoulder!"

"What about our recently elevated young colleague?"

"He'll concur, like it or not, saw him loitering with intent outside number 71 when he was a Junior. That's what I'll whisper in his ear anyway. Ask the usher to fetch Fairpoint out of the Library, tell her to tip off the appellant. No need for anyone to address the court. I'll do the talking."

Everybody in place … the madam quietly triumphant … Davie searching the ceiling for cobwebs, young what's-his-name putting on petted lip … time he learned there's more to law than the letter of it … Lord Advocate complacently awaiting routine ruling in his favour … little does he know …

Here goes …

"Uphold the conviction …"

… Advocate preening himself .

"With regard to sentence, recognising that the appellant, according to the trial evidence, treats her young ladies in non-exploitative fashion, enabling them to provide, in a safe environment, an economic service …"

… squalls of righteousness on my lower right …

"… much appreciated by tourists, presbyterial delegates, MSPs, and our gallant navy … substitute an absolute discharge."

"You mean, you're going to let her walk!"

Bit colloquial that for a senior law officer …

"Certainly! Not a stain on the lady's character! Well, nothing new."

… strolling down the Mound …

"Davie, I'm sending your mother a discreet invitation to lunch at my place this Sunday. Bring the wife. It's high time she met your people – both of us together."

Strange, the way talent runs in families, after all. Father would be pleased.

I am.

The Hat
by Cameron Roach

Longlisted, Scottish Arts Club Short Story Competition 2019

She was sat there, just three pews up. Middle of the pew. Just making sure she was noticed with her fine hat on. It was almost as wide as her forced smile, but not quite. That smile had a vast radius of its own. She would look along each row on her way down the aisle, nodding to this side and that, smiling more and more as she neared her seat at the front. Not smiling to anyone in particular; just a general nod of the head to let us all see that she was there. Each week the chosen hat getting more and more grand, wider and wider.

There were no reserved seats. However, she had somehow managed to gradually work the others out of the front pew. The old dear who is hard of hearing now pushed to the end of the row. This poor soul was now almost covered entirely behind the pillar, cricking her neck this way and that, trying to read the Reverend's lips as she got the odd glance of him moving back and forth.

Retired Dr and Mrs. Smith, both with their leg ailments, no longer enjoying the roominess that the front pew had to offer their aged legs as they too, now pushed to the end of the second pew. They were very gracious in defeat. Never seen to complain and always having the dignity to rise above it. They would even chat as the sermon was ended and they would smile warmly at her. Inside of course, they would be like me, got the measure of that one alright.

Today's sermon was no different. The Hat nodding along with the Reverend like one of those toy dogs on the car dashboard. Not actually taking in what was being said, but eager to be seen to be listening. I watched her as she arrived in the church yard. Holding onto the hat as it blew in the wind as if her very life depended on it. I couldn't put an age to her, as you didn't get to look at her squarely on the face, always slightly downward looking avoiding direct eye contact. Large dark glasses, almost Jackie Onassis style. They are all the rage these days. No need for them of course, just for show.

The rotund woman, who was sat directly behind her in the second pew, was having similar trouble to the old dear. Having to adjust the angle of her head to see around The Hat in front. Today we were also honoured with a matching tweed poncho, just three quarters length, the lower arm and hands just visible. Tweed gloves no less. It was difficult to see where the collar ended and the hat began. She had also brought with her a floral, ladies walking stick. Very countrified indeed. She was almost neckless today as she took the seat and you got a back view. Almost Christmas-tree-like in shape and the hat was shining away as the light shone through the large side window. The Hat tilted to avoid the glare and she would lean to one side, as if the tree ensemble would suddenly balance over.

At the gathering of the collection, The Hat would stand. Looking around her rather grandly lifting the head this way and that. She would raise her neck and look down on those beside her, almost giraffe like as it watched over the land, ears slightly pricking. That should be enough time now for everyone to notice her. Just as collection was gathered and offered up to the alter, the Reverend would look over and she would take her seat. We are truly blessed to be in her company.

Indeed, she had still managed to arrive in the Church yard early today, to get the first car parking space right beside the door. Always managed to be last in though, to make sure that her arrival was noted. Handel's *Arrival of the Queen of Sheba* would play over in my mind as The Hat glided down the aisle. Reverend Jones, much like Doctor Smith always having a kind smile for her, despite inwardly wanting to snatch the glasses from her forehead and urinate on her hat.

Six weeks I've been coming here; and I've got The Hat's card marked for her already. She won't be fooling anyone. They'll be sat here like me, watching it. I've seen her like before you know. Saw them in all the previous churches I've attended. In fact, I've never seen such an unworthy in my life, Lording over the rest of us. Next week I'm taking her seat.

It was a pleasurable feeling as I parked my car just by the Church entrance, almost ninety minutes before the service began. Eventually, the others peering in the car on their way in, as the congregation started to arrive. I looked out and smiled, nodding my head. I knew they were pleased for me, having had the courage to make a stand for the rest of us. Disappointingly, I'd had to miss her arrival in the churchyard so that I could take her place in the front pew. I could imagine her horror as she arrived, looking eagerly for a space to park where the rest of us had to squeeze in, almost door to door.

I could see Doctor and Mrs. Smith just ahead and I smiled warmly as I took my seat in the pew at the front. They were both almost aghast. Indeed, The Reverend was almost taken aback when he saw me. I am sure they too, will be just as intrigued as the rest of us, to see The Hat's reaction when it arrived. I couldn't see her. She would be pushed in somewhere up the back of Church, having to slum it with the others. I could hear the mumblings behind me, feeling rather pleased that they could all see what I had done today, to put her in her place.

I looked at today's sermon on the pamphlet. Today was slightly out of odds with the usual seasonal readings and hymns. The Reverend was almost teary as he began today. We had lost a dear friend to the Church. Someone, who had taken so much time in her own life to spread the word of God around the world. She had so enjoyed her time as a missionary on the continent, helping our Church over the years, developing fresh water supplies and delivering much needed clothing and medicines to the needy. It seems medicine was in the blood, so to speak. Dear Doctor Smith has not only lost a beloved sister, herself a qualified doctor, but an inspiration to us all.

The Reverend told how the congregation had all been thrilled to vote her in as the Churches representative abroad and it was with some reservation and anticipation that she took on the role. She had given up most of her early life to work on the continent. Never had a single person been so loved and had in fact given up her opportunity of love and family life here at home, to take on her role abroad. She was a natural fit.

Life brings with it, its challenges along the way explained the Reverend. It was upsetting to us all to see the toll that her condition had taken on her. She was in pain daily as the muscle degenerating condition took hold. Gradually losing the ability to walk or sit for lengthy periods. Often having to stand each week to get a little breather, as we took collection. Wonderful that everyone was so kind as to leave a place for her outside to get as close to the Church door as possible and knowing that it would take her some time to be able to remove herself from the car to get the strength to walk and take her seat. Doctor and Mrs Smith liked to have her beside them, to keep an eye on the old girl he would say. It gave her plenty of leg room sat up front as even in her weakest moments and darkest days, she would ensure that she hadn't missed a sermon.

Of course, the deterioration of her sight hit everyone hard. Even the slightest of glare caused her failing eyesight such pain as the degenerative condition progressed. She had of course lost all feeling in her face and was always in acute pain. Embarrassed that the condition left her head nodding and her shoulders hunched. We would joke in the evenings at her home that she looked as if she were preparing for a fight as she stretched this way and that to keep comfortable during sermon.

She used to joke, lovingly, that this building was so cold despite all the warmth and love in it. In fact, she had taken to almost covering herself entirely, during service. Reverend Jones would say that he may indeed come in one day to find her in her artic sleeping bag if only the hats she wore to stem the glare, would allow it.

The congregation laughed aloud. It was said that her sense of humour was a joy to all. Next week they will be having a celebration of her life, here in this church, where she had paid from her own pocket for repairs to the roof, so the least we could do was hear the sermon without the constant dripping of water.

At the end of service, there would be something special today just to mark her place in our hearts. As the congregation knows, this is a task that we all love to carry out for those who mean so much to our family here in the church. A gentle reminder of what they have given in life.

I struggled to focus on the Reverend for a while as the old dear at the end of the pew glared at me in the most curious way. At collection time, I put my envelope in the basket along with everyone else's. Although naturally, I made sure that it was done sufficiently so, that others would see that it was rather a full envelope I had dropped into the plate.

As the sermon was nearing an end, The Reverend beckoned me over and asked if I would stand beside him for a little moment. Of course, I looked over everyone, and nodded to them. Smiling this way and that. A blur of faces that you cannot easily see as the light gets you here in the front row. I tilted my head slightly down to one side, to take the glare from my eyes. I knew I must be getting introduced to the Church as its newest member.

I watched as the faces in the second row became more visible and was surprised to see the old dear and Dr and Mrs. Smith arrive before me with a beautiful bouquet. The Reverend thanked me for standing a moment and there at that very moment as I went to put my hands forward to collect the flowers, they were laid on the pew where I'd sat. Doctor Smith himself fitted the small plaque to the seat I had taken, marking his dear sisters place.

It was a simple inscription. In memory of our dear friend May Smith. "Please enjoy this seat, there are no reserved seats in Gods House." There followed a rousing round of applause. The Reverend said how touched May would be to see that the new member had taken her seat today. She would have hoped it brought her much love.

Of course, as I left church today, I realised that I rather much preferred the look of the new church on High Street in the next town. I've not been before, but from what I've heard said, it's all right, but for one or two of the congregation.

Lumbering
by Melissa Stirling Reid

Longlisted, Scottish Arts Club Short Story Competition 2019

It's a quarter past four in the afternoon when Mrs Irene McManus of 5 Applewood Road settles herself, ankles crossed, towards the back of the bus. She stepped in a puddle of ice-lolly outside and now the underbellies of her cream 'comfort-fit' loafers make little sticking, smacking sounds whenever she moves her feet.

"Record temperatures sweep the nation!" the young man's newspaper in front reads. "Sunbathers warned to 'beware the rays!"

And indeed, what fine weather they've been enjoying today! This bus – perfumed with the aroma of stale sweat and orange-scented sun lotion – is almost full-to-capacity and (as it clicks and hisses into motion) Mrs Irene McManus feels a certain tug of pleasure in knowing that nobody here will even remember having seen her.

"Naw, it's impossible," the bus driver – a hairy, pork-faced man – will say when asked later on, "*im*possible to pick out any particular face from the hoards I drive about. Holiday weekend as well, mate. No can do."

His clientele consists of free-riding white-haired biddies like herself, after all. So, it's understandable, indeed expected, that they all blend into one another after a few months on the job. What is wee Irene McManus – dressed in blue-polka dots – among this vast sea of ancients?

Reaching into her pocket, Irene retrieves a lemon bonbon (the packet crinkling) and, when she pops it into her mouth – a spot of powdery yellow sugar brushing against her top lip – she is alarmed to detect a certain fishy scent about her fingertips.

Salmon! she recalls, ah yes, of course.

She'd been washing a filet of salmon under the tap earlier on today – this was about ten past one – rinsing its gleaming pinkness of unwanted smells when Alan, her balding son, had arrived in her kitchen.

"Hi Mum," he'd said, kissing the top of her head, "we're taking you out to Largs for the day. Go put your shoes on."

Alan rarely rings the doorbell when he visits. He just walks right in like he still lives at home. And indeed, Irene supposes, why should he not? He did grow up in her house, after all. In fact, she only recently took down his posters from the spare room – so faded, were they, from five decades of sun.

"I'll take care of this," Alan had said, scooping the fish out of her hands and giving her a slight nudge. "Gerri's waiting in the car and we don't want to get caught in the lunchtime rush."

"Isn't it *gorgeous*, Mummy!" Geraldine – the daughter-in-law – had yelled while Irene was deposited beside her in the back seat (Alan had insisted on fastening Irene in and he patted her knee before closing the door). "Isn't it a *wonderful* day for a jaunt to the seaside! We thought we'd take you a little run, you know, to get you out the house!"

Geraldine was wearing a set of large purple sunglasses which consumed most of her face – some feat, really, for it wasn't a small face – and Irene had smiled, at the time, at how they made the woman look like a giant talking beetle.

"And *how* could I forget!" Geraldine shouted as Alan reversed out the path. "Mummy," she yelled, motioning to a figure Irene hadn't noticed in the passenger seat, "say hello to Trevor!"

"Afternoon," came a crackled voice from the front of the car, and a cock-eyed old man peeked round the headrest and grinned at Irene. "Pleased t'make your acquaintance."

"He's our pal for the day – in't that right, Trev? – so he'll be joining us for lunch!"

When Irene examined "Trevor" through her spectacles, she observed a thick layer of breadcrumbs buried deep inside his beard. The collar of his shirt was slightly skew-whiff.

"Gerri's part of a buddy scheme at the community centre now, Mum," Alan explained from behind the steering wheel. Irene looked up to see his eyes (blue, like his father's, god-rest-his-soul) smiling at her inside the rear-view mirror.

"It's a befriending group for the lonely and infirm!" Geraldine yelled. "*He'd* like a bit of company –" and she kicked Trevor's seat with her flip-flop, "– and I just *love* helping people. So, it's a win-win situation, in't it Trev?"

Even sitting here now – on this bus, rumbling far away from the seaside, fields and fields of sheep flashing past – Irene can't entirely rid her nostrils of the memory of Trevor's breath: the way it hung like a sticky cloud of soured milk in the car, only dissipating when Alan opened a window.

Someone has just opened a window on this bus, and a small gust trickles in. It rustles the pages of the newspaper in front and a few strands of Irene McManus' fine white hair tickle the back of her neck as they slip out of her bun.

Traffic earlier had been *atrocious* – or so Geraldine kept exclaiming at random interludes – so by the time they arrived at Nardini's – "Look, Trev! A Knickerbocker Glory!" – they'd had to queue for close to an hour and were then forced to knock knees under a poky table in the middle of the room. Oh, it *was* a busy place, that café, and so noisy! Cutlery rattling, footsteps thumping, there was even a pianist playing at the front: an old guy in a tux who kept glancing around and grinning while he tinkled showtunes on the keys.

"Do you have a kid's menu, or something like that?" Alan had asked the waitress when she showed them their table. "The real portions will be bigger than you are, Mum," he said to Irene, squeezing her hand. "Only eat what you feel up to, okay?"

Alan, or so she has always thought, is Irene's *kindest* child – the one who stuck around while his brothers and sister all settled overseas. Irene brushes a little speck of dust out her eye with the back of her finger. It is about ten to five in the evening now, and the bus judders along, having finally reached the motorway.

"Mummy!" Geraldine kept screaming throughout lunch. "Mummy!" waving a video camera in Irene's face, "Mummy, look at the camera!"

Irene had looked to Alan, but he was busy wrestling with a sauce bottle, his sunburnt head glistening from the exertion.

"This ketchup," he had erupted, "is a bloody nuisance!" He shook the bottle violently. He tapped the glass with his spoon.

"I've got you on video Mummy!" Geraldine's voice rang out. "Quick, say something interesting, Mummy! Look! Look over here!"

"I've been having a dreadful bought of diarrhoea, lately," Trevor announced to anyone who might be listening. "In fact, if you'll just excuse me –"

"Look at the camera, Mummy! I'm making a video Mummy!"

Irene had closed her eyes at this point. The whole thing was too much to bear.

"Ohhh, she's worn out, Alan," she could hear Geraldine whispering. "And as deaf as a doorknob, she is Alan. As deaf as an *absolute* doorknob."

Oh yes, Mrs Irene McManus is deaf alright. It's been diagnosed. After decades of insisting her hearing loss was simply the 'residue from a bad cold', she has finally conceded this is yet another ailment she cannot bounce back from. If, however, over the years Irene has created the impression that she is just a *little* deafer than is actually the case, it's never been meant as a *lie* exactly. More of a – she twitches her lip – more of an *exaggeration*. A coping mechanism, as it were. A little trick to pull out her sleeve in moments of need.

Irene hadn't actually *meant* to fall asleep. The plan was just to 'garner a little courage', as Alan's father, god-rest-his-soul, would have put it. But – well, these things happen, and it must have been half an hour later when a sharp laugh near her left ear startled Irene awake. She'd opened her eyes to discover that the lunch dishes had been cleared. There was a murmur of conversation around the table and she realised – squinting through her glasses – that they were all now leaning over their wicker seats to talk to some dark-haired woman at the next table – a stranger apparently – about what topic, Irene couldn't make out.

"–and it's not that we *mind* exactly," Geraldine was in the middle of saying. "I've often said to Alan – haven't I, Alan? I've often said it – that some folks get their kicks from drugs and online shopping. Where *I* get mine from making people smile.'

They were eating ice-creams now – the lot of them – no one having thought to wake Irene up. And there they all were – this stranger woman, Geraldine and Alan, and lonely-and-infirm Trevor smiling on like a garden gnome – there they all were talking, while Irene had been asleep.

"– such a great job you're doing," the stranger was saying now, one arm stretched over the back of her wicker chair. "And *how* old, did you say?"

"Ninety-one," Alan said, and – "ah!" – Irene realised they were talking about her.

"She's fantastic of course," Alan went on, sundae spoon held mid-air, "a real trooper," he said. "But you know how it is," and he let out an exasperated laugh, sticking the spoon into his ice-cream, "we've only just got rid of the children, and now here we are: *lumbered* with the parents! So much for luxury cruises, eh?"

They'd all laughed, a little titter going around the table. And Irene had blinked, a crease forming between her brows. They were all laughing – the stranger, with Geraldine and Alan, and even the old fart Trevor. Laughing. And when Irene clamped her eyes shut again, their voices merged into one cacophonous roar.

The bus purrs to a stop as the driver pulls over. She sees him watching her while she stumbles towards the door.

"Alright, love!" he says, the bus lowering, and Irene thanks him with a wave of her withered hand.

Where are they now – she muses, stepping onto the pavement, turning to watch the bus rumble around the corner – are they still in that busy café? Still sitting there, so patiently, waiting for her to return from the 'ladies'?

She shuffles along Applewood Road – her shoes sticking and smacking the pavement.

No doubt they've sent old Trevor off in a taxi by now, his loneliness no longer to be pitied, his constant toilet-stops merely an annoyance now, slowing them down while they scour the stony beach. She should feel mildly grateful towards him, she supposes as sun touches her face (she tilts her head to the sky, feeling the warmth of it on her cheek, the curve of her neck, her jut of her collarbone) – grateful to old Trev for unwittingly alerting her to that little side door, just beside the café toilets.

"Such a cool air," he had said to Geraldine, his blazer creaking when he moved. "Such a cool, cool air came in through that door."

It is about twenty to six when Mrs Irene McManus – missing, feared dead – settles herself in a deckchair out the back. Her neighbours, when asked later on, might recall hearing a small laugh coming from her garden, and the scent of barbequed salmon hanging sweetly in the warm summer air.

Speranza
by Adriana Carlino

Longlisted, Scottish Arts Club Short Story Competition 2019

They had been driving for four hours, they had been married for six, and he had been in the pub for two. Speranza tilts the rear-view mirror towards the passenger side and assesses her makeup. She clasps the tip of her middle finger in her teeth and pulls off the glove on her right hand. She spits the glove onto her lap. She blinks her eyelashes onto the side of her finger to elongate them once more. Her mascara was stiff to touch. It seemed a long time since she had applied it.

***

Earlier that morning she had put on her best outfit: the purple velvet dress with matching gloves, the one she had worn the night she had met Giovanni. She called out to her uncle, who was sitting on the back verandah with a coffee and the Italian paper, that she was going to church with Maria. She grabbed her pre-packed suitcase from under her bed, it was the same one she had journeyed to Australia with two years earlier. The flyscreen-door clanged shut behind her as she hurried down the street, the morning sun warning of the hot day to come. She found Giovanni leaning against his Ford Fairlane by the old bottlebrush as they had arranged. Giovanni had been working on the mines for a year now and he had a string of lavish purchases to show for it. They were married at the Registry Office – not the white-dress, tiered cake affair she had envisioned. Not the day-long celebration that would start with a procession from her house to the church, her family trailing behind her, tears in their eyes and love in their hearts. No, it was simply a matter of paperwork and promises. The newlyweds set off east towards Kalgoorlie and soon the city streets of Perth were swapped for the red dirt roads of their new life together.

Giovanni pulled the car over at Merredin, went into the bakery, and returned with a brown paper bag. He deposits the bag through Speranza's open window, grease stains making the paper glisten. She picks it up off her lap quickly, with a click of her tongue not wanting to soil her best dress. Giovanni raises his eyebrows at this as if to comment that she has overreacted. She giggles and he leans through the window to kiss her on the cheek.

"*Aspetta qui,*" he says. Wait here.

He crosses the road and she strains her head to see him disappear into the pub. She unravels the paper bag to find a sausage roll. It's still warm. It tastes nothing like the food she is used to. As Speranza eats she pays no mind to the niggling she feels somewhere deep inside. She ignores it until she feels it gnaw at her and her eyes fill with tears. She swallows them down with the blend of meat and carrot. She buries it in her stomach to be compacted, processed and digested.

***

Perhaps all husbands in Australia left their wives in the car while they went drinking? Maybe it was customary for men to drink alone on their wedding day? Women probably aren't allowed in the pub. She wouldn't want to go in anyway. She'd had too much wine at her cousin's wedding in Sinagra and the dizzying feeling was not something she wanted to experience again. She didn't like the way Australian men looked at her. Like she was a piece of exotic fruit to be peeled and inspected.

Her Uncle had warned her, "They're not like us these Australiani."

What was an Australian anyway? This she had not figured out. Some were Englishmen, Irishmen, Scotsmen, Germans, Frenchmen, Chinese. And yet anyone who had arrived by boat was not truly 'Aussie'? It must have something to do with the timing. If you arrived by boat a criminal a hundred years ago, then you were in luck – you were Australian. Any arrival after that and you were unwelcome. Maria had visited the men on the mines in Kalgoorlie and she had seen the true Australians. They were the native people who had been here for thousands and thousands of years. They knew how to live off the land, moved around it constantly and could find home within every sand dune, bushland and desert. Maria had said they had the same sadness in their eyes that Speranza had when she thought of home.

Speranza rested her chin on her forearm as she leant out the window. She stared down at the red earth. Sometimes she would spot a tree or a shrub that vaguely resembled the dry foliage of summers in

65

Sicily. If she closed her eyes the dry heat of the afternoon sun warmed the skin of her arm just as it had at home. But the squawk of some native bird would bring her back to the desert she was in. She tried to find home but she could not. Her ancestors lay on some other ancient field, across seas that were too far for spirits to travel. A wooden water tower cast a shadow over the car providing Speranza with a modicum of relief from the sun. A hand painted sign advertised 'Kalgoorlie Bitter' across it. When the lead heroine elopes in a Hollywood film she rarely if ever ends up in Kalgoorlie. Clark Gable never sweeps his lover into his arms and says, "Let's relocate to rural Western Australia. Think of the draughts we could endure together, the snakes, the water shortages …" And yet, Kalgoorlie was where Giovanni insisted they go.

"A new start", he says, eyes dancing.

A new start, away from the disapproving glare of her uncle, free to do as they pleased. She could cook, and keep house while he worked on the mines making their fortune. They would have kids, as many as she pleased! They would be rich enough to feed them all. Here, far away from their own families back in *La Bell'Italia* they would make a new family!

Giovanni Stilatino was a handsome man. He had a thick head of dark hair, a crooked grin and eyes that spun you about in a waltz. Speranza had met him at a social at the Italian Club. A night when the velvet of her dress did not cause her to sweat as it did today in the Ford. Speranza had her photograph taken before the dance wearing the dress. The dress she had made herself, spending hours designing the pattern and cutting its shapes. It was a photograph she would treasure years after when youth had left her and the happy smiling girl had faded with the emulsion. Giovanni had sought her out that night because she was the most capable dancer. Giovanni could tango like an Argentinian and he loved to prove it. Their courtship was short and it was not long before Giovanni was whispering to her of running away. She had other suitors, even a few her uncle had approved, but it had to be Giovanni. Nobody else made her heart catch in her chest.

He was wild and he was thrilling. He knew how to dazzle people and bewitched them with his charm. She had never met anyone who could make friends with such ease as Giovanni – not just Italians but Australians, English, Chinese too! He drank with them and sang with them. He told her stories of the Noongar tribesmen he met working as a labourer down South, told her of the pub fight he'd been in when an Aussie called him a 'wog', and the time his friend Bruno boxed a kangaroo. He wanted to experience everything Australia had to give him. He wanted to travel, to discover and to conquer. But he also wanted someone to care for him, someone to come home to. He wanted a constant and Speranza was a fixed point. Speranza dreamt of family. Family she had lost, family she would never see again and family that was yet to come. She dreamt ardently, feverishly of the family she would create with Giovanni. She was almost glad he had disappeared into the pub because it might delay their wedding night. She had heard tales of weeping virgins and sheets stained with shame. The old women of her village used to swap stories of the sin of marriage and cackle over their husbands bumbling. It seemed to be a thing endured rather than enjoyed.

A truck rattled past the car and the chassis shook from the force. Speranza's eyes brimmed hot with tears. Eloping was romantic and full of bliss until you're alone in a car in the middle of a desert. For a minute she hated Giovanni. She hated him for taking her away, for leaving her here and for convincing her to elope. Nice girls didn't elope, nice girls didn't run away to marry as if they had something to hide. What would they think back home? Her mother, her nonna, her little brothers and sisters all miles away – what would they think? It would take weeks before a letter from her uncle would arrive. Perhaps, if she sent a letter first thing tomorrow, she could beat him to it. She could explain how tempting it was, how much she loved Giovanni, and how she simply had to do it.

She leant her head against the car seat, she squeezed her eyes shut; if she tried hard enough she could send them secret thought messages filled with love. They would be fast asleep in their beds, dreaming of the far-off land where birds' calls were laughter and mothers could carry their young close in their pouches. How desperately she wanted to hug her nonna. That wise old woman from another time, who had lived through poverty and two wars. She would know what to say to a husband who leaves his wife in a blistering car for hours on end. She would have the words to shame a man who leaves his new bride alone and thirsting. She would know just how to comfort Speranza's wedding night nerves. She would have some old proverb or wives' tale to solve the worry. But they would never meet again. They had said their forever goodbye.

***

Speranza is shocked awake by the opening of the driver's door. Giovanni has returned.

The setting sun shines directly into the windscreen. Speranza shields her tired eyes from the glare. Giovanni hands her a bottle of once cold lemonade. Speranza traces a finger down the damp glass as it trickles onto the glove in her lap.

Giovanni, swaying, tucks his shirt into his pants. He takes his seat with a grunt, a cigarette hanging from his lips as he struggles to get the keys into the ignition. He takes the cigarette from his mouth and hands it to Speranza to hold between a finger and thumb. He returns to the business of the keys.

"Disgraziata!" he slurs as they jangle anywhere but into the ignition.

Speranza drops a silent tear onto the upholstery but says nothing. Eventually, Giovanni concludes the tarantella he's dancing with his keys. The engine cracks and sizzles as it expands and idles. Speranza says nothing.

"There was a woman in there today ..." he begins, his breath reeking of cheap booze. He places his hand on the back of her headrest as he checks his blind spot, meeting Speranza's eye with his clammy, swollen face, "Who danced *so* beautiful ..."

He reverses slightly, thrusts the stick into gear and speeds off onto the highway. "... If I met her before today, I would have married her."

With a drunken nod he takes the cigarette back from her and takes a long drag. Speranza says nothing.

It looks as though they are driving towards the brilliant sun. It sits just between the sky and the earth where they can never reach it.

An Orange From Two Miles Away
by Lucy Grace

Longlisted, Scottish Arts Club Short Story Competition 2019

We walked home in the summer heat on the last day, pushing into the road and bashing at nettles with sticks. I'd taken my school tie off and stuffed it in my trouser pocket, but it uncoiled like an overheated snake and slid onto the melting tarmac.

"Aagh," I said, picking it up. "My mam'll kill me."

"Don't tell her, then," said David. David was my best friend and found life to be quite straightforward. He mostly achieved this by lying but seemed to live with it. He wasn't an over thinker – it's what I liked about him.

"But she'll notice," I said.

"Not right away, she won't. You won't need it for another six weeks, and that gives you ages to get it clean. Just hide it until September."

"Hide it where?" I asked.

"Look," said David. "Come to mine."

I followed him into his yard and to the coalhouse door.

"No-one's going to be digging to the bottom of here, not in this weather," said David. "Put it right at the back, and we'll get it out before school, give it a wash, and your mam'll never know."

We left the coalhouse far dirtier than we entered it but after a quick game of football on the field and a scuffle in the grass we were returned to our usual standard of grubbiness.

"I'll come and get you first thing," said David as we parted ways at the bottom of the street. "For the ponies."

I had forgotten about the ponies.

Next morning, David was already sitting on Mrs Bates' wall, swinging his legs.

"Let's get a good place," he said, squinting into the sun. "Last year was rubbish."

Last year had been rubbish – the ponies had broken into a run as soon as they got onto Wharf Road and we couldn't keep up with them as they headed for the field.

"We'll stand near the bottom this time," he said. "We can wait outside the Co-op and when they come past, we can run down with them, and climb on the gate to see."

David jumped off the wall and crossed the road to say good morning to the milkman. When the milky went down the ginnel with Mrs Friar's full cream, David slid past the cart and appeared at the back with a grin and a glass bottle.

"Come on, then," he said, walking down the street. I followed him, looking over my shoulder – although David was my best friend, he didn't half try and get me into trouble.

From the kerb outside the Co-op we could see the pit wheels winding. The collieries closed yesterday, along with the schools, and there had been many celebratory pints shared last night as the two-week summer shut down began. The streets were holiday quiet. But it wasn't miners coming up in the cages this morning – it was the ponies.

The pit lads brought the ponies up out of the ground every summer for their fortnight on the surface. For the next two weeks they would be kept in the field at the bottom of Wharf Road. We had come to watch them be led down the street on bits of rope, their ears flattened and eyes rolling white, like black dragons. They were sticky with coal dust and scared of a sky they hadn't seen for fifty weeks. Last year, when they skittered and slid down the street, close enough to touch, I felt thrilled in my stomach.

One of David's big brothers was a pony lad. They weren't supposed to ride them for the half mile journey to the field, but the daft lads did. They weren't actually supposed to ride them at all, but David had already told me stories about the lads underground, about the manager hiding as they rode past, flicking them with white paint so he could identify the culprits back at the stable. But the pony lads knew to wear their coats inside out.

"Our Jonno's got a secret with his Nipper," said David, kicking a piece of gravel with the toe of his shoe.

"A secret?" I asked. "Who's Nipper?"

"The horse. It's oranges."

"Oranges?"

"Yeah, every pony has a secret, and with Nipper its oranges."

"How do you find out their secret?" I asked.

"Well, the miners share their snap with the ponies every day, and they just get to know. With Nipper its oranges. One shift, our Jonno left an orange in his coat pocket, and when he got back to eat it, it was sucked dry. Not bitten, just empty. Nipper had smelled it through his coat pocket and sucked all the juice out of it. Through his pocket."

I loved this story.

"And what did he do then? Jonno, I mean?"

"Well what could he do? He brought another orange the next shift to see if Nipper would do it again."

"And did he?"

"Of course he did. Jonno tested him all over the pit. He could smell an orange from two miles away."

"But why did he want to know?"

"For the races, of course."

The sun was warm on the back of our necks. I flicked a beetle off my leg and David finished the last of the milk.

"Tell me about the races."

David was good at stories. I loved listening to him, eyes closed, imagining the world he described. I wanted to be his friend forever.

"Well, underground, it's massive, right? There's room for proper stables and everything. And sometimes the pony lads take the ponies to a place big enough to run in and they race them."

"They ride them? But you said …"

"No, not usually, there's not enough headroom for that, but they let them go and see which one is the fastest."

I didn't speak for a minute whilst I thought about it. I looked down at the road – all this happening under my feet, a mile down.

"So, what's that got to do with the oranges?"

"Well, Nipper loves oranges, right? He'll do anything to get at an orange. He doesn't even need to see one, he can smell it. Our Jonno stands at the end with an orange in his pocket, squeezing it, and Nipper runs like the wind. Our Jonno's made loads of money at it."

"They pay him?" I asked.

"No, dummy, the men bet on the winning horse. But our Jonno's not daft; he doesn't take an orange every time, or nobody'd bet on him."

David looked up the street to see if he could see any sign of the ponies. There were children cheering and David stood up.

"They're coming," he said.

Wharf Road was the main street in the village. Several houses down the road from where we stood was a removals lorry. It was a big one from the Co-op, and two men were just undoing the back doors outside Dr Dalton's house. We were getting a new doctor.

"They're here, look!"

David was excited, standing on his tiptoes on the edge of the kerb. Along the street trotted a gaggle of pit ponies. Small and stocky, they were single minded in their desire to get to the field, and I wondered if they could remember it from last year. Pulled along ingloriously on the end of various bits of rope were the pit lads, yelling and laughing as they ran in the melee.

"There's our Jonno. Jonno! Hey, Jonno, over here!"

Towards the back of the group, one of the younger pit lads was riding his pony. Without saddle and stirrups his long skinny legs dangled almost to the ground on either side, but by hanging onto the pony's scraggy mane he was managing to stay on top.

The first ponies were passing us now, nostrils flaring and hooves clattering on the road, and out of the corner of my eye I saw David rummaging in his pocket for something. I had an awful feeling. As I watched Jonno bouncing up and down on what must be Nipper, Nipper's head went back a bit and I swear he looked right at me and David. The frequency of the bounces changed as Nipper increased to fast trot, and Jonno looked less confident. Some of the horses were already at the field gate.

"Come on, David, let's run with them," I said, but David didn't take his eyes off Jonno and Nipper.

"David!" I said, pulling on his arm. "Now!"

As I tugged on his sleeve, his hand came out of his pocket and I saw the orange fly out into the gutter. It didn't stop to rest, but rolled down the edge of the kerb, picking up speed. Nipper flew past us, Jonno wobbling about all over the place and yelling. The pony ran right up the ramp into the back of the furniture lorry, full tilt, as the two men in brown overalls were carrying a red velvet sofa with a tasselled fringe.

Now, furniture lorries are big things, but they probably seem a lot smaller when they contain a large red velvet sofa with a tasselled fringe, a swearing pit lad, a pit pony looking for its orange and two angry removal men.

It was chaos. The men were shouting at Jonno, Jonno was shouting at Nipper and Nipper was unable to go anywhere as he was half over the red velvet sofa. Dr Dalton was standing on the pavement holding his hat and Mrs Dalton was running down the garden path, crying. It was brilliant.

"David," I said, turning, but he was nowhere to be seen. David wasn't daft – he wasn't going to hang about discussing secret oranges with an angry bigger brother. Jonno had dismounted Nipper now, and was trying to lead him back out of the lorry without causing any more distress to the red velvet sofa with a tasselled fringe or to poor Mrs Dalton, but it was too late for that.

"Johnson!" The pit stable manager was striding down the middle of the road on his way to the field. He hadn't seen Jonno riding Nipper, and Jonno thought fast.

"He's a rum 'un, this 'un, sir," said Jonno, wiping his brow. "It's a good thing I'd got him on the end of this rope, or he'd have been right inside that furniture lorry, I can tell you."

"Lad, he was inside the furniture lorry," began the manager, but before he could finish Nipper was off again down the street to the field, pulling Jonno with him.

"Got to go, sir," called Jonno. "Got to get him safe in that field."

And with that, the pit ponies were gone.

***

I'm an old man now, eighty-nine, and I don't get outside much. The pit did for my knees and my lungs, and it turns out they're pretty essential parts. David discovered that first. But where I am, I am warm, and I am fed, and it could be worse. There are too many lights on, and the television is playing every goddamn hour of the day, but I manage.

On the news this morning was something called The Running of the Bulls. It was in a hot street with a relentless sun. It reminded me of David, and Nipper, and Jonno riding on his back, and Dr Dalton holding his hat and Mrs Dalton running down the path, and I started to laugh. I laughed and I laughed until the nurse came to see if I was ok, and I said that I was, and she said but you're crying, and I said these are happy tears, my love. And I wasn't sure if they were happy tears or sad tears, but they all taste the same, so I didn't over think it. I thought about David and his stories and the endless summers and ponies and oranges, and I was glad that I had all that in my head, that I had all those outside days to remember.

Matchy-Matchy
by Maggie Innes

Longlisted, Scottish Arts Club Short Story Competition 2019

It was the cutlery that pushed Norah over the edge.

She pulled open the drawer to discover serried sleek ranks of knives, forks and spoons laid out, identical handles together, like gleaming rigid corpses. Under her breath she counted to ten and in her mind she headed for her happy place. She didn't get anywhere near.

"What's. Happened. To. The. Cutlery?" The question burst out of her like the creature in Alien, when she had barely opened the living-room door. Her strained, fury-simmering tone could just as well have been enquiring, "Did you put arsenic in my kale smoothie?" She was almost scaring herself.

Jed looked up from his book. He smiled – the picture of innocence. Of eagerness to please. For a brief moment Norah felt guilt. Emphasis on the brief.

"It was on offer. In the petrol station," Jed said. "It's called Contemporary Chic," he added – for some strange reason seeming to think this might help.

"Right. So what happened to all the old stuff?" Her mother's bone-handled antique knives, the silver teaspoons rescued from the skip, the ornate dessert forks that were a leaving present from her last ever full-time job … Norah ran through her mental list.

"I didn't throw it away!" Jed protested. Again, like this was a remark of considerable positivity. "I put it all in a shoebox in the cellar." Norah nodded. She didn't yet trust herself to make any verbal response.

"None of it matched, anyway," Jed added, turning back to his book.

Norah returned to the kitchen, and slumped down on a white plastic chair. Her diverse old set of chairs, some from The Crown pub up the road, a couple from junk shops and one wicker-seated cutie left in the driveway of Saint Peter's vicarage with a handwritten sign PLEASE TAKE ME, had been the first casualties of what she was now starting to consider a war.

Jed had 'surprised' her when she got home from a client meeting with the scent of a bubbling pot of soup on the stove, and a set of six matching white chairs ranged around the kitchen table. While out on the patio, a lone beautifully-turned vintage chair leg stuck out of the garden burner, being slowly engulfed by flames. Norah, in her naivety, had reframed Chairgate as an endearing effort by Jed to put his own stamp on the house post-retirement, like a dog scent-marking his territory.

She'd read all the books, the websites, the problem pages – she expected it would be a difficult transition for Jed from busy office, bursting in-box, team of colleagues to manage, to just the two of them at home. A short, sharp shock – that she could deal with. But instead she'd been confounded by this creeping plague of Matchy-Matchy that had engulfed her previously gloriously haphazard life.

They'd discussed the issue post-Chairgate, of course they had – with the polite, clipped tones of two people bumping into each other on a bus after 30 years, rather than living those three decades as husband and wife. She didn't think Jed heard a word she said – and that obviously made her unwilling to listen to his point of view.

So the battle lines deepened.

Norah had never been a Matchy-Matchy person. There was something about a three-piece suite that made her feel dead inside. While nothing thrilled her more than twenty different designs of dinner plates, brought together over time via charity shops and department store remainder bins. She saw herself as something of a crockery saviour, rescuing a raggle-taggle of mongrel dishes and giving them hope, a future, a new raison d'être. Like a superhero movie starring odd saucers.

Jed did occasionally enquire about the gigantic, seemingly infinite Willow Pattern dinner service, complete with two shapes of soup tureen and four sizes of gravy boat, his parents had bought them as a wedding present. Norah reassured him it was all safely tucked up in bubble wrap in the loft, better to protect its integrity. She outlined a nightmare scenario where one piece got damaged and the whole set was traumatised by it. Jed went almost pale at the thought.

The truth was that for years now Norah had taken one Willow

Pattern item per month and released it into the wild. Well, driven it to the next town and donated it to the charity shop that raised money to neuter cats. It was either that or smash it with a hammer. And she might be Matchy-Matchy-averse, but she wasn't violent.

Until, to be perfectly honest, today.

She barely recognised the kitchen these days, with its neatly ranged, frankly hideous ceramic storage jars, and the saucepans suspended in strict order of size on the rail by the cooker. Without looking, she knew the cans in the cupboard were stacked according to their contents, and all the dry goods decanted into identical jars with identical labels. Her plates were long gone – ousted by a bland box set in an insipid shade of grey. Dishes so intrinsically dull her food tasted of dust – and she sometimes even felt nostalgic for the Willow Pattern.

The cutlery had been Norah's last stand – her refuge in the raging domestic storm that was Jed's apparent late-onset compulsion for conformity. Without the cutlery she was adrift.

On one level she acknowledged this was Jed's house too – he was entitled to make changes. Maybe it was petty of her to cling to her concept that mismatched items made life more interesting and creative. But they did! Where was the joy in a table of Contemporary Chic? And wasn't Jed's way just as petty, come to think of it?

Dragging her kicking and screaming towards co-ordinated cagoules and the same mugs pointing the same way in the same place. Forever and ever.

This Matchy-Matchy hell – for however many years she might have left – stretched out ahead of Norah and she baulked at the prospect. She was going to Do Something.

The first noticeable thing about the cellar was how much room there was down there these days. She tried not to dwell on what was missing. All those old, one-off tiles she planned to turn into arty teapot stands and sell for a fortune on eBay, for starters. On the plus side, all the household tools, including a solid-looking set of hammers, were now arrayed in ascending size, primed for easy access.

Norah scanned the orderly cellar shelves for a while. Then, with a cold fury building, she climbed back up the stairs and approached Jed in his reading chair. He'd ordered the 'Minimal Self Assembly' set of two from a trendy online store. And sent back the original package three times till he received two chairs with exactly the same shade of wood on all eight legs.

"I can't find it," Norah said. "The cutlery." Jed smiled first, before he spoke. It didn't go un-noticed by Norah.

"Ah. When I said cellar, I might have meant… charity shop," he said.

Norah swallowed hard. She would not show weakness. "Which one?"

"Neutering cats," Jed replied. To Norah, he sounded simultaneously smug and accusing. But she was already turning on her heel, heading out. "We'll talk about this – later."

"I was just trying to help," Jed's voice drifted out after Norah like a bad smell. The car keys hung on matching hooks in the hall. As an act of rebellion, she grabbed the ones marked JED. Touché.

The charity shop had that musty, unloved smell that spoke deeply to Norah of items that needed her help. But today she was on a mission. Her cutlery had been bundled up and fastened with elastic bands, but most of it was still there, scattered around the bric-a-brac shelves. She also spotted a set of Art Deco cake slices that would fit right in. Operation Matchy-Matchy Fight-back started now. She gathered everything up into her arms and deposited it on the glass top of the shop counter. Then she registered that something familiar was already sitting there – the sugar bowl from the Willow Pattern dinner service. She'd brought it in a couple of days ago.

A woman of about Norah's age stood beside the bowl, handing over a ten-pound note and looking delighted with her purchase. Norah couldn't stop herself. "I donated that," she said. "I'm so glad it's going to a good home." The woman blushed slightly and smiled. She wore shoes and a blouse in exactly the same shade of blue, and a perfectly co-ordinated necklace of blue and white beads. It was like the Willow Pattern was made for her. The shop door jangled as she left.

When Norah exited with her cutlery safely in a second-hand carrier bag, the woman was waiting outside.

"Sorry if I seemed a bit weird in there," she said. "I just wasn't sure what to say."

"No problem," Norah replied briskly. Her mind was elsewhere, already planning her battle strategy. She had to start reclaiming the territory she'd lost at home.

"Helen," the woman smiled – extending a small, beautifully manicured hand.

"Norah."

"Um...There's something I'd like to show you," Helen said hesitantly. "If you've got a few minutes?" Norah started to say no – she had to get home. But she fought the impulse to play safe. Resisted the pernicious influence of Jed's relentless Matchy-Matchy. That way led to madness. It was a one-way street to his'n'hers coffins.

"Why not?" she smiled.

Later, back home, Norah stood in her kitchen and unusually for her, savoured the quiet. Jed didn't appreciate the music station she'd always played. So gradually silence had seeped in. Now the whole house felt heavy with anticipation.

"Something smells good," said Jed, poking his head round the door.

"Chicken stew," Norah said. Jed's smile registered surprise. That was his all-time favourite, while Norah preferred spicier flavours. But she recognised she had to make some short-term sacrifices. Perhaps Jed's retirement had brought their differences into sharp, uncomfortable focus but they could have a future, she saw that now.

Norah's clarity had come as she stood before the dresser in Helen's neat, neutral dining room. A dresser groaning with every single piece of Willow Pattern Norah had donated to the charity shop. Restored as a set and staring blankly out at the world like stunned sheep. In that moment, Norah just knew what she had to do. It was all so simple. It would take a bit of creativity and a bit of time. She had plenty of both.

"Would you lay the table, please?" Norah asked Jed. He slid the cutlery drawer open and could not disguise his pleasure at its contents. Norah's resolve hardened. "Make it for three?"

Jed looked puzzled. "I made a new friend today," Norah explained. "Her name is Helen. I think you're really going to get along."

Norah turned to stir her stew, and hide the sly smirk on her face. Jed was a lamb to the slaughter. Encouraged by Norah, he'd fall for Helen and her Matchy-Matchy charms, and be guilt-tripped into moving out.

Then Norah could turn the house back into a proper home – her home – at her leisure. Maybe it was a bit brutal, but it was for the best. Anyway, Jed had brought it on himself with his inconsiderate ways.

At the table, Jed paused, remembering the once-happy history he and Norah shared. But the future was what mattered now, and he'd had to find a way to claim the house – his home – for himself. Maybe it was a bit brutal, but it was for the best. Anyway, Norah had brought it on herself with her inconsiderate ways.

He finished typing a text message. *You were right, the cutlery did the trick! You've been so patient darling but we're so close now. Love you xxx* He copied and pasted two matching heart emojis and pressed SEND TO HELEN just as the doorbell rang.

The Eighth Day
by Jupiter Jones

Longlisted, Scottish Arts Club Short Story Competition 2019

Dundee was holding its breath. Seventy-five souls were lost when the railway bridge collapsed in the storm and only one body had been recovered and buried. Found by a mussel dredger, on a sand bank, three miles down from the bridge. She was buried in Fife with hundreds upon hundreds of strangers there, each one shaking her father by the hand, saying "Sorry for your trouble." And him speechless and bewildered, his rheumy eyes blank with disbelief. Since then no more bodies had been found, the firth had swallowed them. They were out there somewhere. Somewhere where the sweet water of the Tay turned salt. Drifting in the currents, or caught in the ebb and flow of tides, or on their way out to the unremitting cold of North Sea. Somewhere.

The whalers had a theory.

"They'll rise on the eighth day" said John McBain from *Pride of Dunkeld*, as if pronouncing some ecclesiastical edict.

Donald MacDonald, white-bearded, dour, born at sea, salt to his bones, took his pipe from his mouth;

"Day eight. No sooner. Mark my words."

And the two brothers from Uist, and the strange Norwegian exchanged glances, nodded their heads and muttered their agreement in chorus.

Hamish Buchanan, First Mate of *The Dexterity* could be found holding court in the Hope and Anchor. From the relative comfort of his customary on-shore quarters, in the chimney corner of the snug, he would explain to interested parties exactly why a body washed out into the firth would wash back in again. Exactly why it would rise to the surface on the eighth day. Stand him another drink, and he would recount in some thrilling detail the extent of decomposition to be expected; given the time of year and the temperature of the water. There were those who wanted to know these things; who had the stomach for the details. The town was bristling with investigators, reporters, engineers, insurers, salvagers, mourners, sightseers, mediums, trippers, privateers, embalmers, litigators, and souvenir hunters. Guest houses were full. It is an ill wind they say.

Despite the whaler's timeline, the rescue teams walked the banks each day. The trawlermen eyed the sandbars, and divers working at the site of the wreckage went down and came up with nothing. There was a bounty offered of five pounds for a body, and some of those who searched were desperate with grief, and some were opportunists. No matter. They all searched, walking the high-water lines at dawn and dusk, clambering over rocks, checking inlets and pools. The churches held vigils; the Free Church, the Catholic Church, the Presbyterian, the Episcopalian. Whatever the denomination; no matter. Day six, day seven, the tide turned and turned again. Day eight dawned with a mist that would clear later. Another high tide and Dundee was holding its breath.

Andrew Johnston walked up the street from the harbour to South Tay station. He was in no hurry. He was a patient man. A stonemason by trade and taciturn by nature. But God-fearing, hard-working, and kind in his own way. All this week he had been searching for his brother David. He headed for the Refreshment Rooms which had been commandeered after the disaster. At first, they used words like 'rescue' and 'survivors' and made endless cups of hot tea for the men who went out into the storm and came back exhausted and trying to make some sense of the unthinkable. But gradually as all hope drained, the supplies of first aid and blankets were cleared away and the room was reluctantly acknowledged to be a morgue; a makeshift morgue, waiting for the bodies to come.

Mrs Smith the stationmaster's wife was there, stick-thin and with a reputation for being fierce. Andrew had not found her so this last week.

"Mr Johnston," she said, "I've been looking out for you. Young Malcom bought a boot in this morning, it's a man's boot, washed ashore down by the south road. Come and see."

Along one side of the room was a trestle table bearing an accumulation of objects that had been washed up on the beaches. A macabre bring-and-buy sale of clothing and luggage that could conceivably offer proof of identity of the train's missing passengers and crew. Please don't let it be David's boot. Some hope was surely better than none. But there was no hope left. Please let it be David's boot. He went to look, but the boot was brown not black. Someone else's brown boot. Just one. Half of a pair. How had this boot become separated from its brother? Andrew put his hand inside. He'd heard tell that fishermen sometimes caught a boot on their line, or in a net, with a foot still inside it, preserved when the rest of the body was gone. This one was empty. He rubbed the toe of the boot. For luck? There was no luck left in Dundee.

"You'll take a cup of tea?" asked Mrs Smith at his elbow. "And have ye eaten at all today? Well, whether ye have or no, ye'll take a slice of fruit cake. My sister made it. A little dry perhaps, but it will suffice to keep body and soul together"

Next to the boot there was a broken basket and a parcel of woollens, still tied with string, a walking stick, a book swollen and illegible, a blue mitten. The sight of these lost and found items broke Andrew's heart all over again. How could these incidental items, this flotsam be all that was left? After accepting the tea and cake, he went and sat on the wall outside. And he waited.

It wanted yet another three hours to sunset, another three hours for searching, scouring the margins of the firth, or waiting; waiting for news, waiting to be told something he already knew. The weak winter sun washed over him but failed to warm his bones. He looked out over the Tay. The waters were calm, glassy even. At low tide you could see the stone pillars; the bases of the high girders, sticking out of the water like a row of broken teeth. He had worked on those pillars. He knew them like he knew his own teeth. He watched the gulls; distant specks mobbing the fishing boats heading home. He watched two women walk by; arm in arm, shawls wrapped tight, faces pinched with grief. He watched a boy on a bicycle, whistling. He watched the clouds.

On the other side of the street, there was Father Loyola heading down to the quayside. No bookish cleric this one, but a bull of a man, his long black coat belted high like a prize-fighter, the hem flapping down below and his boots striking sparks on the cobbles. Andrew nodded to him. Father Loyola nodded back and strode on.

A cry went up, carrying easily in the quiet afternoon, and there was a commotion down at the harbour with interested parties all milling about. Folk gathered; drawn to the cry. Some desperate, for news, for closure; some sightseers. No matter. One of the trawlers had brought something in.

Andrew waited. Presently, coming up from the harbour with a small crowd in attendance was Provost Brownlee, looking oddly triumphant, followed by two men pushing a handcart, its wet load covered by a tarpaulin. Some of the women were wailing, they had been wailing for days, and were still wailing. The sound was thin but excessive. It pierced his coat, his skin. Andrew sighed and watched the procession climb the hill. The clouds thickened, the wall was damp, Andrew waited. Please let it be David. Please God, don't let it be David. David was sunny and easy-going, David was a joker, a ladies' man, a bit of a gambler, a tall man; five-foot eleven, a fine tenor voice, a good father to three sons, the eldest not yet eight. You could identify him by the scar above his right eye. A boyhood accident with a swing. David got the scar. Andrew took the blame.

The crowd came up the rise, their pace slowed, their exuberance ebbed as they neared the station. They turned into the yard and unloaded the cart. Four men carried the cargo to one of the tables. Andrew made no move to follow them in. Bringing up the rear of the procession was Father Loyola with two snot-nosed children hanging from his arms. He came to a stop and shooed them away. His face was both grim and tender.

"Away now. Find your mammies." he said, and they were gone.

"Is it my David?" called out Andrew as the priest approached him. "My brother David?"

"Ye'd best come in and see for yourself lad."

Andrew nodded. So, his brother was found. David Johnston, the train's guard, a fine-looking man in his railwayman's uniform, his silver whistle tucked in his waistcoat pocket. Friendly banter with the driver and the fireman, a wink for the old ladies as he clipped their tickets. Size eight boots, an occasional poacher of salmon up the river, sandy-haired with smiling blue eyes.

Still Andrew didn't move. He felt heavy, cemented to the wall. He

84

was chilled through with the damp. There was granite in his veins, and in his heart. He was a man of stone. He tried to speak but his voice was cracked with feelings he could not name.

"But his eyes Father?" he looked up at the priest and they held one another's gaze.

"The fishes? Did the fishes take his eyes? Tell me Father. Did the bastard fishes take his eyes?"

Father Loyola laid his calloused hand on Andrew's shoulder.

"They are God's fishes laddie," he said. "And aye, the wee fishes have been fed. Come away in now."

Greater Expectations
by Katie Burton

Longlisted, Scottish Arts Club Short Story Competition 2019

Date: 10 October
   Reading: *Tess of the D'Urbervilles* – Hardy
   Feeling: Tragic and heroic. Also, quite bored

First, some good news. You of all things know how much I have suffered at the hands of Tony Adams these past three years. It is therefore with great delight that I share the news that he has been suspended (he drew a picture of Buddha smoking a spliff in his R.E. text book).

In less good news, tragedy has befallen us in English. Me, Jess and Charlotte (or is it Jess, Charlotte and I?) were having a nice time, minding our own business during the fifteen minutes allotted to write a diary entry from the perspective of one of the characters in Hamlet. No, I am not joking. Charlotte wrote: "Dear diary, I'm considering doing myself in today," and then we all gave up. In fairness, it was pandemonium around us. By which I mean people were throwing chairs, abusing each other's mothers – the usual palaver you must put up with at schools you don't pay for. Then, Ms Jones just happened to walk past as me, Jess and Charlotte came to the end of our world-famous rendition of You Can Leave Your Hat On from the film The Full Monty.

She *totally* lost it.

"You! And you!" she shouted, pointing at me and Jess. "Pick up your things and move, now."

Jess was made to sit next to Danny Lamb who she said kept brushing her leg with his hand all lesson and I had to sit next to boring, boring Lucilla Brown. Which seems unreasonable when you consider the fact that Michael Jarvis was carving a penis into his desk and he got to stay sitting next to his weird mate who only ever talks about the PlayStation.

So anyway, this year we do creative writing in English and Ms Jones handed out last week's stories. She said "Well done, Chloe," when she handed mine back. I turned it over and almost screamed because she'd given me a B, *again*. The injustice is just so … unjust.

I will copy out what she wrote here, though it will make me angry just thinking about it: "Chloe, this was a great story with a thrilling plot and a clear beginning, middle and end. However, your writing would really come alive with more description. The marking scheme specifies that students should demonstrate awareness of similes, metaphors and pathetic fallacy, as well as a range of punctuation including colons and semi-colons. Try inserting some of these into your writing and see how it blossoms."

I looked up pathetic fallacy in my text book. It said: Pathetic fallacy means attributing human emotions and behaviour to things found in nature that are not human, like the weather. For example: the sullen clouds, the brooding mountains, the dancing leaves.

How schooopid is that?

I went up to Ms Jones at the end of the lesson and said, quite reasonably and maturely: "Ms Jones, I'm disappointed with my mark."

"But Chloe, B is a great mark," she said, all smiley even though she clearly *hates* me.

"Well a B is fine if you usually get a C, Ms Jones, but I always got As in English last year," I said. Which is almost true. "And creative writing is kind of my thing."

She smiled again and tied her hair up and, I know this is beside the point, but she has very boring hair and could benefit from some highlights.

Eughh okay, that was mean. Sorry God.

"Well I'm your teacher this year, Chloe," she said. "Try taking on board some of the advice I wrote at the bottom of your paper." And she started to walk towards the door, almost as if she wanted to get away from me. I followed her.

"But that's not my style, Ms Jones. I'm an economical writer, understated – like Hemingway."

I thought she'd be impressed but she just smiled again. Maybe she knows I've never read Hemingway.

Date: 14 January
Reading: *The Old Man and the Sea* – Hemingway
Feeling: Concise

Drum roll please – I got a B for my story about a scientist who is terribly torn because he finds a cure for cancer, but using the cure means introducing another deadly disease to the world which only kills women. How excellent does that sound? Ms Jones just wrote: "More description please, Chloe. Read the marking scheme!"

"Marking scheme, shmarking scheme," I said to Jess at lunch.

I might have been able to take the hit, if it weren't for the fact that Lucilla Brown got an A. I decided I had to take a look at her story so I made her show it to me (she obviously didn't want to but she is quite a compliant girl). Lucilla's story was about a pony because guess what, Lucilla loves ponies. This is how it went: *Sally Lane was stroking her glossy chestnut brown horses in the stable and the fierce and burning sun shone down on them, a huge gold coin in the kindly sky. She was so happy, brushing Tallulah's coat, brown like the happy, cheerful conkers she used to collect with her papa.*

I won't give in to this nonsense. I am even more like Hemingway than I suspected. I certainly don't need flowery language to write powerfully. Who needs an A anyway? What do I care?

Date: 22 February
Reading: *The Hobbit* – Tolkien
Feeling: Adventurous (what a pity I'm 14 and there's sod all to do)
The crux of the problem is, I really want an A.

I thought Ms Jones might relish the opportunity to read something a bit more exciting. (We've done five stories so far and Lucilla's have all involved domesticated animals). So, when English came around, I wrote a gripping story about a wicked emperor and a common serving girl who owns a beautiful necklace. By complete chance the serving girl finds out that the ring (sorry, necklace), which was given to her by her uncle, is the key to killing the emperor. No luck though.

Ms Jones gave the stories back at the end of day. She wrote: "Chloe, you might have heard of the phrase 'write what you know'. You'll find that most of the best writers write from personal experience and it's an excellent starting point for any would-be author."

I scribbled, "What about J R R Tolkien, J K Rowling and Roald Dahl?" in pink pen underneath her comment and left my paper on my desk.

Maybe a bit petty. But could you really say I don't have a point?

Date: 14 April
Reading: *Pride and Prejudice* – Austen
Feeling: Proud (of myself), prejudiced (against Ms Jones)

We sat on the wall at lunch with our coats over our heads to stop the birds pooing on us. (Lunchtime at our school is a nightmare. The seagulls come down like vultures to get at our sandwiches and if you get pooed on in front of people you may as well kill yourself). I was moaning about my English mark and Jess said she always gets an A in English because she takes the marking scheme so literally. She makes sure to include at least three similes, metaphors and semicolons in every story and she always writes about a haunted house. Her favourite sentence, which she says ticks all the boxes and she has so far used twice (Ms Jones hasn't noticed), goes: *He was as old as time; his hair white as snow; his heart a rotten apple of desire.*

Ms Jones wrote "lovely" under the sentence – BOTH TIMES. It's a good job my parents don't pay for this shoddy level of education.

I feel properly grumpy now. Do I have to sacrifice all my principles for this stupid A?

Date: 12 May
Just finished reading: *Carrie* – King
Feeling: Murderous

I have sacrificed all my principles for a stupid A. I can hardly bear to write this, but I said I'd be honest so I must be honest.

It was already a weird day because everyone was super quiet. No one even got sent out of class for doing stupid accents while reading out loud. I think everyone's run out of energy and just sleeps through lessons now. That, and the fact that all of the worst kids have been suspended, or sent to that hut at the back of the school where they're not allowed to talk to anyone. (By the way, listening to other people read out loud is unbelievably crap. I have started reading each passage backwards and then forwards again whenever someone particularly slow is forced to read out loud and I *still* finish quicker than them). I told Dad this and he said, "Well Chloe, you've always been precocious". I forgot to look up 'precocious' in the dictionary but I assume it's a compliment.

Anyway, we had 45 minutes to write our story and I had something really good in mind. Then, just as I was about to get going, I looked up and saw Ms Jones at her desk, riffling through some papers. And – oh I don't know – I guess it was the weird quietness in the room and then something about her hair. It was the hair of someone who will never understand me, who will always, always, give me a B. Unless …

I took a deep breath, cried a little (internally, although I think I may have made a slight noise because Lucilla looked at me in alarm – then again, she is easily alarmed) and I wrote: *The house stood dark and angry at the top of the hill (pathetic fallacy), its broken windows like the sharp teeth of a mythical beast (simile). The rain was a blanket of misery (metaphor) and the sullen clouds (pt) were as black as Tom Brown's heart as he walked up the hill; (semi-colon) danger was close. The moon shone through the rain like a weeping crystal ball (simile).*

Obviously I didn't actually write the bits in brackets. I have simply included them here as a record of my shame.

Date: 13 May
Reading: *Crime and Punishment* – Dostoyevsky
Feeling: Guilty – I am unlikely to ever finish reading this book

Ms Jones winked at me as she handed my paper back. I couldn't bear to turn it over, I just sat there staring at it for a while. Lucilla turned hers over and I glanced at the mark through my eyelashes so she wouldn't notice me sneaking. She'd got a C. I could see that Ms Jones had written: "A sweet story Lucilla but maybe try and branch out from animals next time."

I didn't even feel smug. I felt like a loser on all accounts. Either I'd got an A, in which case I was a charlatan and a fraud. Or I hadn't. Which would suck.

I turned over my paper.

I groaned.

The big red A looked up at me accusingly (pathetic fallacy?).

Blast from the Past
by Scott Watkins

Longlisted, Scottish Arts Club Short Story Competition 2019

A few weeks ago, I ran into a guy I went to school with, whose name had at one point stung with a significance that could only exist in the realm of teenage myth. This chance encounter in a cheap London hotel closed a long-forgotten chapter in my life. What happened to Fergus had lingered like a dead weight, before the centrifuge of life spun us all to different corners of the world.

It was the first night of my weekly working visit to the capital, in the Hampstead Britannia Hotel, a concrete monolith full of faceless travellers internally cursing their life choices. I was on my third pint at the bar and my day's work had started to slowly blur as Monday Night football served as background noise to my own lager-hazy thoughts. The warmth and glow of the amber nectar was suddenly chiselled into fright when I noticed a man of about my age looking at me from across the bar with the unmistakable eye of recognition. There was a familiarity to the face, which held a horror and desperation he was unable to mask. London is not the place anyone expects to be recognised, no matter how regular a visitor. Instinct would usually make me pull out my phone to look busy, but the surprise of this eye contact and his look of terror had rendered me momentarily dumb. Was the fear on *his* face, or was it a reflection of my own dread? The man had clearly recognised me. And he was now on his feet and heading my way.

This time my natural instinct kicked in and like a flash my phone was out my pocket and was skimming a group chat. He clearly hadn't read the signs, as the bar stool next to me was shuffled into position. "Hi Jamie ..." I drew my eyes up to his and the realisation struck me like a sobering slap from an aggrieved ex. Sitting next to me was the boy I hadn't seen in over twenty years. The boy who left school under a veil of mystery and intrigue, never to be seen again.

I was in third year at high school when I first met Fergus. I was lucky enough to have chameleon-like social skills, honed over the years by a dad with a middle-class background, and a mum with a more salt of the earth upbringing. I could fit in with anyone – boys, girls, neds, Goths, footballers, stoners, you name it. On the outskirts of my social network was Fergus, a waif of a lad with no assets required to fit in at a place like this. He couldn't play football, he couldn't hold a conversation with a girl without developing a tomato-face, and he couldn't play the guitar. No chance. Fergus loved sci-fi and in time, our double chemistry class became a lesson in Asimov, Wells and Clarke. I liked him. He had a sense of humour that took time to get my head around, but he was just smarter than me and once I was attuned to his quirks, I enjoyed his company, even if it got me some unwanted attention from the bams.

One day in class, I couldn't help but notice that Fergus' brow had a sheen of sweat and he had taken on a grey pallor in his cheeks. He was unusually silent – for someone who would generally take advantage of the fact that I (and nobody else) would give him the time of day – and so in the middle of our double-period, when a visit to the vending machine was permitted, I questioned him. "What's up wi you the day?" I asked with what I hoped was a casual nonchalance. He didn't respond immediately, just looked at me with an unreadable gaze.

"I can't tell you. You wouldn't believe me, even If I did," he said, sounding like the proverbial broken man. "Come on, what kinda thing's that to say; you think I'm gonnae leave it hangin on that bombshell??" I said, feeling like I might just have fallen on something particularly juicy. "Honestly, I don't want to talk about it, it's so fucked up, there's no point." A more mature mind would have left it at that and respected the boy's wishes. But I was like a dog with a bone. "Fuck sake, just tell me, what the fuck's wrong with ye the day, maybe I can help?" He mulled this over whilst looking me in the eye like a distrustful hawk.

"Listen, you can't tell anyone, you have to swear that this is between you and me. I can't deal with anyone else finding out." "OK pal, you can trust me" I said, not fully understanding what I had promised. Fergus braced himself, like a stuntman does before impact. "Last night, whilst lying in bed, I was abducted by aliens." "Fuck off" I said, instantly regretting falling for the verbal prank of a boy so much further down the teenage pecking order than me. Admittedly, Fergus often rambled about sci-fi stories, but becoming part of one was a huge side step. "I swear to God Jamie, I was in bed reading …" "Hold your horses" I interrupted, "you didn't happen to be reading one of your sci-fi classics did you?" "What does it matter what I was reading?" I was getting irate. "Jesus Christ mate, you expect me to believe this shite about aliens when you've clearly just dreamt it?"

His demeanour changed from sweaty and nervous to deadly serious as he moved to within two inches of my face. "I'm fucking serious, one minute I was in bed, and the next I was sucked into a bright lab with one of … *them* and I have proof, because he …" He suddenly went quiet. "He what? Probed you for research purposes?" I asked with a wry smile. His eyes, which had been locked with mine, quickly darted to every other corner of the room and seemed to fill before he wiped them on his sleeve. Just at this point, the bell went and Fergus darted off with what appeared to be an awkward limp.

I lived on the same street as my friend Andrew and we would talk shit as we dawdled the pavements home. Andrew wasn't a chameleon like me – he was smart, but he also had a wicked streak that reared its ugly head when anyone different dared to stick their head above the parapet. I knew it was the wrong thing to do, and a feeling that I now understand to be shame niggled at me while I did it, but I told Andrew exactly what happened with Fergus. Not surprisingly, his reactions varied from wild hilarity to sheer disbelief at the drawing of attention to one's self from one so … like Fergus.

I got a lift to school the next day and arrived a few minutes before the bell. As soon as I saw the circle, my heart dropped to the pit of my stomach. A crowd, led by Andrew had formed a ring around Fergus and were pelting him with questions about his abduction, and it's fair to say they were *sceptical*. Fergus was in a state of clear distress: the story was a red rag to a group of teenage bulls. Fergus didn't do himself any favours; he refused to admit that the story was made up.

"It's true!" he yelled at them, "I was taken on board a ship and there was one alien who spoke to me and he just wanted to know about Earth and humans and …" "And then he bummed ye, ya mad

93

bastard!" shouted one of his accusers. "I saw him walking to school today, he's like John Wayne, they must have probed him good!" At that point Fergus, now unable to hide his tears broke through the circle and ran for the school gates, his limp making for the most desperate of exits.

We didn't see Fergus again after that. I heard that his dad had gotten a job down south and the family had moved almost immediately. And like the best high school myths, 'Fergus the alien shagger' had passed into legend. Perhaps fuelled by guilt, this chapter of my life was in time pushed so far into the recesses of my mind that until the night in the Hampstead Britannia, I hadn't thought about him or his strange story in many years.

"Fergus"? I said with a squint that I hoped made it look like a guess. "Aye, good guess." He was a quiet man, with a warmth he seemed eager to share, as if this opportunity hadn't arisen in a long time, the opportunity to share a conversation with another human being. He had continued his schooling in Surrey, where his family moved to, had studied IT and was staying at the hotel where his employer was hosting a function. His life had been blighted by insomnia, since … *the incident.*

By 10pm my curiosity had gotten the better of me, and I found the courage to bring up our last encounter. "Listen Fergus, I'm really sorry that I told Andrew about your alien story. I shouldn't have told anyone." He looked at me, like a man who didn't have a clue what to say. After a long pause, he spoke. "Until a couple of years ago, I genuinely believed that I had been abducted by aliens. After the initial experience of telling you, I never told anyone outside my family again. My parents took it badly, my mum was heartbroken that I would make such nonsense up, but I refused to admit I was attention seeking. My dad seemed desperate to brush it under the carpet and move on – he requested a transfer in his work as a means of a fresh start for us all."

"So, at what point did you change your mind?" I asked with genuine confusion. "My mum died five years ago, and me and my dad were never close, so I stopped seeing him when she passed. He died two years ago, and it was like a light had been flicked on in my memory. The day he died I succumbed to a sleep unlike any I remember having since *that* night. With the sleep came a terrible nightmare, so vivid in its detail that I felt it was real. I was 13 again; it was the night I believed I was abducted. I was lying in bed reading, on the cusp of sleep. My door creaked open and a figure crept in. It was my dad, and he climbed into my bed.

What followed was something only two years of therapy has taught me to understand. My dad ..." "Stop, you don't have to say it ..." Fergus closed his eyes and took an endlessly deep breath through his nose, the type a therapist might talk you through to avoid a panic attack. "In my frozen ... terror ... my brain dreamt up an ultimately more believable and acceptable narrative of being abducted by aliens. This, I believed until my dad dropped dead." My head fell to the bar, before trying with every ounce of strength to lift it to look him in the eye and acknowledge his pain.

Fergus hadn't made up his story. In his head it was real, and it was a far greater reality than the abuse he had faced at the hands of his own dad.

As we parted company that night, we knew that it was unlikely that our paths would ever cross again. He said I should feel no guilt over my part – we were kids, and not even experienced psychologists could fully understand his experience. He was happy to help close a chapter for me, even if it would always remain open for him. And as if nothing had changed in the twenty years since, I went on the group chat: "Andrew, you'll never guess who I just met ..."

The Way of Things
by Tom Gordon

Winner, Edinburgh Flash Fiction Award 2019

How clear the river runs! The noonday sun scatters random jewels on the water's surface, some flashing rainbow colours, some crystal clear. But all transient. It's the way of things.

I should tell him what it's like. But, then, he knows without me saying. This is his favourite fishing spot, after all – just past the wood, beside the fallen tree, on the bend of the river.

A companionable silence will do. He should be used to that. He sees what he sees and knows what he knows, ever the strong, silent type. No words of mine will change that.

He's sitting on the grass, beside me. He likes it here. It's the way of things.

We've been watching the dancing waters for more than an hour now. I have to say something.

"Well, big man. It's time." It's all I can think of saying.

I pick up my bag and loosen the draw-string. The top of the container inside is easy to unscrew and comes off quickly in my hand. And then, it's done. Sandy, my big man, reduced to an urn of ashes, scattered in the river as I'd promised.

He spreads over the surface and the sparkling jewels have gone. But not for long. He goes quickly, and they return. Then they go quickly, but my big man stays with me, just past the wood, beside the fallen tree, on the bend of the river – and everywhere else.

It's the way of things.

Leftovers
by Christine Stanton

Commendation, Edinburgh International Flash Fiction Award 2019

These pottery shards are all that is left of the pie dish from Ned Grout's kitchen. This dip in the land at the edge of the orchard (gnarled plum trees still grow here) is where Ned's wife and maidservant would hide, under the pale grey wattle tree.

Over there, ten paces away, where the scrub grows thick as a hedge, is the spot where a black woman startled them once. She stood quite still, pointing her gaze to a red-berried shrub, shaking her head, one hand pressed to her lips.

Up here on the high ground is all that remains of the chimney bricks, blackened from cooking.

One day the maid let Ned catch her hiding a pie of red berries in the basket of kindling kept on the hearth. After their beating, mistress and servant were made to stand silent, eyes cast down, hearing Ned gorge on the pie until no crumb was left. Then he hurled the dish into the fireplace; bellowing, ordering them to take the shards from the flames with bare hands, to feel what the fires of hell had in store for trollops who'd cheat on their lord provider.

"No," they said. "No."

They waited silent while the fire cooled. They waited until the retching stopped. They waited to be quite sure.

Later they put a dish of plum pie on the ground in the scrub, ten paces away from the pale wattle tree.

"Thank you!" they called. "Thank you!"

Sins of the Father
by Dora Bona

Commendation, Edinburgh International Flash Fiction Award 2019

I'm kneeling in the corner, my nose wedged into the sharp angle between the sitting room and the kitchen.

This time I'm kneeling on my hands, the additional penance driving pins and needles into my knuckles. Father strides past and hurls a stout reprimand, punctuating it with a swipe to the side of my head.

Mother opens the oven and releases the exquisite aroma of the steak and kidney pie that everyone else will be having for dinner.

I'm told to remain in this position for an hour. Each minute that scrambles by turns resentment into angry bile at the back of my throat.

My crime was accidentally dropping father's bible and breaking its ancient spine. The bitter irony sings loud because the desecration of *any* book is to me, tantamount to mistreating an animal.

When it happened, I was horrified, seeing it splayed out on the floor like a helpless cripple, disgorging the hand-scrawled sermon notes father had tucked into its belly. They skittered across the tiles, like parishioners trying to make a hasty getaway after service.

I inhale the slight scent of roses that drifts from the pink note paper secreted in my shirt pocket. I can still feel the soft, silken words curving seductively across the page, the writer unveiling herself to my father, promising to disrobe her desire for him later tonight in the vestry. Mother and I will sit by the fire mending six sets of school uniforms … and we will talk.

Space
by Vanessa Horn

Shortlisted, Edinburgh International Flash Fiction Award 2019

Newly here, you begin – as is your right – with a life-jar of limitless space. Exuberantly, you grab every gem, building your collection with instants: an excitement; a warmth; an awe. Each one a tiny grain hovering briefly for your enjoyment before floating down into the immeasurable vessel of memory. As they settle, they dust the base with their delicate film, only just discernible, but observable nonetheless.

The years pass and your collection builds; the base and the sides of your jar flesh out with moments. Memories. You build them rapidly. You build them keenly. They fit together without gaps, layer upon layer, over years, then decades. Suddenly, you have a full jar. You are complete: a brimming anthology. You.

Then, unexpectedly, a slackening … a mislaying. Strange. But the loss is temporary; the only impairment is a fraying. Surely? A one-off. Yes: happens to everyone. But … occurring again and again, other moments rumple, dishevel, and then depart. Completely this time, with no trace. Confused and frustrated, you claw for retrieval, but it's impossible to recover the memories. They now only sub-exist in the outer rims: a flickering; a frown; a suggestion. And just as you realise they're not as permanent as you once naively assumed, other moments make their escape from the jar, seeping wispily from the smallest of gaps and soaring upwards. Gone. Now, with nothing new to fill them, the voids expand without apology. Unremittingly.

Finally … full circle. You're left with what you started with: space

Lovebirds
by Ann MacLaren

Shortlisted, Edinburgh International Flash Fiction Award 2019

"They were a real couple of lovebirds," said Betty the barmaid. "Always together. He was protective of her – tiny little thing, isn't she?"

Constable Carson followed Betty's gaze to where Mrs Appleby was being comforted by the manager and a policewoman.

"How did it happen?" Betty asked.

"Went off the path to look for birds. Couldn't have picked a worse place to trip over his own feet."

"Poor woman. How will she get home?"

"We'll see to that. Look at her, shaking. She isn't fit to drive."

"She doesn't drive. Mr Appleby took her everywhere she needed to go."

"You know them quite well?"

"Not really. But they've been coming here for years. You learn things."

She had learned a lot, watching them; had seen the husband holding his wife close, her arm twisted up her back, making her lean into him; grasping her arm in mock affection if anyone asked her a question – his hand nipping her skin, warning her to give the right answer. She'd watched him, his lips close to his wife's ear and knew by her terrified expression that it wasn't sweet nothings he was whispering. She didn't tell the constable that the shaking hands and the anxious expression were Mrs Appleby's version of normal.

Betty had been down that road herself.

"Lovebirds, eh?" Carson said. "Her life won't be the same without him."

"No, it won't." Betty looked over at Mrs Appleby, who acknowledged her with a fragile smile then looked quickly away.

Yesterday I Killed a Goldfish
by Glyn Knowles

Shortlisted, Edinburgh International Flash Fiction Award 2019

Not on purpose of course, what do you take me for? Well ok; to be fair, not completely on purpose. I didn't wake up and think, coffee, breakfast, shopping, kill goldfish. If, by accident, you mean not planned, then maybe it was a bit on purpose. A planned but necessary piscicide.

Goldfish are not my favourite pets. Pointless I would say. That is until yesterday. The diminutive carp in question, belonged to my employer – wealthy, ageing, annoying, and as mean as you like. Twenty-six years as her maid and general factotum.

I'm no spring chicken anymore and retirement is on my horizon, but a pension is not. I'm not a dishonest or cruel person, and killing isn't something I set out to do.

Diamonds are a divine yet simple thing, just well-arranged carbon atoms. This diamond, my diamond, is exquisite. Cut to perfection to refract an array of delicate rainbows, a cooling crystalline seductiveness. But how to make what was hers mine?

Taking it from the jewel box was easy. Popping it into its mouth simple. Getting out the house was straight-forward too. After all who would look inside a dead goldfish? It thrashed endlessly but once expired, and with her agreement, I took out the dead thing. And then the plan fell apart. That bloody cat! Down in one and there goes my fish, jewel and all.

Oh well. It's not like I set out to kill a cat that morning either.

Cheap Mother
by Jeremy Tsai

Editor's Choice, Edinburgh Flash Fiction Award 2019
Longlisted for the Edinburgh Flash Fiction Award 2019

Mother Chen's fingers ache, cracked from washing feet and floors all day, but still she hurries home from Boston's winding streets, box of Chinese pears—*Jingjing's favourite*—in hand. In the kitchen, she examines a tender fruit, flushed and pale under the fluorescent light, and brings it to her nose. Its smells perfume her fingers. She presses in; it bruises. Pleased, she angles a knife to the fruit's damp skin. She steadily turns the pear: paper-thin spirals fall to the cutting board.

Mother Chen is not foolish: she sees Jingjing's face fall with each hand-stitched dress; the smelly doufuru, uneaten, disgusting, "like worms" she'd said; Mother's broken English; their crumbling house in Jamaica Plain.

She raises her knife to the air, and in one clean motion, cleaves the fruit. Humming, she pushes the sharp metal into the yellow fruit's flesh again. The pear opens up like a flower, thick white petals plopping onto the cutting board. As Mother Chen arranges each onto the sixteen-layered birthday cake made yesterday—*American, like Jingjing likes*—she thinks back to the motherland: Jingjing clapping, giggling; guiding Jingjing through glimmering street-markets; the two sitting together, rain falling, quietly eating Chinese pears in Guangdong's sleepy countryside.

***

Mother Chen now waits for her daughter to come home and thinks of this new country, so barren and full of melancholy. In the quiet evening, she chews yellow, discarded scraps of pear skin, thinking of when she was still Great Mother instead of Cheap Mother.

A Renaissance Studio
by Marlene Shinn Lewis

Longlisted, Edinburgh International Flash Fiction Award 2019

"Lisa, thou art late!"

"I must needs have my *comestio* before sitting here, 'Nardo. *Prosecco* and *la tortiera*."

"Thou must needs be here when I require. The light, the light!"

"This attic presses on me."

"This *studio* is situated ideally for the light from the north I need to paint."

"How much longer need I sit?"

"Until I am finished."

"How much longer?"

"Thou, *cara*, are simply a bowl of fruit, a mountain, a cow. Thou art an impassive model and *ergo* have no use other than as an object for me to observe and reproduce on this wood panel. A bowl of fruit is blessedly silent."

"Thou, 'Nardo, art a pig. I will complain to Francesco that thou mistreats me!"

"Francesco desires this portrait of thee, although only the *buon Dio* in Heaven and Francesco know why. I would rather paint a cow for him to idolize. Sit still!"

"This chair is hard. I need a soft cushion."

"Thou seemst to carry thine own cushion behind thee. Too much *tortiera*. Move thy hands to the left to cover that *prosecco* stain."

"Have a care, 'Nardo, that I do not tell *Il Duca* what I know about that dinner thou painted for him on Santa Maria's wall."

"Thou wouldst not!"

"I wouldst."

"Here is a cushion for you, *cara*."

"And . . .?"

"Now what, *cara* Lisa?"

"I am not a cow."

"Thou art not a cow."

"And . . .?"

"And I adore thee, *carissima*!"

The Mona smiled.

Life on the Margins
by Shaun Laird

Longlisted, Edinburgh International Flash Fiction Award 2019

The hardback edition of *Persuasion* caught my eye in that neglected old Blackheath bookshop, squatting thickly on the musty shelf, begging my attention. Idly flicking its yellowing pages, I was drawn to an inscription in the margin.

Anne, this book,
a gift for you,
is also, a gift for myself.
Forgive me this test –
the tale in this book has
almost run, and if
you are still reading,
then there is hope
that your heart finds
a mirror in my own and
that my blossoming
love be true;
if you have cast
this book aside,
then by fate's chance
must I too be cast aside.

Over the page was written

Fred,
it is true that
I have feelings for you.
Perhaps I have been
too meek.
I return this book,

with the wish that
you will read this
and know
that my heart desires
you.

Page after page, the slender margins yielded expressions of lives lived
in shared conversation, annotations on the small human dramas of joy
and grief. In time, these two were joined by other voices

I love you most mummy!
But I don't want a brother
Evie 7½

Within the observations, remarks and rebukes (oh, you will SO regret
that!!!), of family holidays, new chapters, fallow-periods then frantic
memos, was love soaked in ink and time.

The entry on the final page was

Frederick Andrew Hollins,
my father
died this January
followed by Anne
my mother
three days later.
My words run dry.
Evelyn 14.2.72

The Sign
by Tom Gordon

Longlisted, Edinburgh International Flash Fiction Award 2019

A Peacock butterfly had landed on his teacup and was flicking its reddish-purple wings open to reveal their huge 'eye-spot' markings, designed to scare off random birds looking for a snack. But it didn't scare *him*. Why would it, when Jennifer had said "You'll get a sign."?

The butterfly didn't stay long.

Neither had Jennifer. She'd promised she'd never leave him. Even when the brain-tumour diagnosis gave her six months, she'd insisted she'd keep her promise. But now? She couldn't be here *physically*, of course. Any fool knew *that*. But she'd insisted he'd get a sign. He'd know, soon enough, that she'd never left him.

He'd picked up a white feather outside the crematorium after her funeral. Was this it?

Surely not! Jennifer had never been the soft, delicate, gentle type. So, no feather, then?

The rainbow over the Forth yesterday? Watery, incomplete, fleeting? If it had been a fat, colourful monstrosity, dominating everything under it, *that* would have been more Jennifer. But a feeble rainbow sign? He didn't think so!

So, was it the butterfly – dramatic, scaring off predators, making the table its own?

More like it! But then, Jennifer never liked tea, so it couldn't be that.

A wasp appeared on his cream-scone. He flicked at it with his finger. Off it buzzed – and returned immediately. He flapped at it with his napkin, but the bloody thing refused to go. "Damned wasp!" he cursed and clapped his hands, but still …

"Shit!" he said. "It's the sign!"

Short Date
by Isobel Cunningham

Longlisted, Edinburgh International Flash Fiction Award 2019

The pernicious hope of a match on a dating site for seniors brought them together. At an outdoor café under a bright striped awning they sat politely sizing each other up.

His kind eyes set in wrinkles followed a young girl passing close by. "Ah, my first wife looked like her. A great beauty."

Across the table she twisted her napkin as a bright spark of anticipation died down. His good looks, his charm, his magnetism were suspect now.

"Looking for companionship." she had written. Lies. She wanted passion, lust, love of body and soul.

Now, jealousy had ambushed her, flooding over her a like a black tsunami. She was jealous of this unknown girl of fifty years ago, she for whom men had turned in the street, she who still haunted this man's heart.

Regret and pity for her own youth as a plain and unloved woman, for solitary years that could never be changed, never salvaged, suddenly made her eyes swim.

She got up. "I think I'll go home now," she whispered to his bewilderment.

Fly, Sissy
by Linda McLaughlin

Longlisted, Edinburgh International Flash Fiction Award 2019

Okay, Sissy's on the streets. But she's doing alright. Got a proper tent, ground-sheet, flysheet, everything, not some skanky old tarp. She keeps it nice.

Alright, sometimes, kids … they throw stuff – bricks, mud, worse things, even … Sissy takes the bat out, waves it about a bit, gives them an earful. She'd never use it, but they don't know that. Gotta show them you're not scared, they're like hyenas, they can smell fear. She's seen skippers trashed, people standing in the rubble, devastated …

So something hits the tent-roof; she's straight out isn't she, but it's not hyenas, it's just a bird, stunned. They do that, birds, think it's clear sky – it's just a reflective window. Bang! Break their necks, usually – but this one: beak opening and shutting, breast quivering, grabbing for air, for life. Can't just leave it there, all undefended – strays'd get it, rats even, maybe.

Doesn't have much space for tears, Sissy. But this thing – so little, so fragile, so easy to break. Breaks her, a bit. It's just trying to get home, to be safe. So she takes it into the tent, give it a chance maybe.

Doesn't make it, though. Sissy's angry at first. Not the bird's fault, though, is it? Things conspire.

So she takes it down the river, watches it flutter down like a dark flag, spiral away on the tide, wings outspread like it's flying. Like it's free. Better, she thinks. Better than just tossed, forgotten, where a rat can find you. Much better.

The Travelling Circus
by Laura Blake

Longlisted, Edinburgh International Flash Fiction Award 2019

The travelling circus is coming to town, to dazzle you with a display of total devastation.

It hasn't a single dancing clown; there are no wild animals or tightrope walkers that glitter and astound. And yet, the circus promises a spectacle the likes of which the world has never seen before. Roll up, and roll out – the show's about to begin, whether you're ready or not.

Forlorn faces peek from windows as the circus rumbles by. It materialises on the horizon at the end of a scope; it cavorts through shell-shocked towns and villages like a venerable parade on the attack. Cannons, pulled on rattling wagons, lead the way. A synchronised battalion march in quick time behind, the brass buttons gleaming on their costumes. We're only here until Christmas, they call out, in dizzy delirium, so make sure you sign up for all the fun!

Here's a fine spot to pitch up, the ringmaster says, and orders the Big Top to be dug out of the frozen earth. The front line offers the best seats in the house! You'll be close enough to graze your fingers on the barbed wire.

That's not smoke that's clouding the air; it's excitement. And that's not the sound of shellfire. It's applause. This show offers uninterrupted, heart-stopping action – the guns roar louder than any lion could.

With a wallop from a mortar shell, the performance gets underway. Tonight, like every other night, there will be fireworks.

Bullet Time
by Gordon Craig

Longlisted, Edinburgh International Flash Fiction Award 2019

The first bullet did not kill Carlos Rodriguez. It passed two inches to the left of his shoulder and embedded itself about the same distance into the wall behind him. It was discovered almost a week later by Juliet Smith, a forensic analyst working her first day in the field. She noted it on her drawing with a red biro.

The second bullet did not kill Carlos Rodriguez although it did graze his right arm, tearing his favourite jacket. Had he survived the day, the graze, without proper medical attention, would have formed an ugly scar. The bullet carried on through the workstation of one Casey Grant, ruining the photo of his dog, Hermes, that he had been forced to leave topside.

The third bullet killed Carlos Rodriguez. It entered at the exact point on his neck where his wife, Christina, had kissed him before leaving for the lab that very morning. He had been too sleepy to say goodbye. It shattered his left collarbone, severing his subclavian artery. The bone sapped enough momentum from the bullet that it did not make it all the way through his body, preventing another hole in his favourite jacket. Before he died, the lack of blood reaching his brain made him lose consciousness, but not before he pulled on the lever that opened the cages.

Not Lost or Drowned
by Jupiter Jones

Longlisted, Edinburgh International Flash Fiction Award 2019

You scan the cliffs, past gulls hovering on thermals. Half-expecting her body spatchcocked on sharp rocks, draggling from a nesting ledge, eye-sockets pecked egg-shell clean. But no; her husband already searched here, expecting the worst, finding only spume, tossed high, sparkling in late-summer sun.

You're staying alone in a caravan. You walk to pass the time. Sometimes you take the bus into town, cruising past trinket shops. Missing posters; signs of desperation, fly-posted along the coast. She has, or had, the same name as you. Unsettling to see it there above a number to call, day or night. You memorise it, test yourself at the next poster, and the next, till you know it by heart.

She looks, looked, a little like you. Do strangers wonder if they have seen the missing woman, striding about the cliff, not lost or drowned at all. You go to the mini-mart for dye. By morning you are blonde-ish. You will not be her.

Your sister rings.

"He's been here," she says. "Says he's missing you. He's sorry, won't do it again."

"Yeah, same old," you say.

The next day it rains, you stay in bed. Raindrops slide down windows. If this one reaches the bottom first, you'll get up. If the other wins you won't. You came to escape a gambler who hurts you when he loses. All gamblers chase the chance; not of winning but losing completely; everything.

On the cliffs again. You throw your wallet, phone, shoes over the edge.

Rich Harvest
by Ann Abineri

Longlisted, Edinburgh International Flash Fiction Award 2019

I creep painfully across the wet grass, aching from the beating that the cook gave me last night. I pause to rest at gravestones with carvings obscured by fat yellow crusts of lichen. Back home people scraped simple plants like that from the rocks on the shore. Knowing what you can eat is key to survival.

My grandfather could not keep me at home on a sexton's stipend once my parents were gone. But as I prepared to leave the island for servitude, he stilled his sobs to whisper his secrets.

I find what I am looking for in a malodorous corner of the graveyard, shadowed by black yews. My quarry glows white in the dark grass. I cover my hands with my apron and begin to pick.

As I approach the kitchen door, a guard demands to see what I am carrying. He peers at the fungi. Despite the fact that there is nothing to raise any alarm and I am averting my eyes, he gives my ankle a vicious kick as I pass.

I smile as I hand the bag of pale fungi to the cook. At tonight's banquet the mushrooms will be served to my masters in a rich dark soup. It will be declared delicious and my foraging skills will be praised.

From now on every mushroom for the high table will come from the graveyard where the arsenic used to embalm the bodies of the wealthy leaches slowly and silently into the damp black soil.

Flash Point
by Sherry Morris

Longlisted, Edinburgh International Flash Fiction Award 2019

Urgency propels Maude to the open window where Herman sits below. Her mouth burns from the bomb that's hurtled down the phone line and landed in her gut. The fuse sears her throat. It'll do worse to Herman, sitting in the shade of the station's awning, protected from the fierce Midwestern summer sun, humming *My Way*.

Old fool she thinks.

His back is to her. The tall pumps with their round, red heads, rectangular bodies, and open faces like slow children stand nearby ready to serve. They're all that keep him company while he watches road and sky. Both are empty. Cars prefer the interstate now. Decades ago people came, buying gas, penny sweets and pop. Now, not even a cloud passes.

His stillness gives her pause. There's no clatter or patter today, no puttering about. Once she speaks, peace will be shattered. Sheltering in shop shade won't be an option. They'll never be happy again.

Maybe he'll blame her. But she's done her part, clipping coupons, endlessly mending, never minding not having new. He assured her they'd be fine handling things his way. All the little sacrifices she's borne for nothing. The sizzle in her stomach intensifies, stings her mouth. She clears her throat, ready to detonate with news.

Without turning, he says, "Come sit with me, my love."

She notices the box of Red Top safety matches on his knee, smells the puddle of petrol, sees the letters in his hand. Realises who's been shielded all along.

"I Would Never Hurt You"
by Bethany Bolger

Longlisted, Edinburgh International Flash Fiction Award 2019

Words are like colours, he told me. They paint a picture of your life. He promised me Monet sunrises.

Words are red.

Strawberries burst in our mouths; juice dribbles down my chin. He laughs. We kiss between bites and drink merlot.

You're too beautiful, he says.

Blood courses through my veins and rises to my cheeks. Hearts appear as he arrives in a vermilion Ferrari. Poppies in my kitchen as passion reigns in my bedroom.

Words are yellow.

Blazing sunbeams illuminate golden sands. I wear a teeny-weeny polka-dot bikini.

Fat arse and tiny tits. He's joking.

I go to the shop. An ochre kimono will do, thank you.

Lemons become lemonade. Apologetic promises given with sunflowers. Forgiveness given with hopefulness.

Words are blue.

Leaves fall from lilies like tears behind ultramarine curtains. I timidly walk the halls in furry periwinkle slippers. Melancholy turns the moon sapphire.

Ungrateful bitch. Old hag. Useless cow.

He's drunk. The words appear with the alcohol. He won't remember tomorrow. I will. Hidden bruises don't heal. We play this game too often.

Words are red.

Lust and rage written in scarlet letters.

Fucking slut. Whore. Cunt.

A hot poker and searing pain. Rising screams match rising flames.

Words are black.

Dressed for death. Onyx umbrellas threatening clouds at a sombre funeral.

Words are grey.

Bitter winds beat cemetery slabs. The granite feels nothing.

*****

He always said: I didn't mean it. They're only words. His words don't affect me anymore. Now he can't speak.

A Christmas Surprise
by Peter Kelly

Winner, Scottish Arts Club Short Story Competition 2020

I hate my life. Everyone will be getting on it at Jimbo's Party, but what am I doing? Traipsing around George Square with my gran. Brilliant. I bet Natalie's there. I bet that clown Tam will be trying to fire in about her. Fuck sake, man.

"Look at this Charles," my gran said, holding up some crap from a stall. "Our Rebecca would look so cute in this. What d'you think?"

I couldn't give a fuck about an elf baby-grow. "Definitely Gran. That would be smashing."

"I knew you'd like it, son," she said, fishing her purse from her handbag.

I sighed and glanced to the heavens. Flashing LEDs of a Santa waving caught my eye. What a prick.

Don't get me wrong, I love my gran, and she's been taking me to the Christmas market since I was a wee boy. But I'm not a wee boy anymore, and did she have to pick a Saturday night?

After getting her change – a whole fucking penny – from the guy at the stall she turned. "Right son, I think that's me sorted. I just need something for Angela's wee one, you know, the young lassie next door. She" —I don't care. I don't care – "but I'll just pick something up next time I" —still don't care. I want to go home – "oh, and I need to get a bottle of gin for Mary, you know, my bingo pal, she" — aww, here we go with the bingo shite. Kill me now. My ears pricked at the word 'home'.

"What?" I said.

"I was saying, is there anything you want to do before we go home?"

"No Gran, I'm good, let's go."

"What about the skating? You used to love scooting around the rink."

I probably did ...when I was five. "Na Gran, think I'll give it a miss. I've got a big game tomorrow, don't want to risk going over my ankle."

She shook her head and tutted. "You and your football. You need to let your hair down once in a while and enjoy yourself."

If I hadn't been dragged here, my hair would be all the way down to the fucking ground by now. "What can I say Gran. I'm keen as."

"You are so," she said with a laugh. "Come here, son." She hooked her arm onto mine. "My old legs aren't what they used to be."

A bit of me died inside as I shuffled toward Queen Street with a pensioner hanging onto me. She looked like ET waddling along beside me, with her brown coat and headscarf. At least nobody would be here to see me.

We eventually reached the stairs to the train station. Two big coppers with guns stood at the foot of the stairs, and two with dogs were at the top. We climbed the stairs slower than one of they tools with the green 'P' plates on their car. I pulled my phone out: 18:25. See if we miss this train.

We reached the top and I nearly shat myself when one of the police dogs started barking and straining at its leash. Must not have liked the look of me. I looked at the copper holding the dog back, and my heart sank. He was looking right at me, beckoning me with one finger. What is this?

The dog shut up when the copper commanded it to sit. He pointed toward a doorway away from the stream of people who were having a right good gawk as they walked past. He passed the leash to his colleague before joining us.

"What's your name?" he said.

"Chaz."

"Do I look like one of your pals?" he barked, scarier than the dog by his side.

The day I'm pals with a copper is the day I become a loner. "No," I said with a shake of the head.

"Then give me the full name your parents gave you."

"Show some respect, Charles," my gran said, cuffing me around the ear.

I had to stop myself asking the big copper to do her with assault. "It's Charles McLeod."

"Officer," my gran said in her best telephone voice. "Is there something wrong?"

"Ma'am, we need to ask your ...?"

"Grandson."

"... grandson a few questions." He turned his attention back to me. "How old are you, Charles?"

"Sixteen."

"Do you have anything on you, you shouldn't have?"

I shook my head. "No."

"Then you won't mind if we search you?"

Actually, I do mind. "Fill your boots."

"Empty your pockets, please."

I rummaged around in my pockets, coming away with a phone, some cash, keys, and a half-empty packet of chewing gum.

"Do you have any sharps on you?" he said as he snapped on a pair of those blue glove's doctors wear.

"What, like needles?"

"Needles, knives, scissors, anything that could injure me."

"Na, this is all I've got."

He either never heard me or didn't believe me as he had a good rummage himself.

"Hold your arms out like this," he said, mimicking the motion.

I sighed and rolled my eyes but did as commanded.

"The less attitude, the easier this will be," he said.

Easier for who? His rubber protected fingers swept through my hair, felt behind my ears, under my collar and along both arms. I gagged at his cheap aftershave as his hands reached around, and down my back. He stuck both thumbs in my waistband and swept around until they met at the front. He squatted as he ran his hands down both legs; his hands coming dangerously close to my pecker.

"Slip your trainers off, pal."

So, we're pals now? Cold concrete seeped through my thin socks. He finished inspecting my shoes and signalled for me to put them on. He stood and looked at his colleague with a puzzled look on his face.

"There's one more thing before you can go, Charles."

The train's long gone, so do what you want. "Sure."

"Is it okay if my dog has a sniff around about you?"

"Officer," my gran said. Her telephone voice gone, replaced by a slight hint of annoyance. "Is this necessary? We have a train to catch."

"Ma'am, it won't take a minute. What do you say, Charles?"

I glanced at the dog then back at the copper. "Does it bite?"

A sleekit smile crept over his face. "Only if I tell her to."

A copper with a sense of humour? They should put him on display. "Fine."

"Ka-ra," he said, clicking his fingers in front of me.

Kara sprang into action and held her snout high. She sniffed the air as she approached and kept doing so as she passed me before coming to a rest between me and my gran. She put her snout against my gran's bag and froze with only her tail wagging. What the fuck?

The two coppers glanced at each other with wide eyes before turning their attention on my gran. "Ma'am," the first one said. "Is there something you—"

"Yes, yes, alright sonny," she said as she unzipped her bag. "You know, I'm quickly becoming a cat person." If looks could kill, then the dog with its snout pressed against gran's handbag would be dead.

"Kara, sit."

She produced a small jam jar from her bag; it wasn't filled with jam.

"Wait till I see that boy," she said. "He told me glass jars kept the smell contained."

"Kara's sense of smell is stronger than you think."

"Is that right," said my gran. "It's a pity she didn't have a cold."

She handed him the jar; he looked like he was trying to keep from laughing. The moment he unscrewed the lid we all caught the scent Kara had picked up.

"Ma'am," he said as his eyes darted to me. "Is this yours?"

"Less of the ma'am, sonny, I'm not the queen. My name's Jean McLeod, and yes, it's mine."

Fuck me, gran likes a smoke.

"Are you aware this is cannabis?'

"I hope it is, else that would be another reason to chin that boy."

The copper stole a glance at his colleague holding the two dogs. He too looked to be fighting the urge to laugh.

"And are you aware cannabis is illegal?"

"Very … I'm also aware it shouldn't be. It's an absolute joke that they can say something so—"

"Look, Ma'am …"

"Jean."

"… Jean, I'm not here to debate the law, I'm only here to enforce it, and right now, this is illegal. Right or wrong, one thing I do know, buying this lines the pockets of drug dealers."

"Sonny, I've lined the pockets of the biggest drug dealers on the planet. For fifteen years I bought their junk – paracetamol, co-codamol, ibuprofen, diclofenac, methotrexate – and what did it do for my chronic arthritis? Not a thing. Sure, they masked the pain for a while, until I built up a tolerance. So, their pushers, I mean my doctor, fed me more and more, stronger and stronger pills, until I became hooked and the only thing numb was me. So yes, you're right, it's not ideal lining dope dealer's pockets, but at least they're honest about what they do."

I was stunned. The coppers looked stunned. Even Kara looked sheepish for grassing on my gran.

"Jean," began the copper. He looked serious. "Does this really work?"

"Son, the first night I took it, I had the best sleep of my life. I woke up feeling like I did in my twenties. Before lunch, I had gutted the house, did the washing and ironing, I even hung they new curtains I'd bought years before. Since using this medicine, I've been pain-free. It really has given me a new lease of life. Never thought I'd say this, but the sooner we follow the Yanks lead, the better."

"And if we confiscate it?"

Her body slumped and she gazed into the distance. "I don't even want to think about what tonight will be like."

The copper glanced at his colleague who gave a slight nod. He screwed the lid on tight and slipped it into my gran's handbag.

"Did you say something about having a train to catch?"

"I did." My gran zipped her bag shut and flashed him a big smile. "Thanks, son."

The police officer nodded and returned the smile. "Safe journey." He turned and resumed his position at the top of the stairs.

We walked through the station in awkward silence and boarded our train. We sat across from one another and our eyes met.

"Well," I said, "at least I know what to get you for Christmas."

"Charles, if I ever catch you buying dope, I'll break every one of your fingers."

I smiled and looked out the window. Turns out gran's a bit of a bad ass.

The Time of his Life
by Neil Lawson-May

Second Prize, Scottish Arts Club Short Story Competition 2020

Mrs Marrak was up early to make Professor Adler a proper hiker's breakfast of fresh farm eggs, local cured bacon and foraged mushrooms. She wished him a good day's walking as he and his German Shepherd, Copernicus, set off on the coast path to Gunver Head.

It had become his habit to visit the West Country at the end of the Lent Term, when the daffodils were blooming and the sea had a magic spring shimmer. The idea was to flex his intellectual muscles away from the restrictions of Cambridge, to enjoy some strenuous hiking and to satisfy his appetite with good local food and some West Country Cider.

A fine Cornish morning thought Adler, humming a few bars of 'Ode to Joy' to himself. A chance for me to consider my work on Einstein-Rosen bridges. The mathematics of wormholes in the fabric of space-time was tricky, but his mind felt especially clear and creative. Perhaps he could make that breakthrough he'd been trying for.

As he neared Gunver Head the path became dangerously narrow and slippery. It was some 150 feet above a wild sea that tore at the broken and serrated rocks below. This was not a place to miss-step or fall and he kept Copernicus on the lead.

A sea mist rolled in and he shivered. He thought he could see the outline of an animal and as it approached he realised it was a dog. Where was the owner? The dog ran up to him in a friendly way. It was a German Shepherd very like Copernicus, but this dog was distressed and its lead had been chewed through so that just a few inches remained. The stray had been in some sort of scrape, but otherwise the two animals were so similar that they could have been brothers.

Adler was concerned about the dog's owner. They might be in trouble, possibly hurt. He walked on and to his great unease saw a hiking boot on the rocks below. It would be quite a tumble for someone to lose their boot thought Adler. The stray ran ahead to the faintest of paths going steeply down the cliff face. He reached for his mobile to call for help, but to his annoyance he'd left it on the breakfast table. He tied Copernicus to a fence and reluctantly decided to go a little way down the path. With some difficulty he held the stray by the short lead. After a while he shouted out,

"Hello, are you in trouble, do you need help?"

"Stay where you are and don't let go of the dog."

The stray slipped from his grasp and shot off, barking furiously. It stumbled on some loose ground and slid madly down the cliff – disappearing from sight. Then, silence.

"Can you see the dog, is he alright?" Adler shouted.

"Don't worry about the dog and don't come any further."

But he was already edging down the path to where the dog had vanished. Then he too lost his footing and started to slide. He grabbed at flimsy bushes growing in the outcrops but couldn't get a hand hold. He swore to himself, this was it – he was going to die.

But he didn't die. His fall was stopped suddenly and painfully by a large gorse bush. Below him the sea and rocks were awful. He took a few deep breaths and looked around. There was no way back up. A voice came from below.

"There are some footholds just to your left, lower yourself down."

He climbed a little way and hands grabbed his legs, hauling him onto a small rocky ledge.

"Thank you." He said turning to his rescuer. But to his utter amazement there was not one person on the ledge but three. And all three were Professor Ulrich Adler of Clare College Cambridge.

"Yes, yes, we know." Said the Adler who had pulled him onto the ledge, "there's three of us and you. All four of us are the same person. We think it's some kind of Morris-Thorne effect."

"A wormhole for time travel. On a Cornish cliff?"

"We've all got the same story. A walk after breakfast, the stray dog, the boot on the rocks, the dog disappears, and then our fall is broken by the gorse bush. We all look the same, are dressed the same and we talk the same. We are the same person. So, yes, most likely a wormhole in space-time."

"Can we climb up or down."

"Both impossible."

"Have you called for help?"

"The only person who ever comes past is ourselves, and you will notice there are no birds or planes in the sky. We seem to be in our own time dimension."

He looked down at their feet, "We've all got our boots on."

"Yes, the boot on the rocks is nothing to do with us, we suppose it just washed up."

"Where's the dog gone?"

"That's the wrong question."

Adler thought for a moment, "Copernicus – of course, time travel. The stray dog is Copernicus. He waits for me to return, becomes agitated, chews through his lead and wanders along the cliff to meet the next me and the next Copernicus."

"Correct, but?"

"Ah! Why are there four of us but only two dogs?"

The answer came from the man furthest along the ledge. "When Copernicus slips down the cliff he tumbles and falls to where I'm standing. He's a big dog travelling at high speed and the impact will topple me and Copernicus off the ledge and into the sea. When the next Adler climbs down off the gorse bush you will all shuffle up one place. The Adler after me waits for Copernicus to crash onto him, and so on and so on."

"Good God. Into the sea. You mean you and Copernicus are going to drown?"

There was a silent pause. The other Adlers looked rueful.

"But surely we can all hold hands or squeeze up together or something."

"It's all been tried. Nothing's worked so far – the Adler on the end always dies. It takes about an hour for Copernicus to get distressed enough to chew through his lead and start looking for me – you – us along the cliff before the next Adler finds him."

"How many? How many have gone into the water?"

"From when we started counting I'm number 473," said the furthest; "this is 474 and 475, you are 476."

"This is appalling. How can you be so calm?"

"Once you've seen your own death you are sort of ready for it. It becomes the opposite of that artwork – you know, the dead shark in the tank."

"The impossibility of death in the mind of someone living?"

"Exactly, here death is not only possible it is inevitable."

"Scheisse. If only I'd…"

"…had more cider to drink last night and was in bed with a hangover?"

"And I felt so alive this morning, I felt the universe opening up to me, such possibilities."

The others nodded.

"Well," said 475, "We are working on a mathematical solution."

They worked together on the maths. It was a thrilling session, the productivity, the ideas, the sheer brilliance of it all. No solution was found, but the work was luminescent. They lost track of time. Then,

"Hello, are you in trouble, do you need me to get help?"

"Stay where you are and don't let go of the dog."

The Adlers stared at 473. A German Shepherd came spinning down the cliff, smashed into 473 and both man and dog plunged off the ledge into the furious water, vanishing completely.

After a few moments a new Adler landed on the gorse bush and was helped onto the ledge. They all moved along one place and the cycle continued. An hour later Copernicus knocked 474 to his death and in due course 475 went the same way. Now Adler himself was on the end of the ledge where the dog would soon take him off. He found the mathematics much less interesting.

Then he had an idea. "What if I lowered myself down from the ledge and you pull me back up after Copernicus has fallen?"

"How can you lower yourself, there's nothing to hang onto?"

"Bootlaces. We have eight walking boots, each with a pair of 60-inch nylon laces, that's 40 feet of rope, 20 if we double it up. We can tie it round that wooden stump – he pointed to a branch at the other end of the ledge.

The Adlers looked at each other – yes, this could work.

They spent more time than was sensible on devising an equation to prove that it would work, and it wasn't until late in the hour that they made the rope. It was passed along between them; one end was tied to the stump and the other around Adler's waist.

"Hello, are you in trouble, do you need me to get help?"

They weren't ready. For this to work Adler should already be lowered off the ledge. But he was still with the others – the rope lay along the ledge, blocked by their feet.

"Stay where you are and don't let go of the dog."

Bang. The impact of Copernicus hitting him was incredible, he was catapulted off the ledge at tremendous speed – whirling crazily. One of his boots flew off and landed on the rocks. The rope tightened and it became clear that the other Adlers hadn't been quick enough to step over it. They were sling-shotted off the ledge. Adler gasped as they were swept away, their arms and legs flailing in the air.

The rope stretched out, Adler held on with one hand, not breathing. But it was okay, it took his weight and incredibly Copernicus was lying on his chest, with the rope holding him in place.

Just as he was beginning to recover, there was a crashing noise above him as the next Adler landed on the gorse bush. But with no one to help him climb off, the bush couldn't hold his weight and it snapped. The new Adler followed the others into the sea.

"Hello, are you in trouble, do you need me to get help?"

"Stay where you are and don't let go of the dog. No hang on, it hasn't been an hour yet. Yes, get help. I'm trapped with a dog. I don't know how long the rope will hold."

By the time Mrs Marrak arrived at the hospital, Adler was sitting up in bed furiously scribbling equations on any piece of paper he could get hold of.

"No visitors, no visitors." He shouted.

"He's a bit delirious," said the nurse, "he keeps talking about time travel. We found very high levels of Psilocin in his blood stream, so no wonder he fell off the path."

"Psilocin?"

"It's what's in magic mushrooms, Professor Adler seems to have a drug habit."

"Magic mushrooms" Repeated Mrs Marrack, thinking back to Adler's breakfast and the foraged *funghi*. Giggling, she added, "he's probably had the time of his life."

Hunger Point
by Gail Anderson

Third Prize, Scottish Arts Club Short Story Competition 2020

Eucalyptus. A clean smell, too damned clean – but underpinned by the pleasing aroma of frying onions, drifting from the valley below. It was on this smell that Eddie Rigel focussed his mind. He could just about taste his mother's *Bacalhau à Gomes de Sá,* salt cod layered with potato and onion. *11.43pm.* Rigel breathed deeply. He was grateful to those onions, savoured them, became one with them. They obliged by keeping his mind off the job he had to do.

Eddie Rigel was waiting. A dark man in a dark suit, sitting in a black sedan in the shadows along a lonely, moonlit ribbon of canyon road, a hundred feet up from the old Mayerling place. He let his mind move past the onions to linger on the crisp sweetness of his mother's fried plantains, the charred lime-and-pepper piquancy of her *Poulet Boucané,* her fiery *Sauce Chien.* The onions that inspired these memories of his Martiniquais mother, long dead, were most powerful sign he'd encountered over these past two troubled weeks. Eddie Rigel, who'd chosen his own surname from the brightest star in Orion's belt, believed in signs.

He basked in the phantom glow of his mother's home fires until midnight, when his watch played a little chime. As if on cue, the tall gates of the Mayerling place swung open. A red roadster pulled out and started off down the hill. Rigel watched the beam of headlights sweep one bend of the steep road, then another, before starting his engine and following at a distance.

The Mayerlings were old money, quiet money. They'd fled the Nazis early enough in the game to bring their fortune with them, and they'd made good use of it. Property speculation. Plantations. Now the Mayerling patriarch had died, leaving his estate to the last in the family line. Louisa Mayerling was twenty-two, pretty, wild. When Philip Silva had first put Rigel on her tail, he'd called it *protection.* Tonight was Rigel's final night of the assignment, because now the order had changed. Silva wanted the girl dead, and Silva got what he wanted.

The twisting road spun the two cars down out of the foothills. It skirted the reservoir, water silver by moonlight, and ran along the floor of the canyon, an avenue of tall palms, before drifting to join the ocean highway. Out at sea, white foam furled like the manes of spectral horses. The two cars passed the scattering of all-night *taquito* trucks, their oil-barrel fire pits ablaze with driftwood. As usual, the taco guys hit their air-horns as the red car passed: *Cielito Lindo* blared into the night, successive waves of sound mingled with the dried-earth smell of *chipotle*, the thick pungency of frying oil, of *chili verde*. Tonight she wasn't stopping, but as usual, she waved back, her slim arm out the window, red nails flashing, bracelets winking.

She pulled up at *Rincon Aleman*, as he knew she would. Rigel parked, watched in his wing mirror. They knew her in there too. She came out of the little shack with both hands full: *bratwurst*, loaded with *sauerkraut*. Rigel smiled, seeing significance in her choice on this final night. He was a *boudin noir* man himself, blood sausage fired with pepper – but after three days of following her, he'd been curious enough to go back and try the *wurst*. It was mild, too mild for his tastes, but he enjoyed the delicacy of the spice – nutmeg? – and imagined that it spoke to her of Austria, a homeland she'd never seen, just as his *boudin* reminded him of the Martinique he didn't know.

From the *Aleman* she turned inland, up the *arroyo seco*. Under a winking neon Pegasus she pulled up to a drive-thru window, picked up a shake. She was a regular there too, bantering with the delighted kid at the window. Louisa devoured her meal as she drove, her long curls and delicate profile silhouetted black against the oncoming headlights, like a Chinese shadow puppet. Four miles inland, up a coast canyon studded with bay cedar, she pulled in behind a busy roadhouse. *El Encanto*, the name lettered in a typography of palm leaves, was one of Silva's many 'investments'. Rigel let his sedan roll to a stop on the other side of the road, killed the engine. Then he lit a smoke.

His own family, like hers, had been transplanted. He and his mother brought to the mainland from their native Martinique by his soldier-adventurer father. Brought to a so-called land of opportunity, and left there. The father had moved on before his son had formed any lasting memory of the man, and his mother had longed to return home, even just the once before she died, but they'd been too poor. Rigel had sworn never to be poor again.

Philip Silva rewarded his faithful. Rigel now made the kind of money his mother could only have dreamed about. His fortunes had risen, while the Mayerlings' had fallen. These days the Mayerling estate was nothing more than a considerable amount of good hill country, and a run-down, Bavarian-style mansion spiked like a puffer fish with turrets and gables. Silva had been throwing loops around the place for years, buying up the old man's gambling debt. Silva, small in stature, was gargantuan in terms of wealth and power. Rigel was glad his mother hadn't lived to wonder at her son's line of work. *Protection, Édouard?* He could hear the doubt in her voice. *What sort of work is that?*

Faint music from the roadhouse: the wavering, old-world melody-line of Cole Porter's *Solomon*. Rigel swung his legs out of the car. The bouncer was built like the Chixoy Dam, but he knew Rigel, let him pass.

The old place was nothing from the outside, but inside it was celestial. A vast room, low table lamps hung like stars over a hundred faintly glowing tablecloth moons. Jewelled necks glittered and studded shirt fronts winked. From upstairs, the whir of roulette wheels, the discreet snap of dice and markers. The first night he'd followed her in here, Rigel had searched the crowd anxiously, thought she had given him the slip, before realising she wasn't seated in the club at all. She was up on the stage.

Rigel took his place at Silva's exclusive table, right up front, and gazed openly at his quarry. Louisa Mayerling had to work for her living, and she was best burlesque performer in the country. Too damned good. Night after night, Rigel prayed for her to drop one of her fans.

A black and white waiter brought brandy and iced champagne. Another brought oysters. Last night Rigel had nearly chipped a tooth on a tiny pearl. Another sign.

The orchestra transitioned. *Anything Goes.* Louisa favoured the old tunes. Rigel, the assassin, tipped a creamy oyster into his mouth, then another. He poured a tot of brandy into his glass, topped it with cold champagne, raised it. One drink would make no difference to his aim at close quarters. He would never see her again after this evening, and he needed something to toast her with, one last time.

Rigel left the roadhouse at 4am and drove towards the glow of the city. Louisa Mayerling would make two more stops that night. He watched from the bar of the Old 35er across the street as the red roadster pulled up in front of Pierre's, a deli with sawdusted floors. Her arrival was anticipated by old Pierre himself, who plated her French dip sandwich as she entered. Thinly sliced succulent beef on a just-baked roll, a little bowl of roasted meat juices on the side for dipping, a smear of Dijon. Rigel tasted every juicy bite along with her, secretly offering her a silent salute. As a last supper, it had merit.

From this point forward, she would be on the final leg of her nocturnal journey. She would leave Pierre's and head into the city, into the hard Angel District, with its forgotten men and women, its burned and boarded-up buildings, its grifters and needles and whores. Anything could happen in the Angel, the police wouldn't even blink. Rigel watched Louisa eat, wishing for reprieve, bidding her to spin it out as long as possible. Pierre sat with her. Simple, uncomplicated talk, the old man rising to fetch her a pickled onion from the big jar on the counter, waving her change away. Rigel watched. People liked Louisa Mayerling. His mother would have liked her. His mother would have liked him to bring a girl like this home.

Down on the Angel she'd stop for a few hours at a dingy hall. She'd chop and slice, cook and serve. One night he'd disguised himself and sat at charity's table with the poorest of the poor, where the bean, rice and pepper confetti of her *gallo pinto* had delighted his mouth, where the steam from plates of hot *huevos rancheros* had washed over him like baptism. He could taste the salt that glistened on her high, fine forehead. Her hair was caught up in a long scarf, tied around her head in exactly the same way his mother had done. Rigel ached at the memory, sorry that this final stop, so indicative of her soul, would have to be missed. The gates of Heaven would open to Louisa Mayerling, this he knew; but time was moving him on, cutting short their final night, and he needed to report to Silva before this assignment was finished.

When Rigel arrived at the high sea cliffs at Hunger Point, forty miles down the coast, there was a pearl dawn on the horizon. *6.14am.* Rigel, always punctual, backed the sedan to the cliff's edge. In the trunk, the fateful bundle awaited the turn of the tide. Rigel hove ropes around the small body, surprisingly heavy, and hauled it free. The sound of the splash was lost in the roar of the surf far below.

Then he drove south, parked his car underground at a cheap block of waterside apartments, dropped his keys and watch down a grate. On the highway, carrying only a small bag, wearing denim and an old canvas jacket, he stood with working men, boarded a bus to the harbour. By the time his ship cast off, the powerful riptide current would have swept the body halfway to Santa Cruz Rock. Rigel had done the parcel up with care, hopeful that a shark would finish with it before it got there. *No trace.* This was what Silva demanded, and this last time Silva had got exactly what he deserved. Far away, in the eucalyptus hills above the sea, Louisa Mayerling would be sleeping, undisturbed. The gates of Heaven would open for her, yes – and God willing, not for a long time to come.

No trace. From here he would travel by sea: through the Panama Canal, then *L'Express des Iles* to Fort-de-France, Martinique. His mind was clear, his hands were clean, and his nose detected a sweet clemency of frying onions on the morning air. Eddie Rigel was going home.

The Last of the Clan
by Sinclair Steven

Winner, Isobel Lodge Award 2020
Shortlisted, Scottish Arts Club Short Story Competition 2020

Why are they aw sae miserable? Huddilt roon the auld man on his nag, convinced their world has shattered aroon them. Hae none of them ony sense o excitement, adventure, am A the only one? Sae the hooses in the glen hae been fired, sae the walls hae been cowpit in, but God A've longed aw ma life tae get oot o that hovel, stumblin aroon in the darkness, bent ower wi nae heidroom, the constant chokin fog o the peat smoke, the stench o the dung and pish o the kye crowding the far end o the hoose. What is there there tae lament?

An ootside ekin a 'living' frae a miserable plot o sodden peat; the numbin labour o diggin in the cloyin morass; knee deep in the cauld sludge hopin a few miserable tatties will survive the blight.

On the other side o that water there's a future, they say: room tae grow, develop, escape the power and control o lairds and their lackeys. Aye, look at auld Lachlan there. Lachlan the lackey. Faither o the toonship he callit himself, but aye keen and iver willin tae dae the laird's biddin, be it tae order the menfolk from their ain desperate plots tae harvest the laird's barley, or bring some young lads tae the laird's 'justice' for poachin a salmon or two frae the river. How can a faither betray his family like that? An there he sits heartbroken, thrown aff when the laird disnae need him ony longer, sittin astride the 'stallion' he rode roon the toonship on. The plough pony that was supposed tae be shared among the crofts tae turn ower the land but, soon as his plot was ploughit, wis somehow needit by him for important business: tae see everything 'wis in order'. Spy his stick hingin at his waist like a claymore, aye the claymore he claimed he'd wieldit at Culloden. Weel he must hae been the only claymore-wieldin fower-year old on the battlefield that day. Many a time, as a young lassie, A've felt that stick across my back and legs when he wisnae paid enough 'respect'. Auld bastard that he is.

Whit future would be here for me? Escape from the grim, hard labour on the land tae become a servant in the laird's big hoose; a chattel, a slave tae the laird's wishes and desires, and his desires are fair disgusting. An then tae be turned aff when he hungers for fresh flesh or, if you were unwilling tae be forced, replaced with more willing, innocent flesh. An a the time tae suffer the petty cruelties of his English bitch of a wife; her knowing full well whit he was up tae, soor and dried up as she is, resentin it and takin her anger oot on the victims, the 'peasant whores', o the disgusting auld man.

An aye trapped in that grim, dreich glen. The high hills hemming it in, almaist ayeways in shadow, wi rare glimpses o the sun, like bein in a big prison, jist nae bars. America A hear is big, open, lots o land tae farm, room tae growe the food you need to live on and then some. Or growing cities you can lose yir past in, away from those that want tae keep you in your place. A chance tae make something o yirsel, an A'll mak something o masel, if I can throw aff this lot of down-trodden cuifs.

Aye cuifs – an the vilest wan, Souter, leaning against the fence there, scorn scrawlit across his face. Souter the sharn-heap. Vicious wee get when he wis young. Shilpit, ugly, never able tae keep up wi the bigger lads who went aff tae be soldiers, and did all he could tae get them intae trouble, carryin tales of who was takin a fish from the burn and who had snared a rabbit tae the laird an loving the punishments they got. Must have wet himself wi excitement when the laird asked him tae be the agent's assistant. Could see the joy in his face as he threw some auld carline oot o her hame tae shiver in the cauld wi nae shelter an then the thrill in his eyes as he set the torch tae the thatch and watched it burn an collapse inside the walls. A mind the day the creature crept up tae me and said he could 'find a place' for me if I was 'kind' tae him. Told him A'd rather be 'kind' tae a pen o pigs. Whit a look o hatred that got me. An whit a kick he launched at my dog. Weel there he is, cock o the midden the noo, although a gey wee midden, but his day will come. Aince the laird has cleared a the crofts and brocht in his southern shepherds, there'll be nae place for shilpit Souter and he'll be doon here again; this time queuing tae get on a ship, no just watchin ithers get on.

At least we've been spared the attentions o the meenister. He's got nae time tae spare tae gie a blessing tae this voyage, too desperate tae sook up tae the English bitch, simperin ower her plans for her Bible Societies tae bring 'enlightenment' tae the fisher folk alang the coast. Aye A'm sure a Bible and some preachin is just whit they need tae succour them when the catches are scant or the storms keep the boats in. He wisnae sae keen tae be absent when he could preach terrifyin damnation tae the folk in the kirk and when, wi the bitch's blessing, he could scourge the lassies caught laughin wi the lads. An you could see the lust and lechery in his hypocrite een as he laid on each stroke. May he find damnation himself when his last day comes.

Naw this boat cannae tie up soon enough and let us on board. They'll aw weep and wail and gnash their teeth, but A'll jist keep ma ain cooncil. Nae word tae ony one about my thoughts and dreams. A don't fear storms and winds. Each storm will just blow me further an further away from this place o desolation an misery. A aye mind those words from that queer-bit poem the travellin dominie read tae us, afore the laird drove him aff for spreading dissent and ideas. 'O my America, my new-found-land'. Weel it's going tae be my new-found-land, my new-found life.

***

The painter stepped back from the canvas after the last few brush strokes to the red shirt of the fisherman. Yes, this was just perfect for his London clientele. Romantic, sentimental, just the touch of wildness in the sea and then the dog in the girl's arms. Yes always put a dog in somewhere. Enhances the sentimental hugely. And he had caught the frailty, but also the tragic nobility of the elderly man on his worn out pony. He felt particularly satisfied with the young woman with the dog: the epitome of maidenly modesty: heartbroken to leave her native fields but resigned to follow the leadership of her elders. Yes, this would do very well. Cleaning off his brushes he called on the men to come and pack the painting to be conveyed to the Academy.

Grace
by Karenlee Thompson

Shortlisted, Scottish Arts Club Short Story Competition 2020

Wednesday's child is full of woe betide anyone who casts a skewed glance at Marika today. She's weary of thick-hearted laundry bags and grimy grout. She washes and scrubs and searches under dark and dusty beds for divorced socks, sometimes finding petrified sandwiches, once a mouse whose game of statues ceased upon her touch. This is just one of three jobs Marika toils at.

On weekends, she wears a truncated and badly-hemmed skirt and serves drinks at a swank boutique brewery. The glass fronted bar sparkles and shimmers from the ground floor of a high-rise nestled between two other buildings at various stages of completion. The zone looks like a giant's Meccano-block amusement, complete with crane and silver-rod scaffolding, but the works don't deter the customers from swanning in for their various froth-topped glasses, chattering about the deep straw colour or the long bitter finish. There's a smattering of wines available but the wankiness is generally reserved for beer talk.

Marika's final money-making venture is Uber-driving which affords her a strange voyeuristic excitement. On designated days, she checks her app and ventures off to high-demand areas. She meets businessmen and call-girls and couples on first dates or old pairs going out for their wedding anniversaries. She drove a famous tennis player clear across town and he said you never saw me as he paid her three times what the trip was worth.

She calculates she is two months away from cashing in for her Greek-island sojourn, to dip her toes into the sea of her ancestors. Snapshots of the Mediterranean and fantasies of dark-eyed lovers help her get through her Domestos Wednesdays. She sings to keep her eyes sparkling and her cheeks dry but today the breath of the old black dog blows at her nape. She is both slumped by burden and pulled taut with stress.

***

Thursday's child has far to

go to hell billy with your karma and your smile and the whole world smiles with you and your life wasn't meant to be easy fucking bullshit that you spout constantly and don't seem to realise that no-one wants to hear because it just doesn't make anyone feel any better and look at you smiling that smug grin and pretending you are some old soul and I have to live a thousand shitty lives before I will reach your level of cosmic understanding and also I don't care about your latest fucking yoga pose in fact you look like you are trying to take a dump and it is gross and by the way who the hell told you mustard is an acceptable colour against your skin and anyway you shouldn't wear those muscle shirts because you don't really have any brawn and I'm thinking maybe if you ate a pie and some chips instead of all those fucking seeds you might look a bit less pasty and then well you could probably even wear bright yellow if you really wanted to and I don't even know how you and I became friends and anyway I'm going for a beer and I'll tell you something else for nothing oh never mind just fuck off.

***

Friday's child is loving and

giving away more than a week's pay is not something Derek is keen to do. His son is constantly discussing the merits of tithing, and his eldest daughter goes on and on about the poor homeless sleeping under the bridge. In fact, Sasha plans to sleep outside all night in the numbing cold which leaves Derek dumbfounded.

"This is Australia," he tells her. "There's no need for anyone, least of all you and your friends, to be sleeping under a bridge."

"But daddy, this is how some people live."

"And I'm saying there's no excuse. They get social security don't they?"

"Doesn't guarantee them a bed if there is no room at the inn."

"Oh don't start talking in religious parables. Please!"

She looks a little glassy-eyed and he can't stand to see her hurt so he pulls her toward his well-fed body and folds his bulky arms around her.

"Sasha, honey, I already said I would donate the money. I just don't see how you help anyone by sleeping out in the cold."

"It raises awareness daddy." She sighs loudly.

It occurs to him that they all sigh at him like that. His wife, when he notices a new hairstyle ten days too late. His son, when Derek admits that he has still not found the time to read the Seven Stages of Happiness book Billy gave him for Father's Day. Sasha sighs at him constantly, almost daily, for a plethora of reasons. And now his youngest has started too. Sooki is only four and when Derek tells her he can't take her to the park because he has to go to work, she lifts her shoulders and syphons in a stream of air before exhaling with a loud whine.

Derek himself sighs as he donates his pay to the homeless but smiles, knowing his daughter will post her pride all over Facebook and then tweet her night-in-a-swag out to the Twittersphere.

***

Saturday's child works hard for a
living like a Queen. High on the Hog. Silver-spooning it.

Lindy has always pretended to work hard but, truth be told, it has never been necessary. She runs a business, in some form or other, at all times. It is good for her ego. And good for appearances. But her real business is the business of taking. With her looks and secret street-smarts, it's a doddle; simple as growing weed under fluorescents. And if the men end up emotionally battered, well that's just their foolishness.

She has thick scarlet lips and wide kohl-lined eyes, perfectly shaped brows and a lush lignite mane. Breasts slightly augmented, sensual hips just shy of lusty, legs elongated, and curves accentuated by the height and angle of her stilettos. She gives the Rolex-wearers a hint of herself, throws clues that are impossible to ignore, carves out puzzles they itch to solve. And then she dances them to her signature tune. She is a puppeteer, perfecting her craft. She preens and promises and they leave wives and jobs and throw real estate and holidays at her and, when she is done, she leaves them alone as wrecks; homeless, alcohol-drenched or drug-addicted. They all end up as puddles of evaporated possibilities.

And, if they come at her, she shifts the money and the real estate, she moves luxury cars, hawks the Tiffany bracelets and changes

137

addresses. She bankrupts herself. Her slate is clean. A new business, a new man. Onwards and upwards.

***

But the child that is born on the Sabbath day is bonny and blithe and good and

gay, you say? My son? But surely not! What about that pretty girl Rebecca in year ten? They went to a weird techno party and he came home tipsy with his jumper on back-to-front and we chuckled behind his back. Remember? Nudge, nudge, wink, wink and all that palaver.

Coop is suddenly terrified. What will his friends say if they find out? Priscilla is smiling, that faint far-off gleam she gets from time to time.

Cilla, this is serious. You've got to keep this stuff to yourself. You can't go telling people. Besides, you are quite possibly mistaken. I can't see how we – two heterosexual liberals – could produce a raging hommo-sexual. Well, of course raging is the right word. They're all raging aren't they? Hommo-sexual? Yes, Cilla, that is how you pronounce it.

Sweat runs down between Coop's shoulder blades. There's an alumni meeting on Thursday. And the reunion next month. He can't cop this. This is just not on.

Priscilla! Concentrate, will you. Please, my love. All right, okay, we will just agree to use that word then. Gay. But what about the football and the rowing and the wrestling … oh – visuals … we can strike that from the record. Be serious, you say? Serious? How can I possibly take this seriously?

He had to get his wife on his team, regardless of where his son was standing with his bat. Billy had gone to Cooper's old school, shared trips with the sons of his illustrious friends. It was a ridiculous scenario.

Gay.

Cooper moved his head from side to side, an eraserhead rubbing out the word.

Gay? I can't believe Billy said that, Cilla, I'm sure you heard wrong. What about the Playboy *magazines we found under the floorboards in the boatshed? What? Yours?*

If Priscilla was going to go so far as to claim porn as her own, then he had a chance. Coop was sure he could convince her to keep her mouth shut. He simply had to.

What on earth would you be doing with pornographic magazines? What do you mean lesbian leanings? Since when, for Christ's sake? Well, that would have been different, I could have watched. Ouch!

The corner of the magazine hit him right in the temple.

That hurt. Bloody hurt. Priscilla, please! Cilla, where are you going? Now you listen to me, woman. I demand that you come back right this minute and we will …

He was talking to a closed door.

***

Monday's child is fair of

face it, Louise, we are living in a zoo. The Wilson's maid has had a nervous breakdown. They found her sobbing in their atrium, cradling a half-dead rodent. Derek's kids put some of his bank statements on Facebook and accused him of syphoning off funds to his mistress while pretending it was a donation to the homeless. The mistress, by the way, is that friend of your sister's. Turns out Lindy blue-chip living in the three-story on the bay is actually a serial bankrupt. She's left a trail of business creditors and ex-lovers mangled on train tracks and pavements all over Sydney and Melbourne.

These are our neighbours Louise. You'd think the whole city has spun around and we are living in the outer west all of a sudden.

Oh, and guess what? Big old ex-rugby player Cooper from two doors down – you know, the one who brags about going to that elite university? His son is gay. Yes, I had a fair idea too Louise. But. Turns out Derek's wife has left him to go to India to explore her religion. Secretly, Pete told me she's gone to Norway. To explore her sexuality.

***

Tuesday's child is full of

Grace feels like her world keeps lurching sideways. Her workmate at the bar has had some sort of episode and quit, leaving behind a cryptic note about being full of woe and she's afraid of mice and something about the Mediterranean being too far away.

Grace is working at triple-pace, multi-tasking on autopilot. Her boss is upset because his wife has left him and he's under enormous pressure due to a forthcoming reunion with his college buddies. Apparently, the stress has something to do with his son being gay.

139

Billy – Grace's friend since grade one – has decided that, after almost twenty years as a vegan, he's going to live carnivorously and therefore can no longer be friends with Grace, despite the fact that she has meat-eating friends. When she points this out to Billy, he says he doesn't care because he is no longer going to wear the mustard shirt she gave him for his birthday and he is ditching yoga for power lifting.

Billy's father is about to lose the architect-designed cantilevered family home that arcs out over the lapping waves so Billy is going to live with a bunch of builders who work on the building site next door.

Grace's boss knows Billy's father and says the bankruptcy will be because of *that fucking Lindy tart.* As if on cue, in walks Lindy, all soft curls and pouting lips and Grace's boss forgets what he's …

Doors
by Robin Lloyd-Jones

Shortlisted, Scottish Arts Club Short Story Competition 2020

Two slim yellow kayaks shuddered on the cobbled quayside. Beyond the harbour wall the Atlantic spumed in the wind. Archie wiped the condensation from inside the rear window of the Land Rover. He caught Martin's eye.

"We've been out in worse."

The younger man nodded, not breaking his preoccupied silence. Another gust shook the Land Rover. The sky was grey. The tip of the lighthouse, seven miles off the coast, was below the horizon. Archie ran his eyes along the lines of their sea-going kayaks. Handled properly they'd come through almost anything short of a fully-fledged gale.

"We've been out in worse," he repeated. "We'll manage OK."

We? Yes, Martin would manage alright. Archie had taught him everything he knew about sea-kayaking, but would he himself be OK? Yesterday had been his sixty-sixth birthday. Paddling a kayak seemed so much more like hard work these days. That was a difficult thing to admit when people looked up to you as the man who'd made a solo crossing to St. Kilda. Admiration and respect were like a drug, difficult to give up.

Two miles out a freighter bashed through the heavy seas. Archie watched its progress.

Martin followed his gaze "Catching a packet, isn't it?"

"Ach, it's not always such a good thing to be big. We're so light we'll bob over the waves like corks."

"The divorce came through last week," Martin said, without raising his eyes. His voice was bitter." Undoing the knot's been a bloody site more complicated than tying it ever was."

"It must be difficult."

"You can say that again!" Martin waved a hand in the direction of the tossing ocean. "At least that will take my mind off things for a few hours."

Archie doodled on the fogged glass. He could visualise the Admiralty Charts spread out on the carpet of the living-room, held down by beer cans. "Treat the sea like your lover," he had once told Martin. "Study her moods and rhythms and there are few places your kayak cannot go."

Martin said, "I've got three letters to post. There's a letter-box down the other end of the quay. Have we got time?"

"Can they wait?"

"Suppose so."

"Better get going."

They stepped out of the Land Rover, pushing the doors against the weight of the wind and began loading the kayaks.

A middle-aged couple sat in a car nearby. He was sketching, she was reading a newspaper. A paper bag scudded by and blew into the harbour between two fishing boats. The husband emerged stiffly from the car, stick in hand, binoculars round his neck.

"You're never going out in this!" he said.

Archie withdrew his head from inside the bows. "Going out to the lighthouse and back today."

The man was impressed. "The steamer trips are cancelled, you know."

He hunched in the wind, a tortoise temporarily removed from its shell. "We're here most Saturdays. We like the sea, the wife and I."

His wife wound down the car window. "Have you told them yet?"

He shuffled his feet. "The steamer trips? … Yes, I have."

"We'll be alright!" Archie called to her.

"I suppose you know what you're doing." She sounded doubtful.

The man hovered. Archie leant on his paddle, waiting for more.

The man said, "I used to have a boat, you know."

"You did?"

He nodded. "Little cabin cruiser." He tapped his right leg with his stick, producing a metallic sound. "Had to give it up. Not quite so nimble after that."

"An accident?" Martin asked.

"Cancer. Puts a lot of things in perspective does something like that."

"Did I see you sketching?" Archie asked.

"Yes. I enjoy the sea in a different way now. I paint seascapes. I can't tell you how much pleasure it gives me. ... Better get back to the car. Have a good trip!"

Archie returned to his final preparations: flares and spare split paddle strapped to the deck, neoprene gloves on. Miriam, his wife, was no stranger to cancer. She'd had to give up her job in the Social Work Department. It had coincided with his retirement as Head of English. They'd planned to hire a van and explore Europe. That was impossible now. Instead they'd joined a choir together.

Martin was jumping up and down. "It's bloody cold! Whose idea was this?"

"Soon warm up once we get going."

Archie tightened the cord of his lifejacket. The waves would be even bigger than they looked from the land. Always were. And there was a confused jobble just outside the harbour where the oncoming sea hit the wall and bounced back. Excitement or fear? Pitting yourself against the elements was all very well ... as long as you won. You could never be quite sure though. One thing was for sure – the adrenalin pumping through his body, the pounding heart.

They carried first one kayak, then the other down the concrete ramp. Archie wriggled into the narrow cockpit. "You don't sit in a kayak, you wear it. You control it from the hips." That had been another piece of advice handed down from the master to the apprentice. Instructing Martin had been a pleasure. Introducing a member of the younger generation to the joys and thrills of kayaking felt like a privilege. He stretched his neoprene apron over the rim of the cockpit, making his kayak watertight.

Inside the harbour's protecting arm they glided past rows of moored boats. They stared ahead, each sizing up the waves beyond the exit, hearing their noise. Archie led, driving his pointed bows at the open sea. Then the chunky, heaving waters were bouncing at him from every angle. "Paddle firmly," had always been his advice to Martin. "Impose your own speed and direction on the waves, or they'll throw you all over the place."

Now the sea took on a different motion, moving northwards with a rolling, surging rhythm. Steep walls of water rose behind Archie's head, lifting and carrying him, swelling beneath him. With every wave a shift of balance, a quick adjustment of the blade, never the same, but all the time the underlying pulse-beat of the ocean. Over and over, riding the crests, dipping and sliding into the troughs. A wave slapped him on the chest, spray flying in his face. His shout was a shout of joy, and the taste of salt on his lips was good.

Already the harbour seemed far away. Archie wondered if the man with an artificial leg was watching them through his binoculars. Momentarily Archie and Martin shared a wave. Martin's face shone with excitement. He pointed to the top of the lighthouse beginning to peep above the horizon. Then he was out of sight in a different valley, with moving mountains of water between. The lighthouse sank from view, then reappeared; sank and reappeared. Slowly it grew taller. A massive wave threw him sideways. Tons of water reared over him. Instinctively he leaned into the wave, riding the welter of foam. Christ! Nearly over then! He'd reacted slowly. He was tiring.

An hour passed. The top half of the lighthouse was visible now.

Another hour passed. The wind strengthened. Twice more Archie reacted slowly and nearly went over. His body ached: His legs, his stomach muscles, his back, his arms and shoulders, all screamed for a rest. The lighthouse seemed no closer. Whenever Martin hove into sight Archie could see he was thoroughly enjoying himself, sporting with the waves. The moment he always knew would come had arrived. Martin was a rising star, improving all the time. He himself was finding it harder each year to deal with severe conditions. This was the moment when their trajectories crossed. The better kayaker was now Martin.

Martin was ahead of him, sculling with his paddle, waiting for him to catch up. He drew alongside Martin and they rafted up.

"That's enough, for me" Archie said. "I'm ready to turn round."

Surprise, disappointment, concern flitted across Martin's face. Archie thought, "He's hiding it well." Doing the lighthouse in a Force 8 would have been a feather in anyone's cap.

"Yeah, fine." Martin said. "Gives us longer in the pub!" He pointed to a small island they had passed not long ago. "We can stop there on the way back and take a rest."

They landed on the sheltered side of the island. Gulls rose, loudly protesting, circling the island in a blizzard of white underwing. Sitting by a driftwood fire, they opened their thermos flasks and sandwich-boxes.

Archie took a gulp of soup. "It's final then ... the divorce?"

Martin nodded. "I ... I never thought it would happen to me ... to us."

"Decided what you're going to do?"

"Those three letters I was going to post ... One is to my boss, resigning from my job. One's accepting the place I've been offered at university."

"Well done, Martin. That's terrific! Electronics, right?"

"Yes."

"And the other letter?"

"To Liz, telling her exactly what I think of her, what a cow she's been." He bit savagely into a sandwich and swallowed hard. "I brought it with me. I wanted to read it to you."

Martin extracted the letter from a watertight box. "You know what? I've changed my mind." And he tossed the letter into the fire, where it curled, went brown at the edges and burst into flames.

"Hah!" Martin shouted. "Hah! Woo! Yay! I feel great!"

"All that anger up in smoke! Good for you, Martin!"

Archie poured himself more soup. "I hear Joe McDermott's group is short of a paddler."

McDermott was the up and coming tiger, the one they talked about these days, the one pushing the boundaries.

"I'll tell him you're interested, if you like."

"Would you? ... Thanks, Archie."

Archie poked the fire with a stick, thinking about his older friend, Doug. When you paddled with Doug and his friends, they weren't bothered about getting anywhere in particular or in conquering anything. They enjoyed the journey, dawdling on the way, seeking the tranquil moments. He was ready for that now.

The wind was dropping, the sea becoming less menacing by the minute. As they set off back to the harbour, running through Archie's mind was Handel's *Messiah* which the choir had recently began rehearsing.

The Kill
by Pat Feehan

Shortlisted, Scottish Arts Club Short Story Competition 2020

The heavy branches of the baobab tree shaded Tambu as he crouched, still as a shadow at noon, observing his prey. He had no need of shelter from the searing heat, but the dappling shadows would trick the eye of any animal that might chance to look in his direction.

Despite the ten-mile trek, his breath made no sound and did not disturb the hot, still air. His legs were folded easily beneath him, poised to launch him in any direction at a second's notice. His bow hung taut and ready over his back, his hunting-spear lay in his right hand. He had honed the blade many times on the black stone near the river bed and it could slice through tough hide and thick muscle without being diverted from its deadly course. He rolled it back and forth between thumb and palm in habit born of decades; he remembered his father showing him the tree from which it had been cut and he offered a silent prayer to the spirits for this gift; the shaft was straight and true, polished smooth by years of use and it would fly swift and hard.

He lifted a pinch of soil and rubbed it in his left palm, testing it for moisture then let it dribble and drift on to the dun earth. He watched its path as it fell almost straight down, diverted only slightly by the whispering air. The ancestors were looking with favour on him today. As he lifted his eyes to observe the herd, the faintest of breezes blew into his face, bringing with it the fierce scent of the kudu.

Before leaving the village, two days earlier, Tambu had painted his body with a paste of crushed berries, yellow mud and saliva before performing the ritual dance with the other men, thumping the ground with their feet as they mimed the kill. He was confident that the hunt would be a success but he also knew, from bitter experience, that the ancestors were fickle. And even when a hunt was successful, men could die. Yes, this also he knew.

His whole body and spirit were focused on the animal. He had tracked it for two days, the size and depth of its prints revealing to his sharp eyes its age. And now that he watched it as it drank from the water hole, he knew he had read the signs correctly. The animal was a proud-looking beast; its coat glistened with health, the eyes alert and defiant, its horns curled out viciously from the massive head, long and sharp and deadly. It would make a worthy opponent, an honourable kill.

He had tracked and killed many kudu but today's hunt was important to him. He let his mind go blank to imagine what the beast might be thinking. His father had taught him this over many hunts. The sounds of the savannah became muffled, the shapes and colours of the landscape became vague and shadowy, he was no longer aware of the sharp, dry grass or the tree that sheltered him. He was now in that alert yet trance-like state that would let him become as one with the beast. His feet, his hands, his whole body did not move, but his mind reached across the parched gap and joined with that of the animal. His body became cold, his mind clear as a lake, his eyes misted over and then, suddenly, he was observing himself through the eyes of the kudu, he was hearing the noises of the birds and insects with its ears, he was sniffing the air for predators with the snout of the animal.

He saw himself watching the animal and he was content. He saw his comrades as they crouched silently nearby. He saw, some way beyond the group, Malvo, who had been set to watch for lions or other predators who might steal their kill or worse. Tambu had spotted lion tracks crossing the trail of the kudu herd and knew by the droppings that the huge beasts were not far away. His eyesight was a thing of legend among the tribe, far sharper than anyone else's and he thought he saw, some way behind Malvo, a brown shape slink forward through the waist-high grass, the flick of a black-tipped tail. He felt the kudu tense, his heart leapt, he looked again but the shape was gone. The kudu relaxed again and he left it and was, once more, in his own body.

High above, in the tree, he heard the birds chattering, the kudu paused in its drinking and lifted its head probing the air for any hint of danger. Tambu stilled himself, his breath waiting patiently in his chest. He detected a faint sound behind him, where he had posted Malvo. But the noise was not repeated, the kudu lowered its head and resumed its drinking and Tambu released his breath.

147

High overhead, a lone vulture slanted through the rock-still air. The bird tilted a wing towards the kudu, perhaps staking its claim, sensing what lay ahead and the air seemed to shimmer with expectation.

Tambu's feet were as one with the ground, the leathery soles and gnarled toes clutching the world like the hawk holds its prey. The events of the next few minutes were under his control. In some part of his mind he was aware of the razor grass slicing and jabbing into his thighs and the crimson scar-beetles crawling over his calves searching out the cuts made by the thorn bushes that morning. But there was no pain or discomfort, his whole mind and body were focused and targeted like an arrow resting on a drawn string.

With his companions he had tracked the herd for two days and finally the animals had stopped at a water-hole. There were ten beasts in the group and he studied his prey as it lifted its proud head once more. He had selected the large male kudu, the leader. Countless generations of ancestors had prepared him for moments such as these, nights by the campfire had schooled him in what to look for, what to listen for; he could identify each animal by its own distinct smell and could assess each one's strength, its health and its value as food; and he knew that he had chosen well.

He turned his head to study the men who accompanied him. They sat, five of them, in a rough semi-circle within a few feet of each other. No word had passed between them since the sun had risen that morning. They communicated by short, jabbing gestures, the sweep of a hand, the lifting of a chin, the raising of an eyebrow, the occasional rough picture traced in the soil. This was all they needed, all they allowed, to share their thoughts and make their plans, to ensure that when Tambu gave the signal, they would move as one. He had hunted with each of these men many times and knew the character of each one, each line on their faces and every one of the many scars they proudly bore. He trusted each of these five with his life. Thirty yards away, Malvo kept his silent, solitary guard.

The insects of the savannah clicked and buzzed and sniped around them but Tambu detected, a little way beyond Malvo, another sound. His hearing, like his eyesight, was a gift from his ancestors and none of his companions showed any sign of having heard the noise. The kudu continued to browse on the sparse acacia leaves, raising its head every few moments, turning it this way and that, testing the air for danger. The rest of the herd watched it intently ready to follow its lead if it should bark a warning.

The kudu had many predators and Tambu's senses were alive to the dangers that surrounded them. Not just the mighty lion but the tireless wild dog and the merciless cold-eyed hyena; any of these could take a kudu or a man for its prey. He knew the kudu itself could kill him with horns, hooves or head. From bitter memory he knew that, even wounded, it was a deadly prey.

But he saw and heard nothing that threatened his prize and he offered a silent blessing to the ancestors. Tambu would be honoured with the first cut of the beast's liver. From the animal's skin, his wife would make a new bag for his arrows and from the horns she would fashion a hunting-knife for Tambu and a birth anklet for little Tala, the joy of his life.

But there was more to the hunt than meat, more than an arrow bag or an anklet. Each time he hunted a kudu, Tambu dedicated it to the memory of his son Talu, killed by a kudu in a hunt three years earlier. And every time he fired an arrow into the neck of a kudu Tambu saw himself firing it into the heart of Malvo, the man who had led that hunt and had caused Talu's death. For months afterwards, each night in his hut, Tambu wrapped himself in a cold cloak of despair and nursed the thorn of vengeance in his heart.

He came back to the present as the kudu shifted position to reach a fresh bunch of leaves. It became almost invisible, its fawn pelt blending with the dry grass and earth. The hunting-party sat like rocks, awaiting the moment, the signal that would come only from Tambu. He heard once more the faint noise to his rear. His head swivelled in that direction and his sharp eyes saw a blade of grass bend towards Malvo. The kudu paused for a moment but continued eating and Tambu knew the time was near.

He eased a poison-beetle arrow from his pouch and checked his bow and spear. He had to get closer to be sure of the kill and in these last few steps the hunt would be won or lost. Tambu remembered his father's words – 'Move like you are walking past a nest of fire-ants'. He let his breath trickle from his lips and a moment later the group oozed forward like the morning mist rolling across the lake.

He was within twenty yards of his prey; the others were as one with him but it was his honour and his responsibility to make the first strike. There was no sound of alert from Malvo. Tambu fitted the arrow to his bow and let his arm draw the string back. Suddenly the kudu froze, something had alerted it. The slightest mistake now could send it off running.

Tambu was still, he became part of the land, the energy of the earth surged through the soles of his feet and he was like a tree growing from the brown soil so that if the kudu should look in his direction it would see leaves and branches, not a man. He let his eyes drift over the rest of the hunting-party, they were as still as boulders.

As his gaze carried to Malvo, fifty yards away, Tambu spotted the movement behind the man. A flash of sinuous brown as the grass parted, the merest yellow glint of the predator's eye. A grim joy flashed through Tambu's heart, he turned back and took aim. As he watched his arrow fly swift and true, the bowstring whipped back whispering the name of his son, Talu. The barbed head sunk deep into the kudu's neck releasing its poison. Tambu surged forward, spear poised and, in that instant, he heard from behind him Malvo's harsh scream as the lion made its kill.

The Academic Wife
by Catherine McDonald

Editor's Choice, Scottish Arts Club Short Story Competition 2020

With hindsight the third request for Box M229 had been a mistake, and now Maudie Grey would finally have to be killed.

This was not a troubling thought; the trail could be allowed to run cold. A last scattering of random searches, the ordering of a couple of books, would throw down a fog and give time for the last traces to be erased.

For long enough Maudie Grey has been among the faithfuls waiting for the reading room to open at 9.30am, every day except Sunday. Coming in with the opening of the front doors, she and other habituals deposit coats and bags in favoured lockers, extracting pencils and notebooks, library cards and spectacles. Maudie eschews the clear carrier bag ('please re-use') with no hiding places, to be checked in and out, library staff on the lookout for theft or torn-out pages for souvenirs and covert sales.

Occupying solitary tables, they wait in the café like satellites programmed to avoid, eyes on any point but each other. Maudie Grey carefully lines up notepad, pencil and sharpener. Her notepad is empty. There is the stir of the rope barrier being lifted, and young researchers slipstream around the old as they swipe at phones, greet, and share signals to meet for coffee before retreating behind headphones in their favourite zones. Once inside the reading room, everyone shrinks into their self-contained space.

There is a pattern. Maudie passes over the reserve slips from the night before and collects her saved books, depositing them at the small table in the alcove she has laid claim to by habit, before pushing out of the swing doors and heading for the computer terminals. Choosing from the catalogue is a slow process. The Indian Empire is vast enough to be lost in and broad enough for tangents. The pattern is no pattern. She displays interest in the subject but there is no predictable cypher for her choices. She seeks out books on open shelves, and from the stacks on and off-site, also pamphlets, bills of fare, old newspapers, adverts, PhD theses and academic articles, catalogues, registers of business interests. She flits between language, history, politics, art, anthropology, religion, literature, travel and commerce. She orders for quick delivery or from the far underground reaches, with occasional complex requests from a series. Sometimes she places an order from Special Collections and travels one floor up in the lift to receive a rare item in the inner sanctum. It is enough activity to make her known but it is routine. She rarely makes a mistake.

She returns to her saved books from yesterday and checks her previous day's work quickly before returning them to the desk. She does not want these on deposit for later. The first of her new orders are through and she gets down to work. Maudie Grey's notepad remains empty. She passes out through the turnstile at lunchtime, her notepad ruffled perfunctorily at the security turnstile and pays a comfort visit before ordering soup, no bread, with tap water, in the library cafe. She keeps her notepad and pencil to hand. She watches, but with a middle-distance gaze which does not invite sharing of her table. Her iron grey hair is cut into a square bob and held in a clasp to one side, she wears a loose cardigan and heavy corduroy trousers which flap some distance above her plain leather shoes. Her hands are clenched in her lap, both from habit but also against Reynaud's disease which forces her to wear gloves in most weathers. She is silent and still, and gives off the air of always waiting; just another wife of a retired academic who never had her own career but carried out research, usually unpublished.

On this day the afternoon is to be passed in Special Collections, always slightly chilly and today more so than usual. A document printed in Calcutta (she refuses to call it Kolkata) contains an engraving of the trip up the Hooghly River by a Governor-General of India. She deliberately seeks out orders of slim pamphlets and single rare books which wait discreetly on the shelves behind the issue desk, and over which she can hunch under the eye of staff who prowl checking for illegal pens, unsupported book spines, and other transgressions.

This time there is no lone pamphlet against her library card. Instead she is handed Box M229. It is filled with letters, maps, and other complicated items as well as the pamphlet – it is a bundle of archive which will demand careful management. She settles on a table close to the window and far from the front desk, propping up the clamshell lid against the foam book supports. Snowflakes swirl outside as Old College dome drifts in and out of focus, and roofs whiten as they begin to settle.

She sifts through bundles of letters, finding loose watercolours and engravings before the pamphlet emerges. Her requests have not yielded paintings before, and she becomes distracted by the images which stray across the written record; a private secretary's amateur sketchings of a journey through West Bengal, the boats and ghats, fishing and temples. She traces over them with her pencil, taking care, exciting no attention from staff and fellow researchers absorbed by the snow globe playing out over the rooftops and Arthur's Seat.

Maudie Grey becomes invisible among the obsessed who return like a dog with a bone to their boxes of rare documents. The staff barely glance at her now. Three times she orders Box M229, frustrated when it is delayed, finally keeping it on reserve so it is there to greet her at the opening of the barrier in the morning. She is lost in its contents, finding stories in the letters and tableaux in the paintings.

Under umbrellas against the sleeting rain, the habituals stand distantly from each other outside the closed doors of the National Library. It is almost 9.40am. The young researchers arrive and set up a stir; why is it closed, when will it open? They Google 'national library opening times', they knock. A member of staff opens the door a fraction, a policewoman glimpsed behind her shoulder. She is agitated. The library is closed due to an incident, and will remain so until further notice.

It will take time for the death to become a murder, but Maudie Grey walks past two bus stops, and in the bustle of the Bridges drops her pencil, sharpener and notepad into a bin. The notepad is still empty but the pencil is blunt, dipped and re-dipped in a clay laced with scrapings of the brown spots from the stems of hemlock gathered on waste ground by railways and abandoned buildings, pressed in the sharpener as an inkwell. Lightly traced and invisible on countless letters, numbers, commas and full stops; on documents, engravings, in book prefaces and pages, marginalia, footnotes and lately watercolours, the ancient poison finds victims who are random but targeted; a Socratic roulette.

For this single death there will have been others who took their palpitations to their GP, complaining of heavy limbs and being out of breath; a virus perhaps. There may be more yet. Whoever touches the residue is an affront to her and deserves their fate; the ranks of retired professors, the aspiring young with their careers before them, the new breed of women bull-dozing their way up through archaic university ranks. However, she does not target all the habituals. India is not a likely field for her kind; the academic wives, who have steered – or been steered by husbands – towards the romance of Jacobites or medieval pageantry, or towards belated degrees in history of art as a quasi-Mothers' Union, cod-academia path which they can supposedly share, unequally, in their quiet houses scattered around the Meadows. Staff do not read the books; she has protected them. No trace was ever left on her empty notebook, riffled through daily at the turnstile. She took no risks herself. She wore gloves, and touched no bread at lunch.

But Maudie Grey made the mistake of becoming interested. Briefly, she stepped aside from dilettantism and stalled her flitting across the catalogue to linger over Box M229, and now she will be remembered. She returned often enough to become invisible but known, a familiar outline among the book supports and bundles of archive.

On Sunday the library is closed. At a church on the south side the congregation meets as usual, a small knot of regulars. She is cashmered and elegantly dressed, her hair is expensively brunette, and she protects her hands with fine gloves. The transformation has been much admired but discreetly; they knew it was the price paid by her ex-husband for diverting to one of the new breed of bullish academic women. A stalwart of the congregation, she lingers for coffee after the service and relieves the burden on the minister by visiting the dying. She seems taller than Maudie Grey, who gained an unexpected second life with the loss of no more than a library card. Her second death is negligible. The grey wig and clothes burn easily, and the body suit with sagging breasts and buttocks is cut up, bagged and left out for with the fortnightly bin collection.

Maudie Grey does return to the library as soon as it re-opens, but only to tease and confuse, ordering a scatter of books which are never collected. Meanwhile despite herself, she is drawn to the library, picking up on fragmented searches and book requests which she has allowed to run throughout her campaign. She frequents the café where she pretends to revise notes while tilting an ear to conversations, or exchanging shocked comments with strangers at tables.

Thus she learns of the death of a 72-year-old woman, who became unwell at her usual place in Special Collections, and died later in hospital. The top floor remains closed, and is now a crime scene, as investigators probe the source of what appears to be a poisoning. Efforts are focussed on the contents of the box still spread around her table, notes on the art of the East India Company neatly filling her pad. Soon after, the back catalogue of books, articles and papers ordered by Maudie Grey will be bagged up for forensics, and then destroyed.

The death of an academic wife leaves few ripples and no obituaries in its wake, meanwhile the grieving husband is identified by his achievements and people nod as they vaguely recall who she was. This devastating perversion of the planned target both destroys and steels her as she walks away from the library down George IV Bridge, her perfect crime compromised by the convergence of herself and her victim around the same temptations. She knows this unknown woman, she had been her, just as she had known Maudie Grey and many others in the shadows of their oblivious men.

Revenge is not yet served and more deaths are required. Hers, nominally, will be the first.

Judith
by Jupiter Jones
A Re-telling of a Deuterocanonical Testament

Longlisted, Scottish Arts Club Short Story Competition 2020

We were sitting on the veranda under the quince tree, drinking chocolate and enjoying the last of the sun's sallow light. The best days of summer were gone; soon the evening air would chill. Hester, always industrious, was knitting rainbow blankets for the orphanage, using up oddments of wool. The faint rhythmical clickety noise of her needles almost but not quite eclipsing the starlings in the branches overhead. Iridescent chatterboxes preparing for the journey south. I was squinting at the newsprint; too vain for spectacles. There was an ad in the personal columns; it was the usual format.

Wanted: Resourceful woman. Please bring own basket.

I said to Hester,

"Look Hes, there's another one."

"Oh Jude! You said no more. Too old now for that caper. Time to retire, take things easy. Enough with the bloody assignments, maybe keep chickens instead."

But I didn't want to retire yet if there was still work to be done. I looked at her over the top of the paper. That look.

"I'll get the basket," she said.

The man they had in mind was called Holofernes, a big man, rugged and fierce. He was the manager of a camping and outdoor equipment place with a good many other unsavoury 'business interests' besides. Hunted and killed for sport; all kinds of creatures with fins or fur or feathers. Handy with his fists too. Macho, thick-skinned; a patriarch they said. But cruel with it, so cruel.

The following day, Hester and I went to see for ourselves. We left Bethulia and travelled on foot over to the next valley, to his emporium. When we arrived at Holofernes Outdoor Gear, they were having an end-of-season shindig in the field behind where the display tents were all strung about with lanterns and plastic bunting, and the yellow grass between the tents walked bald and flat. There were jugs of home-brewed beer and jugs of moonshine, a food stall selling undercooked chicken and overcooked pork. A diddly-dee band had just arrived and were tuning up. Quite a crowd had gathered, and despite all the common signifiers of gaiety, the atmosphere seemed tense and fractious. Some were hoping to avoid trouble, some spoiling for a fight. We slipped in through the gate and mingled.

There were games; tug-of-war, wet t-shirt contest, dwarf-throwing, pie-eating, mud-wrestling, bear-baiting. Muscle-bound dogs in studded leather harnesses with scars criss-crossing their faces were straining at thick chains trying to get at two hollow-chested young gladiators who shivered and sobbed as they strapped on heel spurs. Dwarves, large with braggadocio, foul-mouthed and short-tempered were jeering and hassling girls. The bear wandered aimlessly; he was guzzling moonshine, his big paws clasped around a jug, his fur stinking sour of vomit.

We got our first glimpse of Mr Holofernes, yelling at a blonde in a tight silver dress.

"Stupid little bitch. Brain the size of a pea, a pin-head."

He took a swipe and she cringed like a whipped cur.

"Grrrrrr!" He got right up close, as if he would bite her face, and she broke like a twig and snivelled.

"Sorry, sorry, so sorry. I didn't think."

"Of course, you didn't think Tinkerbelle. Thinking's not your forte. Out of my sight now, or I'll make you know what sorry tastes like."

She scuttled away with her hand to her mouth, stifling sobs.

Apparently, she had fed his dwarf with pie before the contest.

"What's wrong with that?" asked Hester in a low voice, running a hand over her own comfortably convex belly. "A bit of pie never hurt anyone."

He, Mr H, was not as tall as I had expected from the account we had been given, but solid, all brawn. Black-haired and black-bearded with cold corvid eyes. We sized him up, calculating the variables, the risk, and watched him move through the crowds, thumbs in his belt, swaggering just a little, two henchmen following behind, and everyone else showing proper deference. They knew their place. He owned everyone hereabouts, a hand in each and every pocket. We had heard of his cruelty, there were accusations of corruption, pimping, extorsion, racketeering, trafficking, false imprisonment, torture. But still, we had to see for ourselves.

A flunky in a black polo with the HOG logo, the head of a thick-necked wild boar, approached us and tried to hand us drinks. We glanced at his tray of brightly-hued plastic beakers and waved him away. His buck-toothed face fell.

"Please," he said stammering just slightly, "p-please take the beer, it's not too bad, not as bad as the punch. If Mr H thinks I haven't been doing my job, *d-d-diligently* he says, he says he will fire me. And if he hears that you ladies refused his hospitality, he could get ugly."

Things got pretty ugly anyway. Mr H and his cronies were boorish, rowdy with liquor. There were fights, some minor injuries, mostly just cuts and bruises, broken noses.

"Cold compresses and arnica," muttered Hester, rummaging in her bag.

Then a mud-wrestler dislocated a knee, and was stretchered away shrieking in agony, and a dwarf thrower had one of his fingers bitten clean off. Hester, who always seems to be prepared, dressed the wound as best she could; she packed it with lint and wrapped clean bandages around. Told him to keep the hand elevated. He was so drunk he seemed to feel no pain. If we had had some ice to pack it in ... if we could have found the missing digit ... but no, it was gone.

Then a ruckus started. While the musicians were taking a break, Mr H and his brutes started played catch with their instruments. We watched an accordion arc through the air like an orca, again and again, then heard it crash to the ground in a cacophony of jangled wreckage. They jeered and cat-called as it fell and was trashed. Next, Mr H caught a fiddle that came flying towards him. The others called out to him; 'to me, to me', and 'over here boss', holding out their hands in supplication. But seemingly tired of the game, or just plain mean, he shrugged and threw the fiddle onto the bonfire. I heard a howl of anguish, and the brutes laughed and cheered, stamping their feet, whistling. The fiddle player pushed his way through and burned his hands trying to get it out, but it was too far gone. The gut pinged, the maple and rosewood scorched, then flames danced, swallowing it completely. Hester drew the fiddler away and daubed his hands with ointment. I watched her tend to him; a wiry little man in shabby black, with long fingers like pipe cleaners, now charred and blistered. Of course, he was inconsolable. Hester looked up at me over the fiddler's shoulder. Her grey eyes seeking out my yellow ones, and after all the years together, no words were needed between we two old birds.

I had seen enough. He was just as they had said. I felt sorry for the women and the boys; the pretty ones pawed, and molested, the ugly ones jeered at and abused. Sorry for the man in the bear costume who drank to drown his swimming sorrows. Sorry for the dogs with their cloudy eyes and scarred grey muzzles. Sorry for the dwarves, even though they were so coarse in their manners, even though they had been paid handsomely for the night. Sorry for everyone who had the misfortune to work for Mr H, to be caught in his web, sorry for all the small people he bullied.

Anyway, we ate his pork and we kicked up our heels and danced to his jig just as if we were not already past our prime. We drank his beer and we peed in his chemical toilets. Late in the evening I looked for his two henchmen; one had sloped off with one of the hollow-chested boys, the other had passed-out cold beneath a trestle table. I saw my chance to get Mr H alone. He was sitting by the campfire, still burning, but low and red, embers glowing like dope fiends' eyes, and a fine white ash spread all around that radiated a melancholy warmth. The end of the party. He sat nursing a jug, drunk and maudlin, mumbling to himself, bewailing the skinny bitches, the yes-men and the indoor-pussy-types. I hitched up my skirts and sat beside him, and he put an arm around my ample arse.

"Who are you? Do I know you?"

He was slurring, but not so much.

"I am Judith."

"Well Judith, you're not my type, you know? Not my type at all."

"No? Why is that?"

"Too old and too fat. Hey! Do I know you?"

"Not yet," I said.

He was a pushover. Another drink and I led him by the cock to a four-man tent. Him, looking for a fumble. Me, not giving a fuck. Just a job of work to do.

I rolled up my sleeves and drew out my blade. His neck was thick, but my first pass sliced clean through the carotid artery. A parabola of lifeblood spouted forth and I leaned away to keep my dress clean. I leaned away until the blood was no more than a dribble, and the ground was dark, and the air hot and humid like a slaughterhouse. Hester, never far from my side, was standing by in case I couldn't manage, but I grasped his beard and worked that blade back and forth through bone and gristle. She caught his head in the basket. We left it at the agreed spot and the money was transferred into my account the following day.

****

Hester is making quince jelly for the women's refuge, our kitchen is steamy and full of the heady scent and the syrupy bubbling, and the little jars are all lined up, warmed and waiting. She stirs the pan and watches, and stirs again, and wipes away a damp strand of hair with the inside of her wrist. I will write the paper labels, that is my small part. And I have promised her; that was the last time; there will be no more.

Paradise
by Gail Anderson

Longlisted, Scottish Arts Club Short Story Competition 2020

The storms came before the new year was two months old. Late February, 1938. Ruby knew that these were no ordinary rains. The skies poured water onto the steep, bone-dry mountains above Los Angeles, and the floods that followed were positively biblical. Whole districts swept away: houses rinsed down Tujunga Canyon like coffee grounds, the towns of Agua Mansa and Santa Ana swallowed by new lakes, boulders big as warehouses ploughed through Sunland. Finally, the waters rose in Cahuilla Canyon, and the family's little trout farm burst its dams. Thousands of glittering fish spilled onto the red adobe soil of the valley.

Father didn't come home that night. The next morning Ruby and her older sister Beryl set off early, climbing the sodden, sage-scented trail that overlooked the valley and the far-away Pacific. They found him sitting in his wooden chair on the fishing platform, his blue eyes on the gunmetal sky, water on his face.

"Heart attack," said the medic who hiked up with other men from the town to bring the body home. "Sitting there, watching his livelihood wash away."

They had not been rich, the Depression had seen to that, but they got by. Father was proud of his girls, proud to send them to the university on a 'fish scholarship': weekly provision of trout to the dormitory kitchens in exchange for tuition. Barter was a common enough arrangement in the cash-strapped 1930s. But when the funeral and the crying were done, when there was no money to pay her fees, Ruby dropped out of university. Beryl, with only four months to go, was invited to stay on.

Beryl was a swimmer, a state champion, bound for the Olympics. At the last big varsity competition of 1938, a scout showed up to watch. Duke Kahanamoku – The Duke. The Hawaiian was legend: five-time Olympic medallist, movie star, surfer – and coach of the prestigious Territory of Hawaii swim team, full of Olympic hopefuls.

161

"Win it for Dad," Ruby whispered, hugging her sister before the final race.

The 1930s were hungry for paradise, and Hawaii was transcendent. Ukulele, steel guitar, the liquid notes floated from suburban wirelesses to set breezes stirring on airless streets. Bing Crosby, the Andrews Sisters, sang of golden days and tropical nights. Sweet Leilani, Blue Hawaii, Aloha Kuu Ipo Alohai. Grass-skirted hula girls swayed across vaudeville stages and movie screens, pineapple crept into cakes and salads, and Amelia Earhart – a woman no less! – flew a little plane by herself to the Islands. Hawaii was visionary, a new world, far removed from the ravages of Wall Street.

Beryl won her races. And while her older sister sailed to Hawaii to become world famous, Ruby – rudderless, feeling a small and unworthy kinship with the vast diaspora of dust-bowl migrants – drifted one hundred miles south and into nursing school.

Nursing was a living, not a calling. Still, she surprised herself by liking it. The quiet order of the wards, the notion of healing, all this put some ground back under her feet. As her three years' training came to an end, she met Richard. He had dark eyes and an honest face, which Ruby found amusing, since he worked in advertising.

"I heard advertising men are fast talkers who chew cigars," she said, as they orbited through stars of mirror-ball light in a darkened dance hall.

"And I heard nurses carry lanterns," he replied, "and that men kiss their shadows."

At the movies on their second date, Ruby saw Beryl up on the silver screen. It was an old clip, part of the title sequence for a sports feature in the Metrotone newsreel. Late November, 1941. The 1940 Olympics hadn't happened, the war in Europe had seen to that. Germany invaded Poland, France declared war on Germany, dominoes falling. The United States was well out of it – but Beryl's chance was gone. She'd left the team, married Tom, a civil servant.

"What's next for her?" Richard asked over cocktails.

"Their baby's due in mid-December. They'll stay put in Hawaii."

Ruby felt the loss of the Olympics almost as keenly as Beryl had. It was the final link to their former life, to their father. Ruby longed for the certainty of those old days.

"And you?" His eyes held hers. "What's next for you?"

"I'm going to visit her," she said. "I'll register there, and when the baby's born, I'll get my first work experience as my sister's 'private nurse'," she twitched quotation marks in the air, "and spend a few weeks playing with the baby."

Richard smiled. "Nice work. When do you sail?"

"December first – the Lurline."

"So soon." He worried the tooth-picked olive in his drink. "When do you come back?"

Ruby hadn't booked a return passage. Following Beryl to paradise, maybe staying on, finding real work; this had been the plan. Now there was Richard; but it was early days, nothing to count on.

"Not sure yet," she said.

The day of her departure it was raining hard. Ruby's thoughts circled back to that early morning three years ago, when she'd led her older sister over the shoulder of the foothills into the upper canyons, to find their dead father. The memory stayed with her, deepened at the sight of the red roses Richard brought when he drove her to the pier. They ran to shelter under a wholesaler's awning, away from the crowds gathered at the Lurline's gangway. The pounding of rain on canvas, the tarry smell of ropes, took Ruby's words away.

Richard's eyes flickered down. He took off his hat, fingered its brim.

"My agency is transferring me to San Francisco," he said. "I'll be gone, I think, by the time you come back."

A sought-after promotion. Ruby felt a small thread snap, but Richard hadn't finished. He took a breath and looked up at her.

"We haven't known each other all that long, and everything's up in the air for both of us. But San Francisco's a good place." There was a question in his eyes. "What do you reckon?"

It would be at least two months and far too many miles. But he was asking, that was something. She smiled.

"I reckon you could write and let me know?" she said.

Relief on his face. He kissed her, held her. "Reckon I will," he said.

Ruby woke early to the scent of plumeria flowers. Her first morning on Oahu, a heady, exotic aroma, a lapping of small waves floating in at the window. No one else was stirring. She rose and put on her swimsuit, walked barefoot through the cool sand, a red sun on the horizon. The water was warm. Bright, echoing birdsong cascaded from the cliffs. Wading in, laying back, floating, pink wisps of cloud drifting above. Paradise.

They had strolled the beach last night at sunset, Beryl, Tom and Ruby, arm in arm. Beryl more lovely than ever. Tom, dark-haired, charming, a good choice. The baby due any day now. Their bungalow was one of a scattered few at Kaneohe Bay, just east of Honolulu. A settled life. Neighbours, Captain Jaye, retired Navy, and his daughter Kathy, also a nurse. They were invited for lunch today.

Ruby heard a faint humming noise out to sea, paddled to look. Small planes flying a graceful arc. Beryl had pointed out the airfield on Kaneohe point last night. Early morning flight practice, the planes so distant they looked like seabirds, tiny and white. Ruby lay back in the water. The humming continued. She thought again of the plumeria, imagined bees. Birds and bees. Imagined Richard in the water beside her, his hair wet. Then the humming was lost in a percussive boom, like thunder. Ruby stood in waist-high water.

The planes had overshot the airfield. Six of them, engines straining, flying low, were headed straight towards her. She dropped down, her eyes above the water's surface like a frog's. The sea around her ruptured into a million tiny spikes of vibration as the planes roared overhead. Ruby, looking up, saw Japan's round red suns painted on their wings.

At the skirt of the mountains they banked left. A distant siren wailed. And Ruby began to run. Panicking, churning through the water to the shore, making for a cluster of palms, hugging a slender trunk. The planes wheeled, plunged back toward the bay, motors screaming. Tom bursting from the bungalow now, sprinting to the water's edge, shouting after them. The throb of engines fading. The formation drifted in slow motion up and over Kaneohe point. Smoke rising. The second payload of bombs fell, silent silhouettes, the pulse of explosion delayed over distance. And the planes were gone.

A cloud of dust from the road: a car, Captain Jaye at the wheel, his daughter Kathy beside him. The look in her eyes sent Ruby running for her clothes, still doing up buttons as the car door swung open to receive her.

"A hundred ships at Pearl!" Captain Jaye shouted above engine as they sped up the Pali Road. "They've knocked out our planes here, Hickam too, probably. There'll be nothing in the air to fight them."

Kathy turning in the front seat to look at Ruby. "You've only just qualified, you said?"

"Last month." Ruby swallowing fear.

Up and over the pass. Clouds of smoke, knitted black as bundled wool, hid the harbour from view. As they started the descent, the dark lifted once on the wind, long enough for Ruby to see. The water below was an unbroken sheet of fire.

She would struggle to remember anything of that day beyond chaos. Smoke, sirens, shouting, the fevered emptying of warehouses, the raising of makeshift wards just steps ahead of stretchered wounded, row on row, tumbled onto cement floors. She would remember being outnumbered, remember the waxen-red, shining skin of the men pulled from burning water. The Tannafax ran out immediately; they switched to tannic acid; that was gone as well. Raiding the commissary kitchens, rinsing blistered skin in cold tea, wrapping suppurating flesh with baking parchment. The murmuring of the injured and, more powerfully, the fierce and sallow stillness of the dead settled into Ruby's soul like prophesy. Day and night merged, and merged again.

When the flood of wounded began to subside, the civilian nurses were brought to the pier. Two officers, one Navy, the other Army, stood before them, thanked them, praised their courage and stamina, called them heroes.

Ruby looked around her. She and her fellow nurses were an unlikely a group of heroes. All ages and colours, all sizes, all revoltingly dirty. But Ruby felt a spark, felt her place alongside the other women. Felt that something was larger than before.

The naval officer spoke. "The country is now at war with Japan." He let it sink in. "Those of you who would prefer to serve in the Navy, please step to the left. Army, to the right."

February, 1942. Ruby, second-lieutenant in the Army Nurse Corps, aunt and godmother to her sister's baby girl, stood on the pier, scanned the gangway of a recently arrived troop ship. Then a smartly-dressed seaman was closing her hand around a small box.

"Because everything else is up in the air for us," he said.

It wasn't a miracle, this reunion – nearly all Pacific-bound forces passed through the Islands – but it was enough. Richard was gone the next morning at dawn, shipped out to the Asiatic Fleet in Manila.

She'd seen life end with a flood; then came fire, then war. When she told it that way, even to herself, it sounded like apocalypse. Now, waving the departing ship into the horizonless Pacific morning, it was easy to believe that this might be the end of everything.

Except that certainty was something she could learn to do without. Ruby turned and made her way back along the pier. It was time to go to work.

Salt
by Michelle Wright

Longlisted, Scottish Arts Club Short Story Competition 2020

The sun's getting low on New Year's Day, and the last of the town kids shamble home, small arms sandy-sore from digging. The rising tide seeps into the hole they've left behind, and the sodden walls sag and crumble in. Coming in from the east, heavy clouds smother the sky as the coconut palms lean low and rattle in the evening breeze.

Mama Lily hobbles past, her crook leg heavy from the long afternoon of hauling washed up fishing nets off the beach. There'd only been one turtle. Long past rescuing. Sand-stuffed holes for eyes and flippers sawn to the bone. Mama Lily's had enough. She turns her head and whistles to Thud the Staffy.

"Home, home," she yells, yanking the handle of her basket in the crook of her right elbow. Thud stops snapping at the foam on the water's edge and runs after her as she starts the long, slow walk back towards her hut.

On the clutter of stones below the cliff, a newspaper-wrapped bundle flaps open and shut; seagulls squawking overhead. Thud runs ahead of Mama Lily, following the smell of deep-fried fish. He pushes his snout into the bundle, vacuuming up the few soggy chips still clinging to the paper. Mama Lily lumbers up, calling him away, but he doesn't come. He circles the bundle, his mouth wide in a wacky grin, drooling as he licks up grains of salt. She whistles again, knowing that the salt will make him thirsty and that she's finished the bottle of water she'd brought with her. As she gets close to the newspaper, she sees that it's weighed down, full and heavy. She pushes at it with her cane.

"Holy Mother of God," she yells as the bundle starts to cry.

Mama Lily carries the baby home in the basket, her hip-swaying gait sending it to sleep. She puts it on the kitchen table and pushes Thud's dribbling snout away.

"Quiet," she says. "It's sleeping."

Mama Lily pulls the paper back. A red-faced boy, greasy still with matted, flattened hair, salt grains caught in waxy folds, the cut umbilical cord hanging to one side. He looks up at her, eyes unfocussed, frowning.

Mama Lily releases the breath she's been holding in.

"We're keeping him," she says.

Thud grins his wide-mouth grin and wags his tail.

Mama Lily makes a nappy from a towel cut in two and strokes the baby's tummy with her thumb. From the medicine box, she takes an eye-dropper and sterilises it in a pan of boiling water. She dissolves a teaspoon of sugar in a glass of diluted cow's milk, fills the eye-dropper and slips her pinkie into the baby's mouth. When he starts sucking, she slides the eye-dropper in next to her finger and slowly squeezes tiny squirts of milk onto his tongue.

Darkness comes and Mama Lily's mangled leg begins its nightly pounding. The ache loops its way around her calf and through her thigh, then clamps around her hips. She keeps her body in constant motion, carrying the baby pressed tight to her chest, trying to keep the pain at bay; her walk a looping, swinging waltz. After the attack, the doctors had hoped the feeling might be lost, but the obstinate nerves refused to quit, their tiny hooks sunk in. So now, she feels every inch of flesh and skin in her gammy leg, even though there's more of it missing than there.

It was on a New Year's Day, hot and heavy like this one, fifty-two years ago. Her left leg shredded by a tiger shark during a drunken midnight swim. She hadn't ventured far off shore, but it was lurking near the river mouth, hoping for an easy snack. After her boyfriend dragged her up onto the beach, she saw its fin heading back out to sea, satisfied no doubt by the small piece of her calf and the bigger chunk of her thigh that it had managed to gulp down. In the moonlight she could see where the attack had happened, the surface of the water swirling still, pale scraps of flesh carried by the outgoing tide, frantically nibbled at by a swarm of baitfish. Her boyfriend carried her to his car and laid her on the back seat, their beach towels wrapped tight around her leg, soaking through with blood.

At the doctor's surgery, they managed to stop the bleeding and gave her something for the pain. They said she was lucky that the major arteries were untouched. Otherwise she would have bled to death. It was mainly fat and muscle that had suffered. What survived was stitched and bandaged and, later, covered by skin grafts and left at that. When it healed, it looked like a stormy sea – big hollows and ridges in place of gentle swells.

***

First thing the next morning, Mama Lily lays the baby on a towel in the bottom of the basket. She covers it with a tea-cloth, slings it over her arm and makes the hour-long trip by coach into Carnarvon. She goes to the chemist and buys formula, a baby bottle, nappies and a dummy. She pays no attention to the questioning look the pharmacist throws her way.

On the wire stand in front of the newsagents, the headlines talk about a young woman found half unconscious, bleeding in the dunes. Mama Lily goes inside and buys the local paper. She waits till she's alone at the bus stop before she opens it and starts reading. The article takes up the whole of page two. The young woman is not a local. She looks to be in her late teens. She's refused to give her name, refused to say where she's come from, refused to say what she did with the baby. The police are appealing for help to find the abandoned new-born. They hold grave fears for its safety.

Once Mama Lily finishes the article, she tears the whole page out and screws it tight into a ball. She throws it up onto the bus-stop roof and then waits in the shade below for the coach to come and carry them back home. When the baby starts to whimper, she pulls the tea-cloth back and takes the dummy from its case. She slips it into the baby's mouth and watches as it starts sucking, its eyelids fluttering, then closing.

When she arrives home, she prepares a bottle of formula and goes outside to the quiet of the porch. She puts her leg up on a crate. The baby drinks curled into her lap, the suck and backwash of the bottle like the gentle rush of waves. She looks into his face, the blackness at the centre of his eyes. She feels the old familiar sorrow seeping deep within her chest. All these years it has leaked behind her heart, a dripping tap of grief. She leans the baby up against her shoulder and rubs his back in circles like she'd done with her own long-gone son.

When he falls asleep, she holds him on her chest, his palms clenched and pushed against her windpipe. She hums and feels the vibrations pass between their bodies. She presses her lips to the top of the baby's head, tasting the warmth of the downy skin against the tip of her tongue. She draws it away and presses it to her palate. Where she expected sweetness, there's only salt. She isn't sure if it's the chips or the ocean that have left their mark, or if it's a rising to the surface of some elemental substance. She is sure, though, that this baby is where it needs to be. There's no doubt in her mind at all. She'll be the one to fulfil its every need. She knows what their lives will become. The taste of it is on her tongue and it won't go away.

Early afternoon, just as she puts the baby down to sleep, she sees a police car pull up in front of her place. The man in the passenger seat stays in the car and a young female officer gets out of the driver's side. Mama Lily recognises her – Nadia. She's known her since she was a little girl. She used to come around with a gang of kids and spy on her from behind the tea-tree bushes. All the local kids were terrified of Mama Lily. Since Nadia became a police officer fifteen years ago, she's been out here to visit hundreds of times. Mainly welfare checks to make sure she's still alive. Three or four times to follow up on a complaint.

"Hey, Lil," says Nadia, taking off her cap. She pulls a damp strand of hair from her forehead and pushes it behind her ear. "Heard you were in town this morning."

Mama Lily pulls a chair out from the kitchen table and lowers herself slowly onto it. Nadia pulls out the other chair and sits down, not waiting for an invitation.

"Lil," she says. "Can you tell me why you bought a whole lot of baby supplies from the chemist?"

Mama Lily doesn't answer. She rubs her knuckles up and down her aching thigh. Nadia waits a few more seconds before continuing.

"There's a baby that was born about twenty-four hours ago. Its mother left it on the beach." She knows that's where Lil spends all her time, getting rid of ghost nets, rescuing any turtles she finds alive. She leans forward until she's directly in her line of sight. "I know you have it, Lil."

Mama Lily runs her tongue across her teeth before she speaks. "It's a he," she says. "And I've given him a name."

"Okay," says Nadia. "What have you called him?"

"Alfie," she replies. Mama Lily looks away and rubs her thumb across her eyelid. "What'll happen to him?" she asks.

"I imagine he'll be put up for adoption," says Nadia. "There's no shortage of families desperate for a baby."

Mama Lily looks down at the floor, the gaps between the mismatched lino tiles filled with sooty crud.

"Fair enough," she says, laying her palm on Thud's hot, dribbling snout. She doesn't watch as Nadia goes and finds the baby sleeping in the basket on her bed. She doesn't watch as she bundles the nappies, bottle and formula into a plastic bag that dangles from her wrist and knocks against the table as she squeezes past. She doesn't look as Nadia carries the baby out to the car and drives away.

Later that afternoon, Mama Lily goes down to the beach. She walks all the way to the end where there's a pile of orange fishing net washed up on the sand. As she gets close, she sees there's a turtle caught, the net slicing through one front flipper. She kneels and tries to hold it still as she cuts at the nylon net. When the last strand breaks, she wraps her arms around the turtle and struggles to pick it up, but it fights its way free and splashes out through the waves, its injured flipper flailing.

Mama Lily lies back, propped on her elbows in the shallow water, exhausted from the battle. The tide is coming in. With each small wave, the water washes over her throbbing leg, splashing up against her chest, small drops landing on her cheeks and lips. She rests, her eyes on the agitated surface of the sea and lets the sun dry out the trickles of water. Thud lies on the wet sand by her side. After a few minutes, he starts to whine, looking up at her, willing her to move. He pushes his snout against her cheek and licks at the salty tracks the drops have left behind, twisted and pale, like dry creek beds. Mama Lily rolls towards him and lifts one hand from the sodden sand. She looks into his eyes and cradles his head in her dripping palm.

The Biz
by Mara Buck

Longlisted, Scottish Arts Club Short Story Competition 2020

Old Tad Howard's quite the character. I been in the second-hand business for twenty years, and Tad's always got something outlandish to offer. Lives in that rusty doublewide out beyond the abandoned Dorsey place, got sheds and barns and garages overflowing with junk, but every so often he'll pull a winner from that god-awful mess.

Last year I gave him fifty bucks for a dragon he'd welded from tractor parts and bed springs. Right creative she was. Big sucker. Tad was some tickled with the cash. I turned it over to a snotty auctioneer who called it folk art and I come away with one bang-up profit. More like highway robbery, but, hey, that's the biz. So, whenever Tad calls, I get cracking. He gimps around on that fake leg of his real spry. He ain't bad company, always offers me a cup of instant with a day-old donut.

Today there ain't no coffee. Tad's already sprawled in a lawn chair under the trailer awning and motions me to a bench alongside.

"Glad you could make it, Dwayne." Tad whistles when he talks, sucking in air through them false choppers. "Not many would drive out here for an old man. You're a real pal."

I remember all the sinful profits I made off him over the years. I look towards a chipmunk sassing me from a gnarly oak. The chipmunk sees through me like he knows the truth of the matter. That's the way the biz works, right? If not me, then somebody else. "Sure, Tad. My pleasure."

He adjusts his fake leg. The knee hinge creaks something fierce. He winces. "VA was supposed to lubricate the damn thing, but they been putting me off. Bunch of skunks. All of 'em. But you didn't come all this way to hear me whine."

"Got something in mind to sell, Tad? Got an empty truck right here." My brief guilty pang has passed. Now I'm thinking about the profit from that stupid dragon. "Done any more of them sculptures? That last one went over pretty good."

172

Tad spits, creaks his knee joint, lowers his voice from his usual pitch. Looks me dead in the eye. "How much you 'spect a tomahawk's worth these days? Got one of them Cheyenne types out back. Take a look. Tell me what you think. I'd be obliged."

"Jesus, Tad. Where'd you get a tomahawk? Cheyenne you say?"

"Spent some time out west with my first wife Edith. A real looker. Too good for the likes of me and sure enough, didn't last long. But while we lasted, we was quite the pair, I tell you." Tad's face softens from his usual grimace. "We was putting together a collection of relics. Planned to open a shop one day. Plans, you know? Like yelling down a drainpipe to hear the big noise." Tad swats at a cloud of blackflies. He manages to knock off his cap and when he bends over to pick it up, his bald spot shines white as a headlamp in the shade under the awning.

Amazing how many stories folks got. Swirling around 'em like no-see-ums on a summer day. People bob their heads to dodge the pesky varmints, but maybe they're trying to dodge what's inside their heads, too. Trying to shake something back into place that got jostled loose. Like Tad's tomahawk memory of his first wife.

"Tad, you ain't too far from that dream. You been selling stuff long's I've known you. Got that retirement thing down right as rain. Lots of scenery, all the peace and quiet a man could want. If Edith had stuck around, you'd never have met Milly, and she was true blue. Buddy, you've done yourself proud." Why am I babbling like this? Should be focusing on that Indian relic. But maybe something's jostled loose in my own head, too. Something best forgotten.

There's not more'n a decade in age between Tad and me, but I ain't been through the war. Not his war, anyways. But we all got scars. Some don't show quite so much as others.

I ain't never seen Tad's war, or any war for that matter. My older brother's got his name on that granite wall in Washington. I drove Ma down for a visit when they built it. Thought she'd die right there from crying. Gives a body a funny turn to see the name of someone you'd known all your lifelong, who you'd fought with and made-up with and fished with and schemed with and opened Christmas presents with and who's now just a name on a fancy wall. Does a number on your insides. I wasn't no hippie, but I couldn't see no point killing foreign

173

people in a jungle where I didn't belong, so I got a 4-F designation. Wasn't proud of it at the time, and that ain't changed, but I ain't got no fake leg and I ain't got my name on no wall. Not yet, anyways.

Christ. Gotta stop these memories buzzing through my head, jostled loose by old Tad. Best not lose my purpose. Best stick to the biz at hand.

I smother my thoughts and concentrate on that little flower garden lying between the trailer and the barn, just overflowing with a mess of colour. Tad's wife Milly was some gardener before she died and them flowers are still blooming years afterwards. Damn pretty. I mention it to Tad. Figure it's a righteous way to ease back into conversation.

Tad don't open his eyes but a crack. "Yeah. Milly had the green thumb. Them roses was her pride and joy. That smell puts me in mind of her. Close my eyes and I almost hear her voice. My daughter comes by to pull weeds and cut blossoms for her ma's grave." Tad opens his eyes full wide now. Gives me a stare. His eyes are bright as blue water. "That won't be happening much longer, 'cause she's got that same kind of cancer that killed Milly. Runs from mother to daughter. One thing they're right about. They're always right about the bad stuff."

"Sorry to hear that, Tad. They got lots of treatments now. Sheila's pretty young, so they'll fix her up for a good time to come." Poor old geezer. The Howards never had much, but they was a close family, Tad being a good pa to Sheila. Loves his grandkids. Sheila works at Walmart, keeps up the rent on her trailer. Mighty fine gal, Sheila. She don't deserve this by half.

"Damn nice of you to say that, Dwayne, making an old guy feel better, but they ain't gonna waste any new-fangled stuff on the likes of us. My pension ain't what it used to be, and Shelia's got that cancer something fierce. Ain't nothing to pay for that 'cept the welfare, and they're flat broke same's the rest of us, so she's gotta go halvsies on them drugs. Can't go for any more treatments neither. Too frigging costly. Doc says she won't last without 'em. I'll be taking care of them grandkids. Course I am pretty much now anyway. Just hope I live long enough to see 'em off good and proper." He seems more chipper now since telling me about Shelia, like he's reminding himself he's got a purpose.

174

"Damn shame, Tad." And it is, too. Folks like us are always at the bottom of the barrel, trying all our lives to claw our way out and if we happen to, chances are we'll slide straight back down again. "You up to showing me that tomahawk?"

"Yep. Day ain't getting no younger and I ain't neither." The old guy raises himself up out of that flimsy chair, hobbles towards the first solid thing in sight and muckles onto it. "Bear with me, son. Gotta get my balance back."

"Take your time, pal. I ain't in no rush." I recollect he sold me a carved cane before I came away with that dragon. Probably another cane in the trailer and his pride won't let him use it in front of me. Yeah, that's it.

Tad lurches from one tree to another along a zig-zag path worn in the grass. We aim for the barn. It takes a while, but we make it through the big doors without incident.

It's dark in the barn. Thin beams of sunlight sneak through the cracks, like the light's deciding to show us only what it wants to. Real quiet. Puts me in mind of the Catholic church where my brother's funeral was. Where the priest said words over Pa gone before him and Ma gone after. Crosses my mind to wonder if anyone will say some words over me. I'm getting downright sappy and I tell myself, right out loud, "Cut it out!"

"What'd you say, Dwayne?"

"Some no-see-ums followed me in. Damn things drive a man crazy." I shake my head, shaking against the thoughts buzzing inside my skull.

"Yep. Never get away from them things this time of year." Tad flashes a grin and his plastic teeth gleam in the dark. "Got that tomahawk right here, if you want to take a look."

He holds it out to me, like something holy passing from one hand to another. The handle itself is more'n a couple feet long, wrapped in rawhide, the strap covered in beadwork. Hanging off the business end is a hank of hair with tassels and feathers braided in. Quite the fancy rig. Wonder why Tad's been keeping it so long. Memories, I 'spect. Thinking 'bout them days when he and Edith was yelling into drainpipes. Planning.

Tad's keeping up the chatter while I'm ruminating. All part of the biz.

175

"Dwayne, them other tomahawks the government's got? Bet them suckers go for a pretty penny. Million or more apiece, I reckon. Once they fire 'em, ain't much to salvage. Can't exactly reuse 'em. With them planes, subs, carriers, and everything—you got yourself quite the expensive experience. Trillions with a T. And no funds to lubricate my leg? Frigging skunks!"

"Ain't the life we signed on for, is it, my man?" Tad's right. Tomahawks. What they call them missiles. Hell of a lot different from this one in my hands.

"Terrible thing for a body's pride, scraping along, taking handouts. Warn't raised that way, but times is way different today." Tad's speech is winding down, like he needs fresh batteries. Damn shame about his leg bothering him like that. Damn shame about Sheila. Everything's a damn shame.

Gazing out the barn door, I see the chipmunk back on that oak branch, staring at me again, ready to read me my just desserts. Puts me in mind of my ma looking me straight in the eye like she could judge my thoughts. "Dwayne, you do the right thing. Your pa and I brought you up proper." I got memories buzzing in my head fit to drive a man crazier than no-see-ums, but in my pocket I got quite a wad. I always carry cash with me in case of a special opportunity.

Tad spits onto the dirt of the barn floor. The wetness lies there, glistening. "Whatta you say? You think she's got some value? If you ain't into buying, maybe I'll sell her on eBay. Get them kids new school shoes. Pay for my daughter's burying."

My hand closes around the wad in my pocket. "Oh, she's got value, for sure. Indian stuff's mighty hot now. I was planning to head to Bill's auction later, so I got more cash than usual. Would you take a thousand? Got the large notes right here."

I look up and the chipmunk's gone.

Domestic Spirit
by Shannon Payne

Longlisted, Scottish Arts Club Short Story Competition 2020

It begins like this:

words, drip, drip, dripping out of me like letting blood, scraped, scratched, and formed into letters on the page before the scarlet ink dries dull brown.

Here in the entrance hall, where the family would have received visitors, some of the greatest literary minds of the enlightenment were received

under this roof

is where I keep the papers, saturated with sanguine words, in a little wooden house made for dolls. They languish in the dark, unread but for when I take them out to peruse for my own amusement. I don't tell my husband – they're flights of fancy, nothing more. But I keep them close to my heart. Something of my very own.

The lady of the house would wait here to greet the great thinkers. You can see here one of her dresses preserved in this glass case. You can almost imagine her standing here,

smiling

– not too wide, not too dour – I smile and smile and smile and accept kisses on my hand and cheek, and pretty compliments on the house, my dress, my cleverness in securing such a husband. I smile and smile and think about all the words welling up inside that need to be let out or I may just burst from the pressure.

Through here is the dining room, where the men – in these days only the men – would smoke cigars and discuss enlightenment ideas that were to transform the way we see the world. Sometimes I feel like

I can almost hear them

from my hiding place – art, literature, politics are being discussed, I'm sure, but all I can make out is the buzz of conversation. I can't distinguish a single word. And night after night, the papers pile up, bursting at the walls of their little pine house.

Most of you will know the man of the house – still famous even now, centuries after he first put pen to paper to write some of the most iconic works of literature of the era. Though according to his diaries, even he struggled with intense bouts of writer's block where he simply couldn't find

the words

are gone. I notice when I try to add to the hoard of papers and find the pile missing from its little room in the dollhouse. It feels like the tightening of a garrotte.

But he overcame it. And he must have been a genius to come up with ideas for all

those brilliant stories

are mine. I poured them from vein onto the paper and hid them away in the dark where they were supposed to be safe, safe, safe. I didn't ask for anything but to be allowed to keep what was mine. To keep them folded close to my heart. The accusation tears itself out of me like I'm exorcising a demon. I have never felt anger burn like this. They are *mine*.

His wife, of course, was ever supportive of her husband's work, taking upon herself the bulk of domestic labour as he toiled in his study, where he spent his days. He often mentioned feeling

trapped

with his hulking mass blocking the doorway. My words scattered around the room, splattered across the writing desk and pooling on the floor.

There is, however, tragedy that hovers over this idyllic family. How many of you knew that the great author's wife went missing in the summer of 1782? Well, it's true – it was said she went for a walk and was never again seen

within these walls

I cannot breathe. I can only move to scratch helplessly at the pine. I cannot dislodge the cloth in my mouth. It is dark, but I can see at my feet the ground is saturated with my little papers – scarlet dried brown – used and abandoned. It is so very dark. But still I scratch at the walls until my fingers begin to bleed.

Now I know what you're thinking — what happened to her? Well, the truth is, we'll never know for sure. The case went cold and was never solved. It's a shame, really, but a reality of history. Some things fall

between the cracks

I watch him. He writes and writes and writes and writes and I scratch and scratch and scratch. He will have no peace, not while I am watching. Did he think he would get more words from me? That he could tap them like sap from a maple tree, and distil them for himself?

He never fully recovered from her disappearance. His writing declined afterward, as he was overtaken by memories and grief for his darling wife which may have been what eventually drove him from the house where he had last seen her. For many years the house was

abandoned

with the mice, the rats, the spiders, the sound of rain, and the rot. Rot that slowly begins to eat away at this wall. Still I scratch, scratch, scratch, digging my way out of rotting walls

until

our company bought the property and refurbished it, restored the rotting walls, kept the structure standing, and opened it for you people.

The new walls are stronger than the old and I must begin again. Scratching. But I have been here for years, what's a few more? The stories begin. Stories about him. Even the stories about me are really about him. Beautiful lies, dressed up as history

is what we really care about here -- an authentic glimpse into the life of a great mind.

I can see them moving about in the room every day. They cannot see me. They aren't looking.

But I'm here.

I never

left.

Can't

they hear me

scratching at

the walls

… I thought I heard… Never mind. You know those old stories that this place is haunted? Maybe they're not just stories, eh, folks? I'm just kidding with you, keeping it interesting …

I wish I had a tongue to scream, then someone, someone would know
what really happened,

finally

I'll let you in on a little tidbit from my own research. Something I've discovered in the archives… Notes containing some early plot and dialogue written in handwriting that does not match the samples we have of the credited author.

Every person who's stomped past my tomb, tells the same story over and over and over so many times I could recite each lovely lie. But this voice, this woman might be the one who

uncovers

that these great novels, long thought to be a work of singular genius, may have, in fact, been a collaborative effort, or perhaps even stolen. Stolen from who, you might ask? Well, I have my theories…

I begin to scratch again. More insistently.

While we may never know for sure what happened to his wife, or who wrote those notes, or who the true mind behind those books was, we owe it to the unnamed, uncredited other writer, and to ourselves to keep digging for

the truth

only I can tell. I can't speak, can't call out to her, but she hears me.

She's listening.

and it ends like this:

with the silent scream of nails tearing into
pine,
with the splintering crack of breaking
through.

Hare Soup
by Ann MacLaren

Longlisted, Scottish Arts Club Short Story Competition 2020

"I wonder what he's going to give you, Margaret?"
      Edith giggled as she pulled the white lace antimacassar from the back of her armchair and dramatically draped it over her head like a veil.

Margaret was expecting a ring, of course. And Edith's knowing laughter, though irksome, reassured her. If Edward was going to propose he would no doubt have discussed it with his daughter first; he consulted her on everything. Margaret would soon put a stop to that.

"No need to play games," said Margaret irritably. Edith really was the most tiresome of girls. One would have thought that at seventeen she might have acquired some decorum, but her manner was frivolous and often childlike. Margaret hoped that once they were married she could persuade Edward to send her off to a finishing school somewhere – preferably abroad.

"Would you like to hear my practice?" said Edith, rushing over to the piano. "I'm learning the latest Louis Armstrong. It's so exciting!" She launched into a stumbling rendition of a tune that Margaret, who preferred classical music, had no hope of recognising, even if it were played well. Closing her eyes and ears to the cacophony she pondered her future, and prepared to say goodbye to her past.

***

Margaret had only ever had one ambition: to be married to a rich man. Her grandmother, who had been both mother and father to Margaret since the death of her parents, had supported this objective wholeheartedly, but counselled:

"If you want to make hare soup, Margaret, first you must catch your hare."

All well and good – but so many hares had outrun her; so many times she had been thwarted by an overbearing mother, an interfering friend – or even the discovery of an existing spouse. She had assumed, when the war ended and all the men came back, that she'd be able to take her pick, but it hadn't worked out like that. At thirty-two she was considered 'on the shelf'.

"New pastures," Grandmother had advised. So she had applied – successfully – for the post of librarian in another town in the hope that there she would find her future husband.

She had only been in the library for a few days when she met Edith Forbes. The young girl had chattered incessantly as her books were stamped, and Margaret had hardly looked at her for fear this would be seen as an encouragement to linger; but when Edith began to talk about a forthcoming journey to Italy with her father, Margaret felt interested enough to ask:

"And will your mother go too?"

"My mother died when I was born," said Edith. She prattled on before Margaret could express her sympathies. "It's Daddy's birthday gift to me. He's always so generous. Last year he took me to London and we stayed at the Ritz." She prattled on about all the places they would visit in Europe – Lugano, Milan, Rome, Venice …

Margaret thought 'Daddy' must be very rich.

"We have a wonderful book about Rome that you might want to read before you go," she told the girl. There's so much to see and do in the city. It's out on loan just now, but I'll keep it for you once it's been returned."

Two days later Margaret looked up Edith's address in the files and took the book, which had been on the shelves all the time, to her home – a large townhouse at the edge of the park, close to the river. She was, for her kindness, invited to stay to tea.

And so she had met Edward. Not the Adonis she had hoped for. He was middle aged, short, rotund and quite bald – the hair on his head having migrated to his ears, where it grew in profusion. Rather uncultured too, she gathered, as he cut off her discussion of the library's Greek-inspired architecture to explain to her the boring workings of his engineering company.

Still, he was a hare.

As the weeks passed she had found herself more and more in

Edward Forbes' company, although she realised with dismay that their only common ground was his daughter, Edith. However, any doubts she may have had about setting her cap at Edward, any worries about spending her days with this outright philistine, and her nights in expected intimacy with him, were erased on one particular visit to his house: for in a home where the only reading material other than the daily newspaper seemed to be a Bible, a dictionary and a set of encyclopaedias, she had made an astonishing discovery.

Underneath the small bookcase housing the aforementioned volumes, lying on its side and camouflaged by the brown carpet, Margaret had found one of the rarest books in the world. Astonished, she had stared speechless at the volume, caressed the leather cover, admired its intricately embossed lettering; gingerly she had opened the first pages and confirmed her suspicions: one of only two published copies of what was known as the Kaufmann Shakespeare.

She had learned about this book when studying to become a librarian. Dating from 1786, and allegedly illustrated by the famed artist Louisa Kaufmann, only two copies were ever produced. Margaret had seen one in a museum, in a glass case. Rumour had it that the other had been spotted once, somewhere in the Far East. It was worth a fortune.

"I see you've found that old thing."

She had been so absorbed she hadn't heard Edward coming into the room.

"My father gave it to me when I was only twelve. He brought it home from a trip to China. How ridiculous, eh? I had asked for a real ivory mahjong set and he brought me a Shakespeare! I've never read one word of it. Not my thing. Don't know why I kept it."

"It's beautiful," she told him. "Just look at this marvellous cover. Why is it hidden under the bookcase?"

"It wouldn't fit on the shelves. Too big" He dismissed the book. "There's something I wanted to ask you."

Margaret filed the Kaufmann away in her head for later. She felt sure she knew what Edward was going to say; she and Edith had already discussed it.

"My daughter has become very fond of you over the past few

weeks. I wondered … would you be interested in accompanying us to Europe, as her companion? I would pay all expenses and you would have your own room, of course. And," he coughed and looked down at his feet. "I too would be grateful for your company."

***

"Perhaps he bought you something when we were in Italy," said Edith, breaking into Margaret's reverie. She had abandoned the piano and now thumped down beside Margaret. "Or perhaps not," she teased, as she tossed the cushions to the floor and threw her legs over the arm of the settee.

"That really is a most unladylike posture," said Margaret. Then getting no reaction added, "You do know your father asked to see me alone?"

"Yes. At 11am. It's only a quarter to."

Fifteen minutes, thought Margaret. Fifteen minutes and then I'll be mistress of this house. Mistress Forbes. Well, almost. She surveyed the drawing room, imagining the changes she would make, where she would place the paintings she would buy, the vases she would acquire. They would certainly be more tasteful than the existing drab decorations – dull brass candlesticks, grey-black engravings, dark velvet curtains. The bookshelves in the alcove would go; she had plans to create a library in the small bedroom at the foot of the stairs. Thinking of the library made her shiver with pleasure. The Kaufmann Shakespeare would have pride of place. And when Edward was gone – he was thirty years her senior, after all – she might sell it and buy a second home on the continent. Italy perhaps. She had already established that it was worth thousands of pounds.

"Wasn't it a super holiday! Did you prefer Florence or Pompeii?" Edith again interrupted her musings.

"They're hardly comparable," Margaret replied. But if I was forced to make a choice, I'd say Florence. All those exquisite paintings – Raphael, Titian; and the sculptures; our hotel beside the Arno; that bridge from "Dante's Meeting with Beatrice". The place is packed with …"

Edith cut her off.

"Daddy was bored in Florence. He told me so. He preferred Pompeii."

184

"The unusual plumbing I suppose. His leanings are obviously more technical than aesthetic," said Margaret. She wondered if the girl knew what aesthetic meant.

"And what about you, Edith? Which did you prefer?"

"I loved Pompeii too. All those lava encrusted bodies. And the drawings on the walls were quite fascinating."

Margaret knew exactly which drawings the bold little hussy was referring to. It was the only art she had shown an interest in. She had been scandalised that Edward had allowed his daughter to enter the Lupanar and gawp at the blatant pornography. Margaret had waited outside the door; she had already seen the pictures in a guide book.

"But really my favourite was Venice, and the Lido," added Edith. "Wasn't it a shame we just missed the Duke of Windsor and his lady? I might have asked for an autograph – to add to all my other my bits and pieces."

Edith had a huge collection of memorabilia from the holiday: luggage tags, itineraries, train and bus tickets, museum and art gallery entrances, postcards from every tourist shop they encountered – there was hardly a piece of paper or card that she hadn't collected. She even had food and accommodation receipts.

"What on earth do you want all that for?" Margaret had asked, irritated at having to find room in her suitcase for a large bag full of papers.

"I have a plan for them," said Edith. "It's a secret."

***

At two minutes to eleven, Margaret asked Edith to leave the drawing room, adding:

"Please don't think of listening at the door."

"As if I needed to," laughed Edith, dancing out of the room.

Margaret could hear her whispering to Edward, who must have been waiting in the hallway for the clock to chime. She supposed he was nervous.

She hadn't expected it to be so easy, or so soon. They were, after all, only two weeks home. Edward hadn't actually courted her during the trip; but he had, in his awkward, self-conscious way, given her his attention. Margaret had, in turn, but rather more subtly, let him know that she was interested.

She composed her face into a smile and waited.

When Edward came through the door he was proffering a book. It took Margaret a moment to recognise it; it looked somewhat different. The Kaufmann. She could see that it was bulging, that there was something inside it. She didn't understand.

"I know how much you've admired this." Edward thrust it into her lap. She began to tremble; she could see without opening it what he had done.

"It was Edith's idea really," he said, looking indulgently towards the door. We tried to buy some scrap books in town yesterday but we couldn't find any. So Edith thought, why not use this? She's seen you looking at it often, you seem to be very fond of it. We've been up half the night glueing it all in. It's all there. Memories of a wonderful holiday."

Margaret couldn't move, couldn't speak, couldn't believe what this ignorant, uneducated, fool had done. Her chest felt tight; she flushed, began to perspire.

Encouraged by her silent blush, Edward continued:

"I wondered if I might ask you ... the holiday was such a success ... would you consider a change of occupation? I'd be very happy to employ you on a permanent basis, as companion to my daughter."

As the swift blackness of a faint enveloped her, Margaret imagined she could hear the high-pitched sound of Edith's irritating giggle from somewhere very far away. Though in reality it came from just behind the door.

White Christmas
by John Coughlan

Longlisted, Scottish Arts Club Short Story Competition 2020

When the Colonel announced that the battalion would be moving up to Kohima early on the 23rd, I had, as the junior subaltern, stifled a cheer, presuming the thankless task of organising the Christmas concert would no longer be mine. I was mistaken.

Shortly after breakfast the adjutant made it plain to me that the concert must take place that evening. That the Colonel had every confidence in me as entertainments officer and was positive I would not disappoint him. Enough to say that I feared his displeasure more than my scheduled meeting with the Japanese. Appalled, I struggled through the scanty auditions that had been done the previous week and which I had prematurely consigned to the rubbish bin and now had to ransack the rubbish area in order to retrieve.

A dearth of talent stared me in the face. The number of men who thought they could juggle, sing, dance or do magic tricks were Legion. Monologues of varying length and debauchery were steady favourites, Not a few of these lewd ballads had to be refused as the nurses of the base hospital were to attend en masse.

Private Cairns for instance, had trained a dog to bark in unison with his demented screeching on a bugle. Sgt Taylor, who fancied he could sing, thumped two keys of the knackered piano and dirged out what was supposedly a rendering of *Ophelia*, an irritating drone at the best of times. When I inquired diplomatically whether it was appropriate Yuletide fare, he asked nippily what the feck that had to do with it.

I very quickly discovered that neither Kings Regs, nor a small book entitled *Hints for Young Officers*, adequately covered concert parties, and not all bad-tempered sensitive Diva sang in the Royal Opera Company. I was further bemused, confused, and not a little educated by the number of officers who wished to dress up as women and dance in a chorus line. While aware this might be the effect of social repression in certain public schools, I resolved never to shower in their company again.

The Colonel had insisted on a programme lasting at least two hours with intermission but even with dire threats and bribery I was well short of that expectation. Somewhat desperate then, contemplating seppuku with my head already down on the Orderly Room desk I was relieved when the RSM approached me and suggested the inclusion of one of his Bren gunners, one Davie Dick. Told me he could sing anything and sing it like a linty, and being at the end of my patience and sanity, I added him unheard to the list. I informed the RSM he could go on last and sing the bloody telephone directory if he liked. Grinning, he left me with the solid conviction that death at the hands of the Japanese would be preferable to the Colonel's limitless and eternal displeasure.

Time's winged chariot fast approached with myself firmly in the path of its thundering wheels. At 2000hrs prompt, the battalion assembled in the motor pool area where the wooden forms were soon packed leaving the rest of the battalion perched atop lorries and armoured vehicles. Some took to the lower branches of the banyan trees displacing the screeching monkeys. The quartermaster petulantly raised an official objection that the men were sitting on stacks of ammunition boxes in the ordnance lorries and were smoking, contrary to peacetime regulations. Infuriated by this last-minute attempt on my production I dismissed him with a total abuse of my rank and powers as MC invested in me by the Colonel. Smug with this crushing of bureaucracy, I proceeded.

Each man clutched an issue of one tin of warm beer, one melting chocolate bar, and one sausage roll of undetermined grey pasty content which raised questions of where all the pariah dogs had gone from about the camp. Some individuals had obviously got their hands on more than the official beer ration, supplemented by a ferocious hooch brewed somewhere behind the Motor Transport Lines. Highly flammable as a few eyebrow-less smokers had found out to their cost. The transport officer indulged the still as it was useful as a degreaser. The inebriated were studiously ignored on the eve of battle by the Regimental Police and the normally eagle eye of the RSM turned Nelsonian. These inebriated groups were to be the principal hecklers.

I mounted the rickety ammunition box stairs and took the stage though truth be told I would have sooner entered a minefield. Shouting above the clamour of catcalls and barracking I welcomed the audience I thanked the Colonel, thanked the cooks for their disgusting pies and sausage rolls and announced the time of sick-call. Barely making myself heard I introduced the first act.

Everything followed Paddy's Law from the start, then went disastrously downhill.

The lighting failed intermittently, the music, played from scrounged and homemade instruments, was raucous as the screeching monkeys who joined in the chorus, off key even to my tone-deaf ears. Two of the dubious officer chorus girls toppled drunk off the back of the stage, obviously an excess of gin and tonic. In response to ribald heckling of his singing dog Private Cairns lifted his kilt, showed them his tackle and told them to eff off. This brought a storm of cheering.

Certain that nothing could be worse I was confronted at this point by a scarecrow apparition. This baggy-uniformed, balding, podgy, smelly, sweat drenched person turned out of course to be he of the unfortunate name. Davie Dick. His smile revealed tombstone teeth and his twitching hands betrayed his almost catatonic stage fright. I groaned inwardly and told him he would be on last. He nodded his large oversized head which wobbled dangerously. I took refuge in my hip flask and despaired.

At least the communal carol singing led with gusto by the padre went well, not a few getting very misty eyed. The Colonel joined in lustily which I took as a mark of favour for my efforts. From my perch in the wings, as disaster followed disaster, I could see the audience enjoyed every moment of it. Inexplicable!

At last my Calvary ended. The RSM gave me a wink and thumbs up as Dick wandered out onto stage at the mercy of the shrieking mob ... And he just ... stood there frozen, the butt of impossible physical suggestions. The generator came to his rescue and packed in concealing him apart from the oil lamp footlights. As I stepped forward to rescue him and bring things to a close, he lifted his head and began to sing.

"I'm dreaming of a White Christmas
Just like the ones I used to know ..."

I stood amazed, enthralled. Those leaving returned. From this untidy shambles came the voice of angels, tingling as sleigh bells, soft as snowdrift, carrying us all away from the war. The jungle faded away, it's ark of creatures stilled, the song carrying men away across the miles and the seas to their families. Returned them in an instant to a time when they were little, a place of snow and roaring fires, lighted trees. To that delicious moment as a child, when you woke and came down to cries of joy. Back home in mind to wives, children, parents, friends, sweethearts. To Bolton, Carlisle, Glasgow, Aberfeldy. To slum and farmhouse or palace, transported on the wings of his song.

The hecklers fell silent, men began to sing softly along with him, but it was Davie

Dick who soared above them. Strong men wept openly and without shame, held for a while in a small, safe capsule of time, private to them alone. The last song faded into total silence, the last notes melting like frost.

A pause, then they were on their feet, cheering, clapping, whistling, banging on the truck panels, demanding more. They wouldn't let him go. They had him sing every song they ever knew. Davie Dick swept us away from fear and killing, away from wounds and disease, away from what the morrow might bring. Gone from here, over the sea to home.

They laughed, they cried, they had him sing song after song, every Christmas carol we had sung as boys. *Silent Night* broke our hearts. Inspired now from within, young Davie just stood and sang, his voice with more range than a ladder has rungs. He stood with eyes closed oblivious to everything but the song. *The Slave's Chorus* choked our throats and stung our cheeks with burning tears. He held us in his hand, he tore our hearts, he made us laugh, made us weep, he wrung our souls clean.

They stormed the stage and carried him away shoulder high, leaving me alone on the loading ramp with my chest burning and my face wet, the ground littered with abandoned sausage rolls.

I never saw Davie Dick after that night, but I did see his name twice, many years apart.

The first was when the RSM wordlessly handed me a casualty slip and dog-tag inside a bloodstained paybook and went away without speaking. I peeled apart the sticky pages.

'Private Dick. D. 'A' Company. Killed in action, early hours of 24th.'

I entered the event in the Regimental diary, and mourned the fact that, while his death was recorded, his song was not.

The second time was many years later, when I returned to Kohima in the company of other old soldiers but of many more ghosts. Davie has no known grave, lying forever in the slit trench where he was killed. I heard his voice on the wind, saw and touched his name on the memorial at Kohima, under the simple inscription.

For your tomorrow, we gave our today.

24152188   Private David Dick.   Aged 20 years.   7th Btln A&SH
24.12.44

The First Casualty
by Colin Armstrong

Longlisted, Scottish Arts Club Short Story Competition 2020

"We drew straws." I told Gerhard Weber. He looked at me intently with those anxious blue eyes of his.

"Vassilis held them out to us in his stubby fingers. I never thought we should do it, so I dived in first. You know? Better odds. But I drew the short one anyway. Vassilis clapped me on the shoulder and pressed the pistol into my hand." I paused. "Look, are you sure …"

Gerhard was younger than me, maybe in his early 50s. Neatly cut short, grey hair and round designer glasses that were in fashion back then. Under his bottom lip was a sprout of hair – what do they call it, a soul patch? Anyway, I thought it looked silly on a man of his age.

"Yes, yes, I need to know everything." he insisted.

I nodded. "So, Vassilis made the prisoner kneel on the edge of the grave that we had made him dig for himself. He had kept up a constant murmur that I thought might be a prayer. Was he religious?"

I thought that was a nice touch, but Gerhard just shrugged, so I went on.

"He seemed to sense that I was holding a gun to the back of his head, because he raised his voice to make some kind of plea. I didn't know German well, but it was something about his children and his wife. The blood was pounding in my temples. I wiped sweat from my eyes so that I could take better aim, but my hand kept shaking. You have to remember, I was only sixteen. I had never shot anyone. I tried holding the pistol in both hands, but it did no good. I couldn't squeeze the trigger. Like I say, I didn't want to kill him."

"What happened next?"

"Vassilis snatched the gun from me. He hit me across the face with the back of his hand and called me a coward." I pointed to the deep scar that runs across my left cheek. "His signet ring left me with this memento. Then he kicked the prisoner in the back, pushing him into the hole. That was when the German decided to make a run for it."

"He tried to escape?"

"Yes, he started scrambling up the far side of the pit. It had been raining and he kept sliding back in the mud. Vassilis just laughed at him, watching him struggling in the muck. When he finally managed to pull himself out of the hole and stood on the lip, Vassilis shot him in the left leg and he tumbled back in. He was in terrible pain, but he was very determined and tried to crawl out again. So Vassilis shot him in the other leg, then the back. And finally," I pointed at my temple, "it was over."

I was elaborating, of course. Munitions were in short supply. We couldn't afford to waste four bullets on one prisoner. Vassilis had shot him in the back of the head then pushed the spade into my hand and ordered me to fill in the grave, while the others jeered at me for my cowardice. I can still recall the smell of cordite and newly dug soil. The wind rustling the leaves. The humiliating feeling of shame, because I had bottled out of the execution. I got the scar years later, from a bad-tempered sheep that didn't like to be sheared.

Gerhard jotted something into his notebook, a tear smudging the ink. I took the opportunity to top up his wine glass. It would be best if he wasn't thinking too clearly.

"Where can I find other witnesses?" he asked.

"Oh, long-gone!" I shrugged.

"But you said that most of your partisans were local farm lads brought up in the hills. Vassilis had recruited them because they knew the forests and had hunted game. There must still be some of them about."

"Herr Weber, you must understand, we didn't just fight the Wehrmacht. There were also the Italians and the Bulgarians. Then we Greeks began to fight one another – the Communists killed Conservatives, the Conservatives fought the Liberals, the British kept sending us arms so long as we shot Communists as well as Germans. Then there were German reprisals and the Great Famine." I slammed my glass down. "My own grandmother starved to death!" I rose from the table and looked out of my kitchen widow.

"And after the war, do you think anyone cared about our little valley? The young men left for the cities. Found jobs in the new factories and holiday resorts. Some emigrated to America, Australia and, yes, Herr Weber, even to Germany. Perhaps you might find your witnesses amongst the *Gastarbeiter* back in Wolfsburg?" I was quite pleased with my little speech and thought I struck a noble pose staring at the horizon, stroking my moustache.

Gerhard was suitably chastened. "Forgive me, Demitris. I didn't mean to offend you. You can't imagine how overwhelming this has been for me. To discover from old military records that my own father died on active service in the very valley where I had bought a holiday home. And then to find you – a witness to his execution."

Active service? That was a laugh. The soldier we shot that night had been as drunk as a skunk. We had snatched him when he staggered out of a brothel. I had no idea if he was Gerhard's long, lost Papa or not. It was fifty years ago, for Christ's sake. Gerhard had approached me after making enquiries in the village about former members of the partisans.

When he had stuck his dog-eared photo under my nose, what I had recognised was an opportunity, not the German soldier we had executed.

"The only other witness that I know of is Vassilis." I said.

Gerhard nodded, "He refuses to talk to me. He spat on the ground when I approached him."

Ah, Vassilis, as charmless as ever. How I hated the man. Not just for humiliating me that night. A frightened boy, ordered to murder a prisoner in cold blood. But also because, later, he had unfairly denounced my father as a collaborator and organised a lynch mob to string him up in the village square.

I decided it was time to make the pitch. I reached into a kitchen cabinet and pulled out an object wrapped in cloth.

"This is for you." I said, placing it on the table.

Gerhard unwrapped it and sat back in surprise. It was a Walther P-38, the standard issue side arm of the Wehrmacht.

"I took it from the prisoner that night," I said. "Gerhard, it's your father's gun."

I had actually bought it in Athens the previous week from a dealer in military memorabilia. The gun was in working condition and came with a small number of live rounds.

Gerhard picked it up like it was a holy relic. "But this is incredible." I hoped he didn't mean that literally.

"I kept it as a souvenir of the war, I suppose. But now I have heard your moving story, I feel more like a caretaker than an owner. Gerhard, you are destined to be the rightful owner."

"You're very kind, but an item like this must be worth a lot of money to a collector."

"I did think of selling it last year. Money has been short, lately. A dealer offered me 3,000 drachmae. But I couldn't take your money, Gerhard." This figure was actually three times more than I had paid for it.

"Dimitris, I'm a wealthy man. I insist that you must have the true value of the gun. If you don't want to keep the money, then please feel free to donate it to your favourite charity." So saying, Gerhard began constructing a very satisfying tower of banknotes on my kitchen table.

I felt pretty pleased with myself as I watched the tail-lights of his Mercedes disappear down my farm track towards the village. I had made a tidy profit on the sale of the gun and, in exchange, Gerhard had a colourful story and a fine souvenir to illustrate his family history. Wasn't everyone a winner? But the smile was wiped off my face a couple of weeks later when a blue and white police Land Rover bumped its way up the track.

Captain Michelakis accepted a black coffee and a bowl of olives and took the same seat that Gerhard had occupied at my kitchen table. He had a reputation for being effective and tenacious, but he must have been pretty frustrated investigating the drunken brawls and sheep-stealing that passed for serious crime in our little backwater. He was in his early thirties, clean shaven and always wore a smart suit, like a city detective.

"Do you recognise this?" he asked, placing an evidence bag containing the gun onto the table. I thought Weber must have rumbled my con and gone whining to the police.

"It is an old gun; I saw many like it during the war."

"How about three weeks ago, in Athens, in a shop called *Military Collectables*?" The Police had obviously traced the gun to the shop using the serial number. I had given a false name to the proprietor and paid in cash, but he must have given them a description. People always remember the scar on my cheek.

I sighed, "Look, if Weber is unhappy with the gun, I'll give him his money back. There's no need to waste police time, is there?"

"Who is Weber?"

"The man I sold the gun to. Aren't you here because he has made a complaint?"

"Tell me about this Weber."

So I told my story to Michelakis while he drank his coffee and chewed his olives, depositing the pits in a neat row around his saucer. All the time I was wondering why the police were interviewing me if Weber hadn't called them in.

When Michelakis asked me where I had been around midnight on Saturday, I really began to worry. What had Weber done?

I laughed, "I was in bed, Captain – we farmers have to get up early, you know."

"Do you have any witnesses?"

"No, my wife passed away three years ago. What is this all about?"

"I believe you know Vassilis Fotakis? In fact, I have been told that you hold him responsible for your father's death during the war."

"Captain, a great many things happened in the war that we would prefer to forget. I mean no disrespect, but you are a young man …"

"Yes, yes …" he interrupted, " … but, you see, Fotakis was murdered on Saturday night. Shot in each leg, the back and the head. We found this gun in a refuse bin around the corner. I'm waiting for the forensic report, but I think this is the murder weapon. What's more a witness saw a man with a scar like yours on his face running away from the scene."

He told me he would check out my story about Weber and asked me to come into the police station to make a formal statement.

Of course, Gerhard Weber had an alibi. He had returned to Germany a week before the murder. He confirmed to Michelakis that he owned a holiday home locally, but he claimed to have no interest in family history or to have met either me or Vassilis. He denied all knowledge of the gun.

I'm an old man now, too old to run a hill farm. Here in prison I have a roof over my head, plenty of food to eat and medicine for my heart condition. In the world outside the government is in crisis and demonstrators are demanding something called Grexit. People can't withdraw their money from the bank, the pensions have been cut and the health service is in a mess. So maybe I didn't draw the short straw after all.

Her Eyes were Full of Stings
by Mark Chester

Longlisted, Scottish Arts Club Short Story Competition 2020

The book arrived in the post on Monday morning, and by nightfall I was submerged in an avalanche of memories, the mess of guilt and shame lying about me like discarded wrapping paper on Christmas morning.

Jo had chosen to send me a newly published collection of Laurie Lee's writings – *Village Christmas: And Other Notes on the English Year* – and she had written an inscription for me inside the front cover. It was typically thoughtful of Jo.

> "To my best friend, Rosie,
> – a harder life
> – a simpler life
> – beauty in abundance!
> Much love, Jo"

Jo's inscription was right. And it was wrong. Yes, we had possessed beauty in abundance; we were in our ascendancy, urged on by the billowing lines of our flexuous bodies into new empires of possibility. Boys were mesmerized, and like the provocative pain of pins and needles beneath our skin we felt the burgeoning force of the power we could yield in a glance, a word, a movement; we just didn't understand how gently we ought to have held that power, how careful we should have been to avoid the haunting recollections of betrayal that now bloat my thoughts.

But Jo was wrong too because I don't believe they were simpler times. The purple haze of hindsight has made Jo nostalgic, and the fog of deceit has shrouded her view of what really happened all those years ago. I know the truth because I was the deceiver, and I still am.

During our O Level years our friendship had intensified over *Cider With Rosie* which we were studying in English and both adored. Lee's poetic prose smudged our belief that reading was a waste of time, and once we had discovered that both our names appeared in his story we gave ourselves completely to the pearls we could find within the covers of books, especially the passages that in any other context would have been forbidden to us.

I remember the day we read *First Bite at the Apple*, the chapter that teased us with 'the first faint musks of sex'. Our names were the same as those of Laurie's intimate shepherdesses, who ushered him into his sexual awakening. We were in class and Miss Trinder had chosen to do the day's reading out loud herself; with a sensitivity that belied her stern exterior, she was sparing a poor adolescent's blushes when the inevitable sniggering began at the mention of any illicitly scented word.

"So quiet was Jo always, so timorous yet eager to please, that she was the one I chose first" began Miss Trinder. I caught Jo's eye and raised my eyebrows; we both smiled. Later, after school, we walked home together and in my bedroom we read the chapter again, mocking one another with Lee's phrases.

"I have a cool face, speechless grace and secretive prettiness," said Jo.

"But your body is pale and milk-green," I giggled. "You just spread it out, naked, for him to explore. You harlot." We both screamed.

"You're the tart," jeered Jo. "Provocative Rosie. Devious and sly. You've got sharp salts of wickedness on you."

"My body flickered with lightening," I said with mock proudness. "And I was even prettier than Betty Gleed."

"Yes – but I bet you that Betty Gleed had big ears and sticking out teeth."

We howled with laughter.

But it was another of his expressions, one neither of us mentioned that day, that would come to define me and now torment me: 'her eyes were full of stings'. And the stings that filled my eyes were ones of jealousy and spite.

When I look back now I realise that Jo and I became Laurie Lee's Jo and Rosie. Jo – timorous and acquiescent. Me – devious and sly. Would it have happened anyway? Or did he influence us with his words? I don't know, but perhaps Lee's Rosie filled my teenage brain with a dangerous sense of destiny. You see, I stole a boy from Jo because I wanted to be the seductive Rosie under the wagon of grass. She seemed so sophisticated, so worldly, so free, and I knew I too had the capacity for such things. Jo had a boy and I did not, and that was not fair. I wanted to be the one who was desired, the one with the power to manipulate those poor bewildered creatures disorientated by the first flood of lust. I wanted a boy to be grateful to me and to live immortally in his memory, to be glorified, just like the eternal Rosie Burdock.

I have never told Jo what I did, partly through shame and I think because I feared losing her. I guess I have always needed her more than I had realised when I risked our friendship by luring her first love from her with a half bottle of cider and a sting in my eye.

Jo and Robert became something more than classmates at a party in Kathryn Parnell's house. Kathryn's dad was the local bank manager and his groomed wife, four daughters, grand house and manicured grounds all seemed to have been acquired principally to remind the neighbours of his social standing. I was sitting on a deep, soft sofa with John Hepworth, a maths genius and social incompetent, but one with a surprisingly good taste in music, and we were analysing each of the tracks on Pink Floyd's *Delicate Sound of Thunder*. We had reached *Wish You Were Here* when I spotted Jo walk from the kitchen followed by Robert and head through the patio doors into the garden. I can still remember the prickle of jealousy I felt, bristling and piercing like a handful of brambles. John kept talking but I had slipped away into a dark covetous chamber.

At school the following day, Jo was coy about what had happened in the garden. "We got to know one another a little better," she said. "We wanted somewhere quiet." She giggled, nervously.

"So, did you – you know – let him touch you?" I asked, breathlessly.

"A bit," she said, and then the bell went, but I knew she was not going to tell me more, and I resented her for it.

Robert was no oil painting, more of a preliminary sketch, which would need some fleshing out and a few flourishes before appearing complete, but that was not the point. I wasn't driven by any kind of desire for a boy who was picture perfect; I just needed to feel a snatch of power, a stolen sliver of self-worth. I got precious little at home where mum's first love sparkled in a glass and dad had abdicated in favour of his office walls, which shielded him from his wife's sins and the complications of his daughter's needs. I still really don't understand why I chose to betray the one person on whom I could depend.

When I intercepted Robert on his walk home from school, he seemed startled to see me – our paths home did not cross and we rarely spoke to each other anyway – but he did not ask me why I was there. His tongue was tied by adolescence, and encountering a girl with coquettish eyes in an unfamiliar place was not loosening the knots.

"Hi Robert", I said.

He just nodded.

"Can I walk with you?" I asked.

He nodded again, but he looked as timid as an animal who had spotted a predator. Paralysis was setting in and I had to find something that would relax the poor boy. I needed to tame him, not trap and torture the helpless soul.

"I wondered if you would be able to help me with our English homework?" I said. "Jo said you know a lot about Laurie Lee."

I am not sure if it was the mention of Jo or Laurie Lee, but one of them was the substance that congealed the shifting sand beneath his feet. "What are you stuck on?" he said, and all of a sudden we were walking together, rather than me trailing lasciviously in his wake. By the time we reached the back lane we were deep in conversation about Lee's relationship with women.

In a gap amongst the blackberry bushes I jumped up onto the wooden gate to the field with calculated unselfconsciousness. Robert stood facing me and I could sense his eyes taking me in. I took the cider from my bag, unscrewed the bottle top and took a swig, like I had done it all before. I handed it to Robert and he drank too as I swung my legs over the top of the gate and dropped into the field.

"Come on," I said and ran across the scrubbed land, disappearing behind one of the large round hay bales, which were scattered across the field like a giant's discarded reels of cotton. I flung my bag down and sat against the hay catching my breath and giggling. Robert caught me up; I knew he would. As he slumped next to me a strand of hair fell across my face and I gently blew it away. It slipped from its place again and so I hooked it behind my ear as I turned my body towards Robert, drawing him in with a silken thread of desire. We drank more. Then I reached out to smooth away the creases in his coating of unease, and I could feel the wings of butterflies fluttering beneath his skin. The bed of hay crackled and snapped, and the dusty veil of sinking air felt like it was on the verge of catching alight.

I tugged and Robert plummeted and then I caught him and held him softly until all his thoughts of Jo had melted away like snowflakes caught on a warm breeze. I threaded pieces of straw into his hair and then I touched his lips, still moist from my kisses. His eyes were glazed with the sheen of a new world, and I knew I had completed what I had set out to do. We wandered home in satiated silence. When I let go of his hand, I said "See ya, Robert." He just nodded and smiled. Those were the last words I ever said to him.

Our final days of school were spent as if nothing had happened. We passed in the corridor and did not even make eye contact. Perhaps we had both found what we had been looking for. Whatever that was, lost its sweetness – for me at least – as the days, then weeks, then years rolled by. I was filled with regret.

Jo cried when she told me that Robert had gone cool on her, and I told her that he was mad and she should not waste another thought on him. "His loss", I said. But, really, it was mine. I lost an unblemished past, and no amount of citing my immaturity to excuse myself has ever been able to restore my peace of mind. Rosie Burdock seduced me, as she did Laurie, and now it seems I can never leave the trap she laid for me.

After our exams I decided I had had enough of Laurie Lee; I promised myself never to read his work again. And now here I am with a new collection of his writings, loaded with an expectation from Jo that I will read them and then talk about them. I must steel myself. The truth is always an option but too much time has passed. Perhaps the truth would set me free, but would it do the same for Jo? I doubt it. The past was more complicated than she thinks. The present is complicated enough.

So I will read the book and I will analyse it with Jo, and my guilt will deepen about a frivolous teenage entanglement that has no business ensnaring me still. But it does, and I think it always will.

How the Kanji Came to Be
by A. Rose

Longlisted, Scottish Arts Club Short Story Competition 2020

At the base of a Sakura tree sat a young man, with legs crossed, eyes closed and a bowl on a flat stone in front of him. There was nothing distinctive about this bowl, it was tarnished brass and just big enough to fit in the palms of cupped hands. There appeared to be nothing distinctive about the young man either, not the short dark hair on his head, nor the faded, ripped tunic on his back. In fact, the only thing a passer-by would have noticed, should they have glanced his way, was the beautiful tree behind him, that he had come to call home. This tree sat on the bank of a river with waters of spearmint green that that flowed down from the mountains just visible in the distance.

The river babbled past, and the mountains echoed all around, but still the man heard nothing.

In his silent world, he sat by the tree roots and watched the cherry blossom flutter past with each breath of wind. Every now and then a stranger would approach to drop a little coin into his bowl. He would open his mouth, but no sound would ever come forth, so he had nothing but his smile to show gratitude.

Some days were better than others, for some people were kinder than others. An elderly lady with a draw string purse and a face full of smile lines always took pity and gave him whatever small change she had collected throughout the day. Young children too, liked to venture close and watch him watch the mountains. Sometimes they would ask him his name, or why he sat under his solitary tree, but when they received no answers, they soon returned to their games, returned to their homes and forgot all about the silent man who watched the world with longing.

Other people did not forget. Other people learned to sneer at him as they strutted past and liked to throw cruel things in his direction, like stones and words and spit. Yet still he did not flinch, and still he did not waiver. He simply sat beneath his tree, until the clouds turned to stars above him.

The stars watched as he slept. And they watched as a stranger approached him in the dark. A stranger from a proud family, wearing robes of splendour and threads of silk, and full of ill intent. For this stranger frowned upon the poorer man, and believed it was disgraceful for the beggar to spoil the beauty of the park and the tree he called his home.

The stranger had come prepared, with a bag full of stones and lumps of charcoal and pieces of old brick to throw, and he pelted the man with them ceaselessly, until he was bruised and bloody. He held his arms over his head, and he cowered down deep into the roots of the tree for protection, but still he would not leave the tree. Infuriated, the stranger decided that he would come back and have him dragged from the park by force.

The bruised and bloodied man was woken by a hand tugging at his tunic. He opened his swollen eyes to see a young boy pulling on his clothes, trying to wake him up. The boy helped him struggle to his feet and hobble down to the river, where he took some water and helped to wash the red from the poor man's face. Then they returned to the tree and sat, where the man had sat for as long as he could remember. The boy's eyes stayed on his face, full of concern, and he had no words of reassurance to offer, so they sat in silence. Eventually, the man picked up a small piece of charcoal that had been thrown the night before and turned the coal over and over in his hands, feeling the soft black power fill the lines in his fingertips. Then he started to draw.

He marked four lines on the stone in front of him, first to make a cross shape, and then to add two flicks coming from the stem he had created:

木

The shape was delicate and powerful all at once, some lines were thick and some lines were faint, and it resonated somewhere in the man's soul. He didn't know why he drew it, he only knew that it was all he had to offer the boy, to thank him for his help, and distract him from his concern. In that moment, he would have done anything to make the kind child smile.

And smile he did. His mouth parted into a wide, toothy grin and he looked at the shape with curiosity.

"What is it?" He asked, moving his lips slowly so that they could be read.

The man puzzled over this thoughtfully, looking at the four clean strokes on the stone. The shape felt familiar, and it dawned on him that he had seen this shape over and over again. It was as much a part of him as his battered hands or his beating heart. Gently he took the boy's palm and placed it on the trunk of the Sakura tree. The boy was delighted, recognizing the long trunk and the thin branches of the tree in the symbol he saw before him.

"Please, draw me another" He begged.

This time the man knew what to draw before he even set charcoal to stone. The symbol was already there in his mind. He raked three strong black lines side by side and then joined them together at the base by another, thicker one.

山

Each stroke represented one of the three peaks of the mountain that stood sentinel in the distance, and the fourth was the earth that kept them grounded. When he had finished drawing, the boy contemplated the shape, looking around him for the source of inspiration. After a while, it clicked.

"Mountain?" He suggested, pointing at the shape. The man's face creased with joy.

The final symbol that he drew that day was the river rushing past. The three lines for this symbol were flowing and wavering, just like the water itself, they curved slightly at the end, to show the bend in the river and how it was always changing. The man's life had been a bit like that symbol, never quite staying in one place, and never knowing where it would end up next.

川

Over the next few days, the boy came to sit with the man under the tree, to see his drawings and learn their meanings. The more he drew, the more the boy could guess what he was trying to say, until the symbols turned into words, and the words turned into stories. For the first time in his brief existence, the man could talk to the boy, and the boy could hear him.

Then one day, the boy brought along his parents to see the man with the sketched-out words. First came the mother, she had a young face that looked much like her son, with long black hair braided down her back, and a silk kimono with golden thread embroidered in the shapes of flying cranes. She knelt beside her son, who knelt beside the man. Then came the boy's father.

Here was a face the man recognized. The father's face flashed with surprise, but he was practiced at hiding his thoughts, and he watched the man with an emotionless expression settled over his features. The man glanced up at him, and then down at the coal in his hands and the words he had drawn. He knew in that moment that he could tell the boy the truth, that his father had been the man to pelt him stones and beat him with rocks all those nights ago. Instead, he bowed his head respectfully and left the truth unspoken, for he chose to believe that the father had given him a gift in the form of the charcoal that had finally allowed him to speak.

At this, the father was once again shocked, for he knew that the man could have revealed him. Hesitantly, he bowed his head in return and an understanding passed between them. The couple sat with their son, looking at the symbols and learning the stories they told, long in to the night. From then on, they came to the park at the same time every evening, bringing hot soup for the man to eat and chunks of bread and butter, and in return he drew them some characters, until the stone slab in front of them was so full that there was no more space.

The family brought their neighbours to see, and they in turn brought their neighbours, and soon the word spread to villages for miles around, of the strange new language that had been drawn under the cherry-blossom tree. People started practicing the letters themselves, passing symbols from person to person and sharing in the wonder of this strange form of communication. And all the while, the man sat beneath his tree. He watched the people talk with the words he had created, and he accepted all of the love and the admiration that the people now showed him. He no longer had to watch the world with longing, for he was a part of it, completely.

People returned to their homes, and returned to their beds, and as the sun set, they dreamt of the strange man and his strange symbols. When they woke, they rushed to see what the man had drawn next, gathering at the Sakura tree where he always was … but he was gone. All they found was an empty bowl, a blank stone resting between the roots, and the Kanji he left behind.

Déjà Vu
by David Wiseman

Longlisted, Scottish Arts Club Short Story Competition 2020

It is late September and what passes for autumn colour in the city is already fading. The leaves in the park are churning to brown mush under leaden skies as the writer scuttles back to her apartment. She is small and wiry and despite her years she is, as yet, unaffected by the ailments of age. Her eyes are bright and enquiring, she walks with vigour and a smile. In her bag she has a magazine from the news-stand by the Metro steps. A successful career stretching back over nearly six decades has never dulled her appetite for a good review. She anticipates the latest with a familiar frisson of excitement. It is a small and secret vanity in an outwardly modest life.

She settles with tea, her Lapsang Souchong, which she likes as much for its name as for its taste. Slowly and deliberately she turns the pages to the reviews, taking pleasure in delaying the climax. Her latest collection of stories, *Present Tense,* is the lead in the section, as befits an author of her standing. The reviewer likens the writing to a champion boxer returning once too often to the ring, to the retired politician wheeled out to pronounce on world affairs long after losing touch with them. Words such as tired, rehashed, worn-out, litter the review. Clichéd is the most hurtful.

In alarm the writer recognises the review as being identical to one she's seen before. Her misery is compounded by the thought that two reviewers have felt exactly the same. But surely they couldn't be the same review, perhaps she has picked up that other magazine by mistake. Quickly she checks. No, it is definitely the one she has just brought home. She looks again but the moment of recognition has passed. It was a false impression, an aberration. There is only one review, only one voice raised in regretful but cutting criticism.

A month passes, during which the writer has other tantalising flashes of bogus memory: a bus driver greeting her as she climbs aboard on a freezing morning; a stranger turning to smile as he steps into the elevator; two women arguing in the street, breaking off to stare as she passes. All trivial, all moments she might once have tucked away, cataloguing them in her storehouse of incidents from which she creates her wonderful stories. Now she can only stare in momentary confusion.

In November she receives a letter from her publisher, her only publisher since they took that gamble with her all those years ago, a gamble which has paid off so well for all concerned. Before she even reads it, the process of opening the envelope, of unfolding the paper, has the same shock of recognition as accompanied the bad review. They write to say *Present Tense* has poor sales and wonder if she would undertake a series of appearances to boost the title and breathe new life into her older ones. She has never received such a letter before but the déjà vu persists right through to the signature at the bottom. The feeling is so strong that the sense of disappointment doubles, as if a second book has failed exactly as a previous one has done.

By Christmas, the episodes – she calls them that because it is a word she likes and it saves properly identifying them – have become more frequent. Once a week, twice a week, daily. Some remain no more than flashes, but gradually the longer experiences that started with her publisher's letter have become more common. She has politely refused the speaking tour and the annual office party. It is the first she has missed since they began forty-three years previously. She has rejected all further contact with the publisher and her agent, claiming that she is working on something new. She has become a recluse.

Snide commentators whisper that she is a spent force, that she is overdue a lifetime-achievement award before her decline becomes terminal. What they do not know is that the ideas, the characters and plots, the unexpected twists, the sideways looks at life which are her trademark, all continue to flow as richly as ever, but as each appears, fresh and original, the writer finds them instantly familiar. From which story she is not sure, she has written many stories, but worse thoughts trouble her – they may be fugitives from another writer's story.

Before the end of January, she has ceased the regular rhythms of eating and drinking, of walking and working. These are the good habits which have sustained her all her adult life and without them she meanders listlessly through the days. Life becomes a mystifying succession of what she might have called double takes, had she still been writing. But she is not, she has ceased to be a writer.

She takes to her bed. Sleep offers her no respite; her dreams repeat themselves endlessly. Only in the shifting no-man's-land between sleep and waking, wrapped in the cocoon of her bedclothes, does she find any semblance of peace. Here, briefly and without the taint of repetition, scenes and characters continue to appear fully formed. These have always been the most fertile moments of her day, a place where she could hold a few of the brightest images long enough to taste them, long enough to smell the tar or the salt or the pine needles carried on the wind, long enough to hear their stories whispered in the grass. As a child, before she thought of writing a word, she could hold these waking dreams in trance-like suspension for as long as she wished.

Within a week this last refuge collapses, the fruits of imagination tumbling over themselves in quick-fire chaos, tears and laughter merging and melting in an instant. They form and fade and re-form so quickly she can no longer be sure they are there at all, lost in an incomprehensible blur. Searching for meaning in her own thoughts requires huge effort. It utterly exhausts her.

Time loses its shape.

On the second Thursday of a bitter February three men stand at the door of the writer's apartment. One is a policeman who, twenty years ago, often exchanged good-mornings with the writer outside this same apartment building. The second is from the building's owners. He too has memories of the writer when he first started in this brownstone block as a glorified janitor. The other is the writer's agent and it is he who has convened their gathering. He has stood at this door many times as her friend for half a lifetime and, in the long ago, as her occasional lover.

The uneasy trio bang and shout at her door. Then they wait in awkward silence, their wet boots making pools on the polished floor while they hesitate. The former janitor has keys that do not fit the lock, but they have come prepared with a battering ram. They exchange expressions of regret and resignation before the policeman smashes the lock with a single blow. The writer's home is dark and fetid. Her lover hangs back, covering his mouth and nose with his hand, unwilling to be the one to find her. The policeman and the property agent move with more purpose. They know where to go and what to expect. They've seen it all before.

In late March the magazine which so injured the writer's pride and witnessed the first of her episodes, publishes the last of the wave of eulogies which have followed her death. The circumstances of her lonely passing were announced a day too late for the March edition, so their fulsome tribute has had to wait for April's. The delay has allowed for more depth and better research, but ultimately they have nothing original to add to the thousands of words that have flowed over and round her life and work.

On the page following this outpouring of praise, the magazine has its regular list of best-selling titles. The writer is responsible for no less than five of the twenty listed, an achievement trumpeted as being unprecedented. There at the very top of the list is *Present Tense*, decried in this same journal only six months previously for being derivative, lacking spark or originality. With her death, those crabby judgements have morphed from negative to positive, for the collection is now proclaimed as accessible and familiar, her style is once again trademark and engaging. She would recognise the listing as describing her rightful place in the literary hierarchy. She would probably not recall that exactly twenty years previously the same magazine had also shown her top of the pile with four more of her books close behind.

Unprecedented then, as now.

The Pig
by Sue McCormick

Longlisted, Scottish Arts Club Short Story Competition 2020

There was never enough to eat. It was a day after day struggle to put food on the table. A miner's wage only ran to rent, bread, candles and soap. We lived on potatoes and cabbages from the garden, fruit from the trees and hedgerows and, in summer, watercress from the stream. Once a week the schoolmaster's young wife, who kept chickens, gave every house two eggs. Anything more had to be robbed from them who had plenty to spare. Now and then, when clouds smothered the moonlight, some of the men would gather in the dark and creep stealthy into the Squire's woods, coming back with rabbits or trout and, on rare and happy nights, a deer. A grown stag would feed the village for weeks, butchered in secret and handed out in newspaper parcels from one end of the street to the other.

That's all Arkley was in them days. A single row of small houses with the church and schoolhouse at one end and the pub at the other. On the road to the Manor, round a curve and out of sight, the Vicarage sat safe behind its high hedges. Further out still, Floppy Whittam's cottage was the last house in the village. From there it was three miles to the pit. The men walked to every shift, six miles there and back, and for the hours in between they sweated in the dark, crouched in the black seams under the weight of rock and earth.

Not many years before, the women had worked down there too, and the children. I gave thanks every day that I was spared it. No one knew how the idea of a life underground gave me the terrors. It was second nature in a pit village, but not for me. I was ashamed to admit it, even to myself, but the thought of being buried in that hot darkness made me shudder. Sometimes I'd lie in bed with the night pressing in on me till I couldn't breathe. I'd struggle to sit up, gasping and shaking, my heart fluttering like a trapped bird, sweat pricking under my hair and between my breasts. Then Jim would stir beside me, reach out and pull me to him without fully waking and I'd fold myself into the warmth of him and feel my heartbeat steady as it measured itself with his.

I know what started the fear. I was seven when my dad was buried alive in a cave-in. They dug him out, brought him home and laid him on the kitchen table. He was naked to the waist, bruised, bloody and filthy. His dead eyes were awful. But what filled me with the sickest horror was his open mouth, full of coal dust, the hard, black glitter of it on his teeth and tongue. I can still see it now when I close my eyes. And something else was born that day in the kitchen with my father's corpse. The anger that swells in me like a tide, that men slave in the dark and still go hungry at the end of it, and that their children are imprisoned in the same hopeless life and nothing changes.

All the bairns in the village were small for their age. They ran and played as children do and, in the summer, they looked well enough, freckled and pink cheeked with the sun. But in the grey of winter, they seemed to fade and shrivel. The Squire's children were a head taller than any miner's child. They rode by on their glistening ponies and they seemed polished from head to toe, shiny hair, shiny faces, bigger and brighter and better. I hated them. I'd watch my Molly and Tom scraping their plates and looking for more when there was none, and the anger would rise up and choke me. I'd look across at Jim, his hair still wet from scrubbing himself in the tin bath, the coal still ingrained on his hard hands, and I'd see it in his face too, the pain and the fury of a lifetime burning in his eyes.

I was carrying another baby when the Squire dropped dead on the cobbles in front of his stables. A sudden bleed in the brain, they said. He was buried in the churchyard, a brass and mahogany casket and the vicar spouting the usual rubbish. There's a great stone angel with folded wings watching over his grave. My firstborn is in the pauper's pit at the edge of the cemetery. I pass the squire's tomb every time I take some wild blossom or evergreen for my baby boy and every time, I wonder that some are cradled in life and in death when most are left to suffer.

The Manor and the mine were sold off to a millowner from the next valley. He cut the miners' wages and when the men complained, he

211

threatened to close the mine altogether. He didn't need it, he said. His mills were profitable. The mine was an act of charity and he could just as soon take his charity elsewhere. I don't go to church, but my neighbour, Ellen, said he was there in his pew at the front, every Sunday, with the vicar smiling down on him from the pulpit.

New walls and fences were built round the estate and extra gamekeepers hired, with orders to shoot poachers. We didn't see meat for months. Winter set in and the land offered less and less. We stored as many vegetables as we could, but they were soon gone. Oatmeal was cheap, so we ate a lot of gruel. I had jam saved and I'd stir a spoonful into Molly and Tom's bowls to make it easier to eat. There came a time when they were so starved, they swallowed it gratefully. I worried the baby inside me was dead. Sometimes I thought it would be for the best if it was.

With the first snow settled over the valley, like clean white sheets on washday, it was decided that somebody had to risk a bullet on the Squire's land or there'd be funerals before the end of the year. The men drew straws, sitting round the fire in the White Hart, with the women watching from the shadows, the glow from the coals flickering over fearful eyes in solemn faces. My Jim was among them and when he took his turn, my heart seemed to stall in my chest, but he drew long, and I could breathe again. It was young Matty Roberts who got the short stick, just turned seventeen and the banns being read for his wedding every Sunday. That night, him and his two brothers were caught trapping rabbits in Low Spinney. Matty made a run for it and they shot him in the back. His brothers got six months hard labour in Carlisle jail.

As Christmas approached, we gathered together every small possession that might fetch a few pennies and me and Ellen walked the five miles into town to sell them at the second-hand shop. It was a crisp, bright day, the hawthorns heavy with red berries, the frost sparkling on the fields and in the frozen carriage ruts beneath our boots. The rooks were circling the tall trees lining the road, their sharp, cracking cries and the crunch of our footsteps echoing through the early morning quiet. The world is beautiful. It's the greed of men that makes it ugly.

In town, we passed windows full of white geese and golden pies, sausages and hams, puddings and pastries. They looked like Paradise, but we turned away from them and spent the few shillings we made on a box of small toys, one each for the children on Christmas morning.

As we walked home, Ellen said we should kill the schoolmaster's chickens and have them for Christmas dinner. It was tempting, but that would be the end of the eggs and they were precious, so we cast the thought aside. It was then, out of nowhere, that I remembered Floppy Whittam's pig, in the pen behind her cottage. It was her man Seth's pride and joy at one time, before he died of miner's lung, coughing up black blood, propped on pillows in a bed brought downstairs. Floppy worshipped him. Even when he was alive, she was known for wearing his old slippers, like boats on her thin feet. Flip-flopping around the village, you could hear her coming, know it was her with your back turned. With him gone, she never walked in anything else. Someone called her Floppy once and it stuck. A small, grieving woman in tartan slippers, and an old pig snuffling in her back garden.

I reminded Jim of it that night when the children were in bed. She might give it up, he said, if she was approached right. A deputation. An appeal. If only for the sake of the little ones.

The next day, six of us stood at her door and asked to take the pig. She looked at each of us in turn, her eyes wide with surprise. Sorry, but she couldn't give it up. It was all she had of Seth now. We said we understood, but what would Seth do, if he was here? Would he see the village starve? Would he leave the children hungry at Christmas? Her eyes filled with tears, but she shook her head. It was no good. She couldn't part with it.

The others turned away to go home, dejected, but I didn't move. I stared into her face, watching the colour come and go in her cheeks. She was clutching the flowered cotton of her apron and her knuckles stood out white against her rough, reddened hands. I should have felt sorry for her, but I didn't. The anger was shooting through me, rooting me to the spot.

I told her she was selfish, greedy. I said we could take the pig anyway and how could she stop us? She looked past me to the others, hovering on the path. Go and get it, I told them. Go on. Jim's face

213

twisted with uncertainty, but he moved off round the house and I stood waiting, as cold as stone, till he came back, leading the pig on a length of rope. Floppy said we'd pay for what we were doing. She said she'd get the law on us. She was as pale as death, even her lips white, a muscle twitching near her mouth. She looked hunted. I kept my eyes fixed on her, though it hurt me to do it. She didn't say anything else. Just closed the door in my face.

I didn't catch up to Jim and the rest, and he didn't wait for me. I walked behind him and the pig, all the way back to the village. The six of us butchered it and wrapped up the packages in silence. Once or twice I caught them looking at me as if I was a stranger. Later, I took Floppy's share to her cottage. She didn't answer my knock, so I left it on the step.

Floppy never set the law on us. By the time we sat down to Christmas dinner, she had packed up and gone. We never saw her again. I remember, as I bent to leave her parcel by the door, I heard her slippers on the flagstones in the hall and my heart gave a little bittersweet twist of hope. But the footsteps shuffled away into the back of the house. I stood there in the silence for a while then turned for home, slowly at first then faster and stronger. I remember, as I strode out under a sky bright with stars, a full moon behind the silver shadows of the trees and my breath misting in the winter cold, I felt the first kick from the child curled in my belly.

Lost and Found
by Marlene Shinn Lewis

Longlisted, Scottish Arts Club Short Story Competition 2020

"Hello?"

"Who are you?"

"That's a rude way to start a phone call."

"Rude! You answered my cell phone!"

"It rang."

"I know that. I called my phone."

"Oh, this is your phone? Why didn't you ask for yourself politely, then?"

"I want my phone back! Who are you?"

"Who are *you*? How do I know this is your phone? What if this is a scam call and you're fishing for personal information?"

"Look, Whoever-You-Are, it's *my* phone. I'll describe it. It has a black cover—"

"Not very creative, are you?"

"—a black cover and a piece broken off the lower right corner."

"Did you drop it or throw it at someone?"

"I'd throw it at you if you weren't holding it!"

"What else?"

"Nothing else."

"Not good enough. Every cell phone has a broken piece in the corner."

"Well, I'm not going to give you the password just to prove it's mine!"

"What about the back of the cover?"

"What about it?"

"There are a couple of paint spots on it. What are they?"

"Oh, maybe when I was repainting the bathroom it splattered."

"What colour?"

"Red."

"Red! In a bathroom? I retract my statement regarding your lack of creativity."

"Well?"

"Yup, they're red splatters all right."

"Then it's my phone and I want it back."

"I can understand that."

"Turn it in to the police station and I'll pick it up there."

"Which police station?"

"Where are you?"

"Where did you lose your phone?"

"How should I know! If I knew that, I'd have gone back for it."

"I could be miles away from you by now."

"Look, take it to *any* police station then! Have them call me."

"They can't. Your phone is locked. It can only answer a call, so you'll have to call them on it. Isn't this fun?"

"No!"

"Let's retrace your steps for the last day or two, and maybe we can figure out where you lost it."

"You *know* where I lost it, you pervert! You found it!"

"Oh, no! Do I sound like a pervert?"

"Arghhh! Well, just at a guess, I'd say probably not."

"Thanks for the vote of confidence. Now, when did you first notice the phone missing?"

"Five minutes before I called you—called it."

"Midday today. Then you might have lost it Saturday and just didn't notice. You had the phone with you when you left home yesterday?"

"Yes, I know for sure I did."

"Where did you go first?"

"I went to the bank."

"Lobby or drive-through?"

"Drive-through."

"Then you didn't lose your phone at the bank. See how easy this will be?"

"Arghhh!"

"You're repeating yourself. Where to next?"

"Yoga class."

"Any men in your class?"

"What?"

"Are there any men in your class? Is the instructor or guru or whatever male?"

"No."

"Any classes before or after yours?"

"No."

"Then your phone wasn't left at yoga class."

"How do you know?"

"Because I'm a man. I couldn't have been there to find your phone without being painfully obvious, could I?"

"You are ridiculous! I don't have time for this nonsense!"

"Do you want your phone back?"

"Yes."

"Then you have time. Where did you go after yoga? I hope you took time to walk your dog."

"How did you— Oh, that was just a wild guess, wasn't it?"

"Only the dog part. You just got a text from the vet reminding you of an appointment Monday. I can see the text preview without unlocking the phone, you know."

"Okay, okay. So, yes, I went home to pick up, uh, Crusher, my bull mastiff, and we went to the park."

"Good try. Now I'm supposed to be impressed, or worried, that you have a bull mastiff you named Crusher? Can't see it. You sound more like a Border Collie owner. Am I close?"

"Who *are* you anyway? Do your conversations always sound like this? Actually, he's a Sheltie named Arnold."

"Arnold?"

"Hey, he was a rescue! I was stuck with the name."

"You could call him Arnie."

"I do."

"Gee, I might ask you to say that to me some day …"

"I just changed my mind. You are a pervert."

"Darn, can't you go back to 'ridiculous' instead? I relate to that better."

"How much longer do we need to do this?"

"Until we find your phone. So, you went to the park. Were there other people there while you and Arnie played?"

"Of course."

"Did you use your phone at the park?"

"I checked my messages once. But I'm sure I stuck the phone back in my jacket pocket."

"What else did you do at the park? Talk with anyone?"

"No, I threw sticks for Arnie a couple of times, but since he didn't bring them back I just sat down on a bench and waited for him to browse around under the rhododendrons."

"As I see it, then, your phone might have slipped out of your pocket while throwing sticks or sitting on the bench."

"Were you at the park? Did you find my phone there?"

"I'm just noting that as a possibility so we can narrow down the final location."

"Arghhh!"

"You're growling again."

"I'm thinking that I don't want to know you if you were hanging around the park watching young women with or without their dogs."

"So you'd want to know me if I weren't at the park?"

"I didn't say that."

"We'll see. Let's move on now. The phone may or may not have been lost at the park. Where to next?"

"I went to the library to return a couple of books and look for some more."

"What did you return?"

"Why?"

"I'm curious to know what you read."

"Oh, good grief! Would you believe *Lives of the Saints* and *Lady Chatterley's Lover*?"

"Almost!"

"You're laughing at me!"

"I'm laughing *with* you, my dear!"

"I'm not your dear."

"But I already feel as if I'd known you forever. How many others know you take yoga classes, have a dog named Arnie, get up early to go Saturday banking, read a wide range of books, and—"

"And what?"

"Nothing."

"You're holding out on me! How can you do that to someone you've known forever?"

"Did you go anywhere else on Saturday?"

"You just ignored me! And you still have my phone! That doesn't give you the right to ignore me, you know."

"I could just hang up now."

"No! Don't do that! This is absurd, but it's beginning to feel like a lifeline—I don't know—a connection of sorts. As if I might stop breathing if we lost the connection. How's the battery, by the way?"

"I'm at 63%. Well, more accurately, you're at 63%. Better hurry this up. Did you use your phone at the library?"

"I don't think so. I don't remember."

"Well, then, let's just add library to our list of possible places you might have lost your phone. Because if you didn't lose it at the park, it could have slipped out of your pocket while you were reaching up to that high shelf for a book."

"Hah! No high shelves. You guessed wrong on that one. But, yes, it could have fallen out onto the rug and I wouldn't have noticed it."

"So you see, I might have been in the library and found it there. Which definitely raises my standing to literary pervert instead of plain pervert."

"Okay, I'm sorry I said that. Forget it. I'm frustrated and you are so, so—I don't know. So out of the ordinary."

"You must mean I'm extraordinary!"

"Don't push it!"

"Okay. Any more stops you made Saturday before going home?"

"I stopped for groceries."

"Oh, the market is a popular place for lost cell phones. Everyone chatting away as they shop or looking up online store coupons or checking with the wife at home to make sure the peanut butter should be crunchy instead of smooth."

"Humph!"

"My dear, you are improving! That's much nicer and more lady-like than 'arghhh!'"

"You'll notice that I'm ignoring you."

"So we've narrowed it down to the park, the library, and the market as possible places where you lost your cell phone, right? You've been nowhere else between then and now?"

"No."

"Your battery is down to 28% now. You'd better hurry up. *No* where else?"

"Well, I did go to church this morning, but that's all."

"How did you like the service?"

"Our new vicar is enthusiastic and not afraid to tell us what's what, but in a pleasant way. He's— What do you mean how did I like the service?"

"Just curious."

"Who *are* you? You need to finish this before your—my—battery dies! Hurry up!"

"Do you always sit in the third pew middle?"

"You were there!"

"Sure, sitting behind you in the fourth pew. Saw your phone on the seat after you left."

"Don't stop! Tell me more—quick!"

"I'm your new vicar's brother, just visiting to see how he and his wife are settling in and catching up on their news. My name, by the way, is Paul Scott."

"Paul! Oh, dear, I've sounded horrible, haven't I? I'm Jenny Ashland. Oh, and quick, before my battery is gone! How can you return my phone?"

"I'll return it to you at tonight's services. No need to hurry now. I lied about the battery and the visit. I'm moving here, and it's really at 94%!"

The Daily Mile
by Alice Clifton

Longlisted, Scottish Arts Club Short Story Competition 2020

Mrs Greta McDonald was, according to her usually reticent husband, probably the maker of the best tattie scones in the whole of Wester Ross. Possibly he might insist, the best in the whole of Scotland. Every morning she made them, freshly formed, rolled then fried on a spitting hot griddle. Eggs flash cooked, precisely arranged alongside the three rounds of fatty homemade black pudding. All topped by the four rashers of meticulously crisped hand-reared bacon.

She set the newly polished bone handled cutlery, on the starched plain cornflower blue tablecloth. After which, she systematically positioned the cruet set with the matching plate. This early morning ritual put everything as it should be, exactly in situ, exactly on time. As the clock struck out its seventh chime, the back-lobby door opened, the falling of his heavy boots met her ears.

Without a word, he moved across the tiled floor, swaying his hips slightly. Careful to avoid contact with the chair, pulled out from the table, ready for him. In his two-purl two-plain hand-knitted socks he padded to the sink and ran the tap to clean his hands. Rubbing vigorously with the bar of red solid Lifebuoy soap. Rhythmically scrubbing with a soft bristled nail brush to remove the taint of silage, soil and dung from his rheumatic fingers. His eyes roamed over the fifty fenced acres through the sash window. Regretting that the ground was so deceptively green for soil that was so very poor. Savouring the smell of the spat fat and charred edges, freshly baked rolls, the promise of the well-kent flavours wet his lips.

Turning to find the hand towel, he found it. Conveniently placed in his hand, her gift as she walked on by to feed the cat. Ginger, tom, patiently awaiting his turn at her altar of attention under the well laid kitchen table. Passing her again he connected this time with a whisper of a touch, a feather light brushing of well-known fingers. Beyond each other now, he moved to sit, she to manoeuvre the jug of milk into its proper position. Steadying it at ninety degrees to the matched sugar basin, she nodded silently and left. Silently pulling the kitchen door shut behind her. As the door clicked shut, he nodded his head in silent acknowledgement. In recognition of her first gift of the day. The effort she had made to prepare this feast for him to break his fast.

Leaving the yard, she tucked her flowered headscarf into her anorak collar, her head held down against the morning frost. Frost, icily hanging heavy in the expectant air of a new dawn empty of any promise of change.

With the aromas of sheep and cow dung freshly spread on the breeze failing to distract her, she walked along their lane towards the sea. Passing between the rowed fields now green over brown, patched with the tops of the turnips. Acknowledging almost unconsciously to herself that the sheep would welcome them when the winter set fully in again. A slight shiver ran down her back as yet untouched by the sun, weak, only rising still. Having left John McDonald to his eggs and bacon, she would have an hour of freedom for now.

The acid yellow of the gorse and the fat red rowan berries shining in the hedge failed to attract her attention. Nor did the cow that stuck its head over the fence as she approached, gain her interest in the slightest.

This time of day was always reserved, only for Herbert.

Since before she could walk, her Father had taken her to the schwimbad. They would leave their three-storey town house pulling the gloss black painted door quietly behind them by the brass letterbox. Ensuring with their near silence that her Mother remained blissfully unconscious of their loss in deliciously ignorant sleep. As the rising sun rouge tipped the clouds, they made their way along the early morning street. A landscape of town houses and small shops, all filled with people and dozing domestic pets. Frosted rooftops, the tall brick crenelated chimneys not smoking with early morning fires yet to be lit. There was something exotic about walking amongst it, in the grip and snap of the frost. When most of the town were still enjoying their dreams, tucked up in their warm beds. For just a while longer, safe from the cold winds gathering through the lanes.

They walked, Greta skipping alongside him. Him striding as he carried the large canvas bag with her costume, swim hat, their flask of tea and thick fluffy towels. Quietly greeting with a smile, the milchmann with his jangling bottles. Their knock knocking in the crate echoing, their slight jostling movement enough to shatter the slumbering silence. The hooves of his newly shod horse ushered the dawn into a slowly awakening town. They passed the black-framed and sugar-frosted windows of Der Bäcker. Each morning there he was, with his beard neatly combed, stood smiling. He would wave acknowledging them, flour flying in a misted arc as he raised his hand waving them past his window. The tiered front of the shop was as always, overflowing with baskets piled high with fresh bread and sweet pastries. The smell of heaven wafting down the street behind them. A life unfenced, but secured through familiar sights, sounds and smells of their morning walk to the pool. A haven of solitude with the rows of cornflower blue tiles. Their time, with their own routine, their own world.

Greta could smell the sharp tang of the chlorine before it assaulted her sinuses. The expected hot rush of adrenaline surged through her body. She stiffened as she pointed her toe into the cool blue pool. A breath, then she relaxed to meet the flat as yet undisturbed water. This was her element, where only she and the water existed. Just them, until Herbert's voice intruded as she surfaced for air. "Swim Greta, swim." A mile before breakfast.

A mile, length after length after length of clear blue water on cornflower tiles. Her whole being submerging and resurfacing until she was just at one, a part of it. Becoming entirely attuned to the weight of it, it's pressure and release until he shouted. "Enough now Greta, that's a mile."

More water, this time to rinse away the chlorine and warm her. He would be waiting, leaning against the wall with smiling exaggerated impatience outside the showers. Languishing in his workday suit, his spit and polished shoes tapping out the minutes. While she inside tugged impatiently at her tortoiseshell comb. Damply struggling with her thick black curls dried and knotted by the daily bath of chlorine.

She swam for Herbert, for his joy, every day, all the way to the glory of Olympic gold. Glory, in the wonder that was Berlin in the summer of 1936. She had stood on the winner's podium, held captive by the intensity of the vibration from the exultation of the audience. The roaring of the crowds echoed around the auditorium, the nation cheered in rapture, the world applauded. Everyone loved a winner. A tumultuous homecoming followed, with a felicitous crowd happily packed into their narrow street. All clapping, shouting and cheering, wanting to be seen to know the golden girl and her golden family. A celebration chocolate torte from Der Bäcker for tea with double helpings of thickly ladled cream from the milchmann. Then the cold winds of change blew harder down the lanes.

The old feeling of being in the empty streets turned from being exotic, to a foreboding, to naked fear. The nation stopped cheering as the jeers and the hatred crystallised in one night. The intensity of the vibration from stamping jackboots held her captive as she hid behind the lace curtains. But above the roaring and screaming of annihilation the worlds voice fell strangely silent. The schwimbad was closed now, but only to her and the others like her. The ones with cloth pointed stars sewn on their coats.

Der Bäcker's shop was also closed, not just to 'them' but to everyone. He, his family and his shop obliterated in a frenzy of venomous fury that burned hotter than his bread oven. There were no more baskets of piled dainty pastries or soft rolls there to savour. Just a masterpiece of a jagged crude star painted on a wooden panel where the window had once been.

The last time she had seen Herbert, he had been waiting outside of the showers. Stood stiffly upright, he was scuffing his worn shoes against the rail line. Herbert, he was just stood, waiting with such a profound lack of impatience. He waited one part of a long line: a gold star sewn with invisible stitches on the arm of his best suit jacket. His eyes, that had once shone as they impelled her to greatness, now implored her to just survive. Her thick black curls were long gone now, replaced long ago by the straightening iron of life and loss. So, she walked, carrying her own bag, walking religiously every day to the shore.

Greta stepped onto the sandy beach of the small sea loch. She stiffened as she dipped her toe in the cold clear blue water. As she stretched in her one-piece blue suit and flowered hat, she heard an echo. The ever-resounding echo that had reverberated down the years to greet her every morning. The sound of her Father's voice as Herbert implored her "swim Greta swim".

Armed and Semi-Dangerous
by kerry rawlinson

Winner, Edinburgh International Flash Fiction Award 2020

Our ragged brigade set off to battle the Rez boys hours ago. Our weapons: wooden spoons nicked from our ma's kitchens; sticks; chipped cricket bats. Harry Fallon pilfered a precious cigarette which got smoked down to our fingertips minutes into the march; and I stole combat-rations (three larded crusts). But with the smoke-break, then Harry puking, then piss- stops for the smaller boys, it's taking forever to forward the troops. In the changeling mist and needling rain, we wonder: what more do our fathers and brothers have to face Over There?

We're desperate to be just like them. Heroes.

Far across the waters, colonial Canada's token contributions to the Great War are leaving pieces of themselves behind in trenches and blood-drenched mud. Slivers of soul; folds of lost reason; whole bodies. We haven't yet realized that heroes seldom come home … only strangers, wearing our father's old skins.

But these thoughts are fleeting. Drenched, lacking enemy contact, we decide to turn our stamp-rationed boots towards home.

Approaching the muskeg designated 'no-man's-land', a thin, banshee screech suddenly splits the twilight. We skitter like startled chicks. But what? – it's Harry's ma! It's Missus Fallon, stumbling towards us, wailing, high fists clawing for her only son.

"Harry! … father! … Your father!" We shuffle, disoriented by this naked display of adult grief.

And as the blood-soaked sun sinks slowly on dead fathers and brothers, comprehension dawns, routing our childish acceptance of the ordinariness of war. Something of our tenuous innocence, along with the daylight, snuffs out.

Lost In The Woods
by Michael Callaghan

Second Prize, Edinburgh International Flash Fiction Award 2020

I am lost.

The thought, once crystallised, paralyses me. By day the woods are filled with light and smells and sound. They caress and soothe and comfort me. I feel at one with these woods. Part of them. But I walked so long that I didn't notice as the darkness came creeping.

And now I stand in the stillness and the darkness. The pools of light and colour in the woods have hardened and vanished. Turned into cold, malevolent shadows. The warmth drains from me.

My phone bleeps.

Are you nearly home?

It's mum. She worries, and she would worry more if she knew where I was.

Because someone stalks these woods at night. The tabloids have dubbed him the Full Moon Killer. Thirteen victims in three years.

I text back. *Home soon.*

I don't want Mum worried. But I am worried. Indeed, I am afraid. So very, very afraid. Something is going to happen. The darkness is closing in. Enveloping me. Suffocating me.

And then, at the moment I think my despair will crush me, the moon rises. It breaks the spell of the blackness. Sends my terror scuttling with the shadows. I look above at the moon, at its beautiful golden yellow light. I close my eyes, letting it bathe and heal me.

A twig cracks. Someone is approaching. Disturbing these sacred moonlit woods.

I trace my blade across my thumb. Feel the hot sharp burst of blood.

"Fourteen," I whisper, and step from the shadows.

Snakes and Snails
by Rachael Dunlop

Third Prize, Edinburgh International Flash Fiction Award 2020

The boys had the dog backed up against a fence, its timidity opening a seam of sadism in their adolescent brains. I pushed them aside. It was a bitch, teats raw with milk, belly saggy.

"We need to find her pups," I said, and turned to find all but one of the boys had melted away. The remaining lad nodded and scuffed off, his eyes stuck to the ground. He soon returned with a squirming heap of puppies nested in his hoody. He held the pups against his tee-shirted chest for warmth – both his and theirs. His biceps, hard and narrow, pressed against the bones of his upper arms. He was still constructed of parts, this boy, not yet resolved into a man.

The mother lifted herself and followed unsteadily as we made our way to the nearest vet's surgery. She pulled her freckled nose up towards the scent of her pups, and her whimpers hurried our steps. The boy told the vet to keep his hoody, it was ruined anyway. He briefly rested his fingertips on the bitch's back, between her too-sharp shoulder blades, and then he was gone.

I see the boy sometimes in the street with his friends. He tips his chin to me in both greeting and warning, and folds his bare arms across his pigeon chest. Not ruined yet, I think as I lower my head to hide my smile.

fourteen
by Paul Walton

Winner, Golden Hare Award for Scottish Flash Fiction 2020

He's mibby fourteen, bairns prowling round the long legs, and he just rushes you there on the towpath, polybag held high and you know something is in there, something with mass. Shoves it in your chest and the fingers start to work open twisted polythene. You're thinking aw christ don't let it be body parts or shite or a vibrator. See this he says. The pike is there in a half-inch of canal water. A youngster, jaws clamped, furious and still. You say ya beauty and he nods, and you become fourteen with him there. And a boy jumps up and grabs at the bag and to save breaking fin or gill he just lets it go. Laddie careers about with the weighted prize. There is no reprimand as a lengthened palm extends unfolding upturned and the bag is returned to it and they laugh thegither and that wee one is made fourteen too.

Euston, We Have A Problem
by Malcolm Timperley

Editor's Choice, Edinburgh International Flash Fiction Award 2020

Hello everyone, welcome aboard the 2019 Conservative Party service to Hell. I'm Boris Johnson, your service manager, and I'll be with you until the end of the line. This service is the Great Britain, calling at Bellend, Middle England, Weekend on Speed, Upper Rentboy and Little Bigot, arriving at Hell around 1945, where we terminate.

Passengers for Old Empire and Brexit change at Bellend; there is no return service from Brexit until 2150. For Smallmind, Uptight and Twitching change at Middle England and change at Weekend on Speed for Methhead (Main Line). For Grunting & Wilting, Blackmail and Closet (Low Level) change at Upper Rentboy. Change at Little Bigot for Seething, Wogsout and Armchair (General).

First-class accommodation is in Coach A. Any Conservative Party member travelling in First-class accommodation without a First-class ticket will be obliged to claim expenses for one. First-class passengers are entitled to complimentary refreshments including our Everyday Dog's Breakfast. Refreshments are available to sub-Standard-class passengers from the 'off our trolley' service.

I'll be running a full ticket check, so please have your traditional blue passports ready for inspection. Scottish tickets to all stations between Equal Standing and Respect are not considered valid by the Conservative Party.

This service is about to depart. Any passengers on board travelling to Scottish destinations with connections to Reality, please leave the Great Britain and transfer to the Flying Scotsman which leaves at 2022. Thank you and have a peasant trip.

After the Fire
by Ann MacLaren

Shortlisted, Edinburgh International Flash Fiction Award 2020

Helen lifted the box of photographs onto the table. She took out a large handful and sorted through them, examining them closely, discarding some, keeping others. When she had a sufficient number, she put the box aside and laid the photos out in front of her, shifting them into a sort of chronological order.

There they were then. She talked herself through them.

Great-grandparents, in sepia: stylish and elegant. One pair formidable-looking, stern. The other two more relaxed, comfortable in front of the camera.

Some black and white photos: maternal grandmother, leaning on a garden gate; a large country house, same garden; a pretty girl on a bicycle – mother; grandfather in naval uniform; aunts and uncles; paternal grandparents in their Sunday best; family friends.

Colour ones now: elderly parents, posing self-consciously; siblings – brothers, alike as twins; a baby in knitted pink; a schoolgirl in oversized blazer, arms around a large dog.

A young mother bending to speak to her smiling baby in its pram, face obscured; the same mother placing a younger baby, shawl-wrapped, into a car seat; a handsome husband, a toddler straining at his hand, an older child on his shoulders; two little swim-suited girls on a beach, building sandcastles. Elizabeth. Molly.

You must build a new life, they had said.

Helen gathered the photos and took them to the desk. She paid the assistant a few pounds and left the junk shop, clutching her family in a paper bag.

All the Times he Tried and Failed
by Ian Nettleton

Shortlisted, Edinburgh International Flash Fiction Award 2020

The car was slewing in the deep snow when Charlie jumped out of the back window. He was not long for this world and, as we drove to the vets, out he went through the gap between the frame and the glass.

Dad slammed on the brakes and leapt out.

"Tom! Tom! The traffic!" mum said. A bus was bearing down in the opposite direction. As the wail of the horn went by and all those faces pressed to the glass, I looked for dad and when the bus was gone, I saw him, running down the pavement by the barber's.

He ran like a man in a river, as though his trousers were waterlogged and he was floundering in his black coat. The cat – Charlie – I couldn't see. He was long gone and to this day I don't know where he went.

I sat in the quiet and waited. Mum tapped her nails on the wooden dashboard, full of irritation even then. I had my face to the window and listened to the hush of the snow falling out of the sky and it was a picture. I see it now. The whole world was quiet and when I saw dad walking back and stopping, bending over, his hands on his knees, I saw the same man I would see through the years, all the times he tried and failed to place his hands on something he loved that was just out of reach.

Bill the Tramp
by Shaun Laird

Shortlisted, Edinburgh International Flash Fiction Award 2020

It's odd: they always take their shoes off before they go.

A bell tolls in the darkness. A young blond man in a grey suit removes his shoes and socks. He climbs onto the bridge's parapet, inching his legs over the waters far below.

Bill the Tramp coughed.

"Jesus shit," cried the man. "I thought I was alone." "No, not quite," replied Bill. "Are you doing okay son?" The man said nothing.

"Just you and me out tonight," continued Bill. "Except for the stars, that is." He smiled because it was true. "So why don't you tell me what's up?"

The man turned to the newcomer – ruddy bearded Bill, wrapped in his nest of cardboard and rags. He rubbed his temples, kneading his eyes closed. "Everything. Is. Up," he hissed. "The job, Susie, everything – it's all fucked." His eyes opened: "And yet I'm still not as fucked as some pissy old tramp."

"Bill the Tramp – yes, they do call me that. I'm not offended."

"Okay Bill," he sneered, "As you're so wise, you tell me; what should I do?"

Bill rose heavily to his feet. "These are nice shoes," he said, picking them up carefully. "A real waste if you're going to off yourself, don't you think?" He held them out slowly, smiling. "Maybe I can help?"

Later Bill placed the shoes next to the others in his collection: the stilettos, the trainers, the work boots. They looked nice.

It's odd: sometimes they jump, sometimes they fall.

Feathers
by Kirsty Venters Marks

Shortlisted, Edinburgh International Flash Fiction Award 2020

The limestone split easily. Sometimes it didn't even need the chisel and the hammer, but she liked the sound, so she used them anyway. Heat hummed, the spiders clambered over the rocks in the old quarry and Irma tapped, tapped away. She tapped away the time, trapped in its layers and left to fossilise. She could relate to that. It was good to liberate these lost remains and open them up to the light again: ammonites in need of emancipation. Maybe there would be a dropped feather, left by an archaeopteryx and drawn on to the stone.

Finding feathers meant the angels were with you. That's what he'd said to her and she'd smiled when he did. They both knew she didn't believe in any of that, but it didn't matter.

A single red poppy bowed to a breeze Irma barely noticed against her skin. It was growing in the tracks left behind by one of the great machines, those monsters with claws strong enough to cut and carry huge hunks of marble and limestone slabs. They were gone now, too.

Everything just goes, she thought.

From a nearby beech, a jay flew across that moment and took the thought away. Irma followed the line of the flight, then watched a pink feather fall from its body, twirling slowly to land on a heap of cracked boulders.

Might as well.

The chisel found a groove. She hammered it apart. An archangel or an archaeopteryx stared back at her; released.

Help Me
by Barbara Leahy

Shortlisted, Edinburgh International Flash Fiction Award 2020

You know by the way his hand is twisted that the arm is broken. He gulps for air. One beat, two. He half sits up, opens his pink mouth and bawls. Noise bothers you. There are long nights when he cries at nothing, for no reason, as though you've done something terrible to him.

But of course, this time, you have.

You touch his face and he flinches, howls even louder. Stop, you say. Stop it. In your head something is tightening, whining like straining metal, and he's screaming now, dragging himself one-handed across the floor, away from you, his arm limp and terrible. The sound gets bigger, fills the room, and it seems like his cries are your cries, like it's you on the floor, white and shaking, and when you lift him he shudders with exhaustion, doesn't buck or kick, just lies in your arms, his eyes full of everything you've ever done wrong. You start to run.

Outside on the road you kneel in the dirt and the fumes, cars stopping around you, and you clutch him close, so close his face is hidden against you, and when a woman touches your shoulder you forget that he's the one who is hurt, and you look at her and say, help me.

'I've killed George'
by Bob Shepherd

Shortlisted, Edinburgh International Flash Fiction Award 2020

"What?"

"You heard."

"No. Not sure I did!"

A look of incredulity sped around Elly's eye as she stared hard at him. Tony swirled his brandy nonchalantly.

"I said I've killed George and I am glad!" He began laughing.

"No! You don't mean it! You can't have!"

Tony shrugged. "Too late. It's done."

"It's not too late, Tony. Change it."

Tony took huge gulp letting the warming liquid satisfy his tongue and gums with its spicy taste. "There's no turning back."

Elly stooped to kneel at his feet. "But he's your star. Your biggest earner. Five million viewers will hate you. He is Canterbury Avenue!"

"He's gone!"

Elly stared pleadingly. "Tony please. Do a rewrite. Peter won't mind." Tony threw her a look of indifference.

"We'll spin out his death. It'll double the ratings." He took another gulp.

"We'll have a fight that goes badly wrong. He falls, hits his head." Elly felt lost for words.

"Trouble is, he's disappeared. Missed two rehearsals. We might have to use doubles and old clips."

Elly walked away and stood silent for a moment. "You know, don't you?"

Tony nodded. "How long?"

"Long enough."

"Is that why you wrote him out?"

"What do you think?"

"That's pathetic Tony. I had to put up with you and Janey."

"That was different. Just a …"

The doorbell interrupted him. Elly walked across to the window.
"It's the police.
What do they want?"
"Obvious, isn't it?
"Not to me."
"Told you. I've killed George."

Knock, Knock. Who's No Longer Here?
by Sharon Boyle

Shortlisted, Edinburgh International Flash Fiction Award 2020

It began with a snigger. The solemn faces lining the pews? Couldn't help myself. It grew to a giggle when the minister spouted fairy-tales of your life. I left your cremation with a clownish guffaw, wondering if God was ready to meet someone more glorified than Himself.

Knock, knock.

Who's there?

Coffin.

Coffin who?

Coffin up my guts.

That's what you did for months, spinning Mother witless until, at last, she ushered me in to watch your fingers being peeled from Life's hem. You'd certainly put the moan into pneumonia and felt you'd earned the right to lecture me on duty – you, who'd controlled Mother with a mean wallet and sly slaps.

"Whit're you smirkin' at?" you heckled, bones clacking, (but not the funny one, of which you were bereft).

It was the pyjamas you were wearing. The striped pair Mother bought and you claimed were 'concentration-camp efforts not fit for the dead'.

I straightened my face.

"My ashes," you wheezed, "are to be scattered over the Spacific, a place I never sailed over, seeing as I was trapped."

Trapped? There was a joke. Saddled with an inconvenient baby and resultant marriage you took revenge by spit-polishing your spite and sailing over the seas of easy living while Mother and I floundered in the doldrums.

***

Mother booked us a hysterically expensive first-class cruise to New York for the deservedly bereaved.

And your ashes?

Left in the bedside drawer. Next to the striped pyjamas. To be specific.

Our Ghostly King
by Sandy Forsyth

Shortlisted, Edinburgh International Flash Fiction Award 2020

On a northern beach a myriad of standing stones wept, as they are wont to do, keeling into the cool ocean breeze, held upright by the shadow of a spirit kneeling against its tethers to the living world — one thousand, two thousand years pass — the salty water seasons the air into dryness and a middle- aged, lipsticked woman lays a checked picnic blanket to soften the shifting sands; our spirit cocks a whisper of an ear to the bored drone of her husband's hunger and lifts the point of a forgotten finger to turn the man's jaw to face the ocean, the ocean which laps in a different kind of hunger at the shore, its foam white as a ghost, this hunger reaching to the moss of the stones which still hold themselves in an aged royal dignity; the collapse of a kingdom — the spirit's kingdom is that of third-man-syndrome, forced complacency, and eager contact with the living — leaving nothing but rubble on a beach, to be viewed in unaffected joy by picnickers who care more for the horizon than the other-worldliness at their feet, a feat of trapped desire which led our ghostly king to cling like the creeping moss of these graveyard standing stones to his tenure of land: ambition latched to one abode that will require a key more eternal than turning eyes to unbounded sea in order to unbind, and, caught between the living and the dead, our ghostly king forgets what it is to end.

These Walls
by Julie Meier

Shortlisted, Edinburgh International Flash Fiction Award 2020

She has learned to move with a cat-like softness, so as not to awaken the monsters living within these walls.

Wearing slippers to silence her footfalls, she pads softly down the hall towards the kitchen.

Dawn slowly draws out the shadows, exposing walls that bear their signature – smears of strawberry red, muddy grey, and grass-stain green.

She picks her way through the debris scattered after yesterday's attack. A lamp lolling on its side, couch-cushions strewn haphazardly.

Gently easing a mug from the shelf, she pours the steaming liquid with a steady hand. Winces as a spoon clatters to the floor. Cursing herself for her carelessness, she holds her breath and waits.

Nothing. Breathe.

Take a sip – scalding hot, tendrils of warmth. And then, as if by clockwork, it begins.

First, a rustling, which to a less trained ear could be mistaken for the wind rippling through the trees.

Then, a low murmur. Nearly imperceptible at first but growing steadily in volume. She flinches as a door is whipped open in the bowels of the house.

A sharp report – announcing the monsters' release.

As they begin their approach, careening down the hall, she crouches in preparation for the incoming attack.

Moments before impact, she opens her arms wide.

"Good morning, my little monsters," she calls in a sing-song voice.

And two little boys, smelling of warm beds and sweet dreams, tumble into their mother's loving embrace.

Torn
by Lisa Verdekal

Shortlisted, Edinburgh International Flash Fiction Award 2020

The boy sat in the back of the parked car watching drops of rain race each other down his window. Running errands with his dad was mostly boring, but he liked the candy he bought him afterwards so he never complained.

Across the street a woman lurched out of a doorway and stood in front of it swaying. The boy sat up, his heart pounding. A glance at the pharmacy window assured him that his dad was still waiting looking in the opposite direction

Quickly, the boy rolled down his window and waved vigorously. The woman peered at him, then a smile burst across her face and she waved back.

"My baaaby," she called, and staggered out into the street. She stumbled, stopped and continued towards him.

Hurry up, thought the boy, please.

She reached out her arms as she neared. "Maamaa's heeerrre?"

The song of her voice seemed to engulf the whole town and the boy whipped his head around towards the pharmacy. He could see his dad putting his wallet away oblivious to her approach. "My beauuutiful boy. Come let me hold you."

The boy thrust his arms through the window, stretching, seconds from her touch. A hard hand grabbed the collar of his top and wrenched him backwards.

"Didn't I tell you not to talk to that drunken whore."

His dad rolled up the window, got into the driver's seat and drove off. The boy watched her standing in the rain until she was out of sight.

Weathering
by Amanda Forsyth

Shortlisted, Edinburgh International Flash Fiction Award 2020

It was a lovely day when you died.

We'd endured weeks of rain that even the heathens in the print press had agreed to recognise as biblical. The grass was saturated, the weeds rampant, and with that, summer in Scotland was over. We loved it, you and I, because we could nod knowingly and smile, and say that you didn't come to Edinburgh for the weather. I held your hand, and it was chilled, but you pressed my fingers now and again, and we nodded.

Knowingly.

Then the rain stopped, the sun came out, and the temperature dropped. In Forties, Cromarty, Forth and Tyne, the wind was no longer cyclonic and the nice man from the Met Office promised us Fairness.

You left me part way through The Archers, though, and that was desperately unfair. But I suppose you know how it ended, now, anyway. Do you? Can you pass a cloud across the sun at two-thirteen next Thursday, to reduce the pressure?

I looked out of the window at the crisp, clear afternoon. Everything was still: the leaves on the trees, my head, your heart. The sun warmed the glass, because it didn't care one way or the other. The kids in the playground opposite would care, one day, but not now, because conkers take precedence when you're eight, so they wept about that instead.

I gave you your hand back and went to the telephone. Personal forecast.

Visibility: Good. Occasionally poor. Rain at times.

Priorities
by Birgit Gaiser

Shortlisted, Edinburgh International Flash Fiction Award 2020

She looked at me. I looked at her.

She was fifteen, maybe twenty years older than me, tall and stocky and reasonably fit- looking. I reckoned I could take her in a fight if I had to and would probably win by some margin.

Even though I had been there longer than her, her seniority had to be taken into consideration. Others stayed out of the encounter that was about to happen:

The couple with a bull terrier appeared decidedly uninterested, aware that they had no stake in the outcome.

The short woman with East Asian features, who could have rightly claimed priority over either of us, deliberately kept in the background, not wanting to be involved.

The hipster in shorts looked pointedly ahead.

I was unsure what to do. In these ten seconds so much can go wrong, impacting the way others perceive you, making or breaking someone's day, triggering amused, annoyed or exasperated posts on social media.

The bus stopped.

She nodded at me.

I said, "No, on you go."

She said, "Don't be daft, you've been here longer."

The driver watched, barely managing to keep from rolling his eyes at this scenario which plays out day after day at Britain's bus stops.

I smiled and stepped on, followed by the older lady, the short woman and the hipster. The couple with the dog remained at the stop, still waiting for their bus.

Heartbeat at Morar Bothy
by Lyn Towers

Longlisted, Edinburgh International Flash Fiction Award 2020

I awake shivering in the night; darkness claws at my soul draining my spirit, evaporating strength instilling frozen terror. How can night be so dark? Morar Bothy, welcome haven at dusk after a long trail is now my place of nightmares. I feel trapped, immobile, even the fire has died.

My heart thumps wildly as I attempt to focus on the door. Where's Jim? He's been away for ages. He was only going to dig peat to keep the fire alive.

My breath stops. I hear the muffled sound of a boat engine on the other side of the loch moving closer. Not daring to move in case I'm seen, the boat engine nears. Loneliness hits me.

The boat continues on an arc around the loch, its tiny light glimmering, dragging something in its wake. The far shore's thin white line of sand exposes dark shapes bundling a body onto a tiny white pony.

Suddenly a helicopter shatters the silence with headlights sweeping across the loch, it circles and heads towards the far shore, landing for a few minutes before taking off. Stuttering loudly, flying low towards the bothy, it rises over the mountain. In horror I hear boots thump towards the door. I flatten against the wall, eyes tightly shut. The door creaks open. Jim steps through the door closing it carefully. "Bit of poaching going on t'other side of the loch."

"Poaching?" I relax with relief. Jim has returned.

Mythologies
by Alison Woodhouse

Longlisted, Edinburgh International Flash Fiction Award 2020

The house is a shrine. Photos of Papa in his crib, at school and University, with my mother before they left for England. Here, he is Christos Gregoriades.

Grandmother is unpredictable. She wept when I arrived. "Adrienne! All grown up! And you have your papa's eyes."

The goats in the yard smell musty, like wet leaves and hay; the dogs snarl, until Grandmother barks at them; a rising crescendo of cicadas falls suddenly silent.

Tonight there's a feast. Grandmother is dressed in black serge. She's assembled a battalion of cousins, aunts, uncles.

I'm hugged, kissed. "You're home! We'd given up on you!"

Me or Papa?

She finds me upstairs, nods at my rucksack. "How long will you be travelling?"

"Six months, maybe a year. Papa thought ..." She waves her hands, brown as walnuts:

"What does he know? When he left me to go to England, he said it was to make money, then he'd build a house in the plot next to your Uncle Dimitri. Your papa has a silver tongue."

"He's built a good business. He's an important man ..."

"What of it?"

"In England he's Chris Gregory." She nods.

"You must return, Adrienne."

"He ..."

"Hush, child. Bring your mama first. Your papa will soon follow."

Downstairs, I drink a beer, pick at roast lamb with rosemary, breathe jasmine and heat. Something locked tight, loosens. When I hear Uncle Dimitri playing the lyra, as mournfully as Papa, I know Grandmother is right. Christos must come home.

Sibling rivalry
by Sally Arkinstall

Longlisted, Edinburgh International Flash Fiction Award 2020

Elena stood up, smoothing the skirt of her black dress. Stepping forward, her long legs lengthened by her heels, she took a deep breath. Their mother remained seated, head bowed, hands clasped firmly in her lap. Elena began to speak, reading the carefully prepared words. Her voice was steady, betraying no emotion. The words told of happy times; of the successes and achievements of her perfect sibling: how pretty she was, how talented and hardworking. How she could be whatever she chose, and make a success of it.

Elena knew that she would never match the level of success that her mother believed had been Karen's destiny. And Karen would never be required to deliver the perfect eulogy for her sister, as Elena did now.

At the afternoon tea, those who gathered around Elena applauded her composure; admired her calmness at such a heart-breaking time. Elena maintained a steady smile, keeping a lid on her cynicism.

It had always been this way. The game of happy families played out for all to see. Behind closed doors the sisters were rivals, pitched one against the other by their mother's words. Elena knew that she could never please her mother. Elena understood that she was a disappointment. She hadn't known that Karen, with all her success, felt the same.

Karen had known that the illness would win. She'd left a letter for Elena. A letter, and her wealth. She had set her free from their mother's judgement.

The Grief Vampires
by Rachael Murphy

Longlisted, Edinburgh International Flash Fiction Award 2020

They come in droves—a drove of Grief Vampires. They flock to the Corp House.

They perch on chairs, on borrowed stools. They drink tea and ooze sympathy.

They wait their turn, line up to stare at the body in the coffin. Head to one side.

Sorrowful faces—shake the families hands, expressing sorrow, devouring grief.

The family —are they crying? Are they sad? Are they weeping and wailing? The Grief Vampires suck at the atmosphere like smokers taking the last drag of their last cigarette.

They are sorrowful. They are mournful. They are … appropriate. They consume tea and devour sandwiches made by neighbours and cousins. They pass appropriate remarks in hushed voices:

—Isn't it awful sad?

—Desperate

—Will they ever get over it?

—They won't. Remember Kathleen Brady? Her son done the same thing. She hasn't been right since.

—What happened to him?

—Over in London, he'd been there years.

—They done well to get him home so quick..

—Francie Brady was three weeks over before he came home.

—I heard he hung himself.

—I heard the same. They say don't know why.

They sit past the respectful time. They convince themselves that it's only right to wait for the priest to say the Rosary. The Sorrowful Mysteries.

—Did he have depression?

—No

—Well, wherever he is now he's at peace.

—I hope so

They leave the Corp House. They are disappointed. But tomorrow there is the funeral and the burial. They exist in hope.

Published in 2020 by the Scottish Arts Trust,
Registered charity SC044753
Any proceeds from the sale of this volume will be used to support the
story awards and the arts in Scotland
www.storyawards.org

Printed in Great Britain
by Amazon

51040386R00149